ALSO BY MARK FRUTKIN

FICTION

*Slow Lightning*
*The Lion of Venice*
*In the Time of the Angry Queen*
*Invading Tibet*
*Atmospheres Apollinaire*
*The Growing Dawn*

POETRY

*Iron Mountain*
*Acts of Light*
*The Alchemy of Clouds*

# FABRIZIO'S

# PRAISE FOR fABRIZIO'S RETURN

"*Fabrizio's Return* is a virtuoso performance of music, drama, faith, temptation and love that dazzlingly subverts the boundaries of time, while binding itself to humanity through the streak of a recurring comet."
—Joan Barfoot, author of *Luck*

"[I]f Mark Frutkin's *Fabrizio's Return* isn't counted among the best Canadian novels of 2006, then it should figure among the year's more ambitious experiments with story. . . . Enjoying a bottle [of good French wine] with *Fabrizio's Return* wouldn't be a bad idea. The two complement one another in flavours and effects."    —*Calgary Herald*

"Woven into the threads of Fabrizio's universe, where time and space fold with the ease and beauty of a passing storm, is the quest to find one's true self, and to glimpse the life eternal. Mark Frutkin is a wonderful and generous writer."
—Madeleine Thien, author of *Certainty*

"[A] good book for a Sunday afternoon. Part historical romance, part fairy tale and part detective story. . . ."    —*Winnipeg Free Press*

"*Fabrizio's Return* is a grand novel full of ossuaries and telescopes, gargoyles and magic potions, apocalyptic paintings, angels, comets, violins, of murmurations of starlings, and characters—such characters!—to make you fall in love."    —Alan Cumyn, author of *The Sojourn*

"Mark Frutkin still hasn't heard that novels rarely enchant any longer, or that the form can't match the seductions of the screen. *Fabrizio's Return* complements all the usual Frutkin dares—the stylistic bravura and erudition, the imaginative occupation of distant times and places—with a wit and charm that makes this story his most delightful, and slyly serious, to date."
—Charles Foran, author of *Carolan's Farewell*

"[*Fabrizio's Return*] weaves in and out of a series of fascinating characters. . . . There is a Shakespearean quality to the dramatic, dreamlike events that recalls *A Midsummer Night's Dream*."
—*Books in Canada*

# RETURN

 *MARK FRUTKIN*

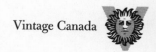

Vintage Canada

VINTAGE CANADA EDITION, 2006

Copyright © 2006 Mark Frutkin

Published in Canada by Vintage Canada, a division of Random House of Canada Limited, Toronto, in 2006. Originally published in hardcover in Canada by Alfred A. Knopf Canada, a division of Random House of Canada Limited, Toronto, in 2006. Distributed by Random House of Canada Limited, Toronto.

Vintage Canada and colophon are registered trademarks of Random House of Canada Limited.

www.randomhouse.ca

LIBRARY AND ARCHIVES CANADA CATALOGUING IN PUBLICATION

Frutkin, Mark, 1948–
Fabrizio's return / Mark Frutkin.

ISBN-13: 978-0-676-97728-2
ISBN-10: 0-676-97728-6

I. Title.

PS8561.R84F32 2006A      c813'.54      c2006-904615-8

*Book design by* CS Richardson

Printed and bound in Canada

2  4  6  8  9  7  5  3  1

*for Faith*

## LIST OF CHARACTERS

*17th Century*
Don Fabrizio Cambiati, candidate for sainthood
Omero, his manservant
Agostino, Duke of Cremona
Maria Andrea, Duchess of Cremona
Rodolfo, Man of the Reeds
Niccolò, violinmaker

*18th Century*
Monsignor Michele Archenti, devil's advocate
Pietro, Duke of Cremona
Francesca, Duchess of Cremona
Elletra, their daughter
Maria Andrea, Duchess Mother (*duchessa madre*)
Man of the Reeds, Rodolfo
Padre Attilio Bodini, a Hieronymite priest

*Commedia dell'Arte players*
Arlecchino
Pantalone
Aurora and Ottavio, lovers
Ugo the Mantuan

## CHAPTER ONE

### THE TOWER

*26 August 1682 / Cremona, Italy*

"Omero, awake!"

Towards the east, Mercury, Saturn, Jupiter and Mars climbed one by one from the horizon, forming a straight line across the sky. The moon was not yet half full and Orion the Hunter came leaping over the walls of the city, the three stars of his belt throwing spears of light. Padre Fabrizio Cambiati leaned over the parapet high atop the tower to see the clock on the tower's face. He read it upside down—4:45 a.m.

And then he saw what he had been waiting for. The comet. Out the corner of his eye—almost behind him. He turned.

"Omero, awake!"

A small man with an enormous head which barely reached as high as the priest's elbow, Omero clambered to his feet and stumbled to the parapet, his mouth hanging open in awe. "*Dio mio,*" he breathed as he cringed in fear of being doused with the comet's ethereal vapours. "I see the face of the goat-footed one! Save me, Don Fabrizio!"

"Calm yourself."

Low on the horizon, the head of the comet shone silvery white, its tail a haze of glowing feathers, as if someone had set fire to a dove and tossed it over the city wall.

Together they watched and wondered as the comet coursed up and across the heavens—a slow-moving acolyte, lit taper in hand, passing down a row of candles, lighting them one by one. The light of a great comet would normally have weakened the brilliance of the stars, but this was not a normal comet. Far from it. The comet ignited the firmament. It refreshed the constellations, brightening the stars as it went, irradiating the hard diamonds of Orion's belt, the glints from the surface of the water in the Water Bearer's bucket, the shards of light in the eyes of the Lion, the sparks from the hooves of the Bull, from the horns of the Ram.

Late that afternoon, the priest and his manservant had begun their ascent of the *torrazzo* that stood on the main square of Cremona, the tallest tower in a city of a hundred towers.

Omero, who had been sleeping at the tower's entrance while he waited for the priest, had struggled to his feet as his master arrived out of breath. Fabrizio Cambiati's rich hair, as black and shiny as if it had been dipped in ink, was combed straight back. Oddly, his brown eyes, set in a face of weathered skin, didn't seem to match—one was happy, the other sad. With his black cassock to his ankles, Cambiati looked taller than he actually was. While he could not be called handsome, when he smiled he displayed a warmth that made him appear more youthful than his middling years would warrant.

The priest glanced back the way he had come. "I have been all afternoon with a patient. Amazing, the efficacy of castor beans and ground senna pods in dealing with a serious blockage. Come quickly now, Omero." Fabrizio stepped into the shadows. "I believe his wife was about to thrust a basket of bread and cheese upon me as payment—a gift she can hardly afford to deny her family. I saw her coming after me down the street. Hurry."

They mounted the worn stone stairs within the tower, the staircase turning ninety degrees at each corner.

Omero lugged a basket of food. Chunks of ham, a fresh loaf of bread, Nebbiolo grapes, a brick of hard white cheese, a bottle of lively red wine and a green melon the size of a man's head. The servant stopped often to catch his breath, putting the basket down at his feet, leaning against the cool brick wall.

Fabrizio carried a sheaf of papers in one hand, and in the other a long, thin object wrapped in cloth.

"Come a little more quickly, Omero. At this pace, she will catch us with ease." The priest glanced back down the stairs, turned and started to climb again, but noticed a window cut in the wall. "No, wait." He looked out the window, scanning the piazza below. A number of stone buildings surrounded the rectangular square—the tower in which they stood, the massive cathedral next to it, an eight-sided baptistery at the far end, the town hall across from the tower, a small fortress-like armoury next to that and a row of small shops at the other end, including a baker's and the workshop of Niccolò the violinmaker. A few people conversed in the piazza but there was no sign of the wife of his patient.

They climbed again and soon Omero was puffing. "It's heavy, this basket."

"If you hadn't insisted on that huge melon, and the largest bottle of wine you could find, it would be easier. You have only yourself to blame."

Omero grumbled, and climbed ever more slowly. He halted, thinking to steal a rest by making conversation. "Why are we climbing this tower? This day's too hot for climbing."

"You know perfectly well. I told you yesterday. Do you not remember?"

"I wasn't listening."

Fabrizio sighed. Omero stared at him. The priest's eyes were watering, as they always did, day and night. "What guarantee do I have, Omero, if I waste my breath telling you again, that you will listen this time?"

"You are indeed a cruel master. Can we not stop here and eat?"

"No. Cease your whining. We must mount to the highest point for the best view."

"If you could take a turn with the basket . . ."

"All right. Give it to me." Don Fabrizio took the basket from him. "First you fill it to the brim, then you get me to carry it. Here, take the sky maps." Before lifting the basket, he placed the long object on top of the foodstuffs.

They trudged upward through the tower, its walls and ceiling of reddish-brown brickwork.

"Well, are you going to tell me what we are going to see, or am I to remain in ignorance for this entire . . . ascension?" He said the last word with his finger pointing in the air, as if he had just discovered something new.

"Yes, yes. We are going to look upon a comet high in the heavens. Rodolfo told me there would be a great comet coming tonight. Do you recall him? I saved his life, remember? An altogether strange fellow—people call him the Man of the Reeds." The priest paused. "Are you even listening?"

"What's that? Oh, I was thinking—do you suppose we could stop by the *taverna* later, after we are done with all this?"

Fabrizio halted and stared at his servant. "Usually a capacious forehead is a sign of intelligence . . ." The priest continued, "We will view the comet through this instrument called a *telescopio*. With it we will bring the stars close to earth. The Englishman, the scientist of the heavens who was here last year, recently sent it to me as a gift."

"I remember him well. The two of you spent many a night talking of mad things about which I know nothing." Omero gave him a blank look. "Tell me, which is it that moves through the tube—the distant object or the eye itself?"

Fabrizio laughed. "That is a question I cannot fully answer. While I am sure that neither eye nor object moves through the tube, my understanding of the science involved is severely limited. I know there are mirrors inside, and somehow . . . but come, look."

The priest paused and, with care, placed the telescope on a wide, waist-high stone ledge before a window. He unfolded the indigo cloth and revealed an instrument about three feet long, constructed of pearwood and bearing three rings of brass.

It looked to Omero like a musical instrument—a pipe or woodwind. He stared at it, and as he did so it seemed that a ray of sunlight shot through the nearby window and sparked off the middle brass ring. He imagined the object filled with stars and tiny comets bouncing off the interior walls of the tube. He wondered it did not explode before his eyes.

"Does it work by means of magic?"

"Science, not magic."

Omero, looking confused, nodded.

They started mounting the steps again. Omero groaned. "They say that comets are the smoke of human sins. They rise into the heavens and spew their venom over the lands and everyone below." He halted. "I don't like them. I don't favour comets. I don't."

The priest nodded patiently. "I know, I know."

They continued spiralling upward in silence, both huffing now, the only other sound the scraping of their shoes on the stone steps.

Long before they came upon it, they heard the steady persistent tick. They turned the corner to find an open doorway off the staircase, leading into the chamber that housed the mechanism of the huge astronomical clock on the tower's face. They stopped. The priest again glanced back down the way they had come. "I believe we have lost the wife—she won't be following us this far."

They sat and rested awhile and watched the complex gears, weights and levers of the clockwork.

"Who made it?" Omero asked.

"A lock blacksmith named Giovanni Divizioli. You know his descendants? They still live in the parish of Santa Lucia."

"Of course. Divizioli—the name itself like gears and levers."

"Yes. An astute observation. Sometimes, Omero, you do amaze me." The priest stared at the mechanism abstractedly. "What does it remind you of? Hazard a guess."

The little man stared at the guts of the clock, his face twisted up as if he was thinking hard. "I don't know. A waterfall?"

"Intriguing. Myself, I liken it to a mill wheel. And what do you think it would be grinding up, this mill wheel, with its relentless turning?"

Omero shrugged.

"Time, my friend. It is grinding up time."

Omero grunted; they stared a few moments more, and then started up the tower again. Slowly the ticking of the clock grew fainter and fainter as they moved away from it, mounting the stairs. Finally the tick faded from their hearing entirely, and it was as if they had passed beyond time, their heads going deeper and deeper into the silence of the heavens, into the mute clockwork of the stars.

After an excruciating climb marked by numerous rests along the way, and a drone of constant lament from Omero, they came upon another door, on their left. Pushing it open, Fabrizio revealed the immense bells of the tower—seven altogether, hanging still and ponderous in a line, each bell dedicated to a different saint. Fabrizio, removing a tiny hammer from the front pocket of his cassock, tapped each of the seven bells in turn and tilted his head, listening. He struck the Saint Agata bell a second time. "D-flat. Did you know Agata was young, beautiful and rich? A noblewoman."

"Like the duchess."

Don Fabrizio smiled to himself. "Indeed. Like the duchess." He added, "Saint Agata is the patron of bell-founders, and cures sterility." Again he reached out and tapped a bell. "And did you know that Saint Teresa experienced transverberation of the heart?" At Omero's questioning look, he added, "In a moment of mystical ecstasy, her heart was pierced by a burning arrow."

"Perhaps it was a comet that fell from heaven and entered her."

"Omero, please. Your imagination runs away with your good sense, such as it is." He bent over to pick up the food basket. "Let us continue."

They began the final climb that brought them to the high stone terrace with its crenellated parapet near the tower's peak. As they came out into the fresh air, the sun just beginning to set over the horizon, a murmuration of starlings blew into the sky, black as a puff of noxious fumes.

"We have reached our destination. At last," said Fabrizio, setting the basket on the floor.

Omero, panting, started rummaging in the food.

After their feast—Omero's face still buried in half a melon—Fabrizio drew the *telescopio* from its cloth. The priest looked out on the dusky light settling over the city and prepared to put the instrument to his eye. He hesitated, gazing southward.

"Come look at this."

"Hunh?" The servant staggered to his feet, wiping his mouth on his sleeve. "What?"

The sky to the south was stained with a faint cinnamon mist, a cloud floating towards the city.

The priest squinted. "I believe a sirocco is blowing this way."

A sirocco wind carrying fine sand from the Sahara was moving towards the city. Known as a glassy wind, it reflected the light and made objects in the distance appear close.

"Is it a good sign?"

"We shall see." Fabrizio turned and looked through the telescope at the square below, seeing Cremona's streets radiating in a star shape from the main piazza. The city was far from extensive but densely packed within its circling wall—houses, palazzi, towers, churches and a warren of workshops abutted each other from end to end. More than a hundred of the workshops belonged to the makers of violins and other stringed instruments for which the city was famous. Few green spaces were visible, and except for the main square and the streets leading to it as spokes lead to a hub, the small city was a chaos of lanes and alleys, a tumble of stone and wood structures, like something organic and unplanned, throbbing with humanity. The smell of woodsmoke came to Fabrizio from the chimneys below.

He gazed down the telescope again. "Do you see the players? They seem to be setting up for a play on the square."

Omero looked over the edge, trying to quell his dizziness and fear. "I see nothing. A play? They were not there when I crossed the piazza earlier."

He handed the instrument to Omero, who placed it gingerly before his right eye. Gasping, he tumbled backwards and shoved the *telescopio* back into Fabrizio's hands. "Devilish instrument! The city is upside down!"

"Yes, of course. Everything seen through the spyglass is inverted, I believe due to the special mirrors within." Fabrizio raised the telescope and looked into the distance. "*Per Dio!* I feel as if I could see forever." He scanned over the city and out to the horizon, pointing the telescope towards the River Po in the distance.

"Oh, look, Omero, a stand of mulberry trees by the river. Reminds me of my childhood spent collecting silk-worms . . . What's this?" Fabrizio sighted a white horse with two riders streaking along beside the river. Not far behind came half a dozen soldiers on horses as well, and a carriage throwing up dust. Reflected in the river, the line of horses and the carriage appeared right side up.

Fabrizio watched as the two riders dismounted from the white horse. The man helped the girl down with tender-ness and deference. Despite the distance, it was all impossi-bly clear through the glass, even down to the drops of sweat visible on the horse's flanks. Suddenly the soldiers arrived and leapt to the ground, the man fell to his knees as the car-riage swept in and an old woman stepped down—it was like watching a scene from an opera. And then everything was lost in a flood of light.

The priest removed the *telescopio* from his eye, held it at arm's length and stared at it. *What exactly am I seeing? A strange and marvellous instrument indeed.*

Omero, for his part, leaned against the wall and quietly enjoyed his wine. "*Vivace,*" he mumbled, smacking his lips, his eyes closed in ecstasy.

Fabrizio ignored him. Something else had caught his eye. A midwife he knew was hurrying down a narrow street, her skirts swishing as she scurried. Fabrizio lost her for a moment and then she reappeared on another street, heading for the tall double doors of the ducal palace just beyond the tower and near the square. As soon as a servant answered her knock she slipped in, before the door was fully opened. Raising the telescope to view a second-storey window in the palace, Fabrizio saw, through shutters thrown wide, the beautiful young duchess in her room, lying in bed. The midwife entered the room and came into his view, approaching the bed as the duchess arched her back and cried out—he could see her mouth stretched open but could hear nothing at this distance. His heart leapt. He bit his lip as he watched. *The child is coming!*

Through the telescope he saw Duke Agostino strutting about the streets below, his barrel chest puffed out, celebrating, his face aglow in anticipation of the birth of his first child. Lowering the instrument, Fabrizio smiled to himself sadly and stood lost in thought.

Again Don Fabrizio raised the glass to his eye and looked out. Under the light of the sun in its final radiance, the world was shining and luminous. There was Rodolfo walking along the river—the skeleton upon his back—and suddenly there was Rodolfo again as a young man. *How am I seeing this? How is it the instrument allows me to see such a thing?* Again he saw Rodolfo in another time, among the reeds by the river, lying inert, seemingly dead—and he saw a cart pulling away.

"Omero, listen. There is something most unusual about this instrument. Truly, I do not know if I am seeing past, present or future. Or perhaps all three at once. Come, look again." He held the telescope out and Omero took it. "Do not be afraid." The little man lifted the telescope to his eye. "What do you see?"

"The play in the square is about to begin."

Dark had fallen, with its icy sprinkling of stars, but no comet. The night wore on and still they waited—Fabrizio with forbearance, Omero with mounting impatience.

"Where is it? The cock is soon to crow, and I've seen nothing. Where is this damnable comet? It's not coming, is it?"

"Patience." Fabrizio scanned the heavens with the telescope. "In any case, it has been a marvellous night. Look at those stars—they will still be here long after we are gone, were here long before we came . . ."

Omero yawned. "I must sleep." He made himself comfortable against the inside wall of the tower. Soon Fabrizio heard his snores.

Meanwhile, the priest watched the sky and waited.

And finally the comet had come. In the pre-dawn darkness of the Feast of St. Felix, the little-known hermit of Pistoia, the priest had happily awakened Omero, and now the two of them regarded the comet in its slow knit of the constellations, beginning with the twins of Gemini, and heading southeast for its eventual date with the Virgin.

Omero's fear dissolved in the beauty of the celestial sight as he and Fabrizio stood enraptured.

Suddenly, Fabrizio lowered his gaze to the square below. "Do you hear something?"

Omero peered into the distance. "It is almost morning. Perhaps the gatekeepers are opening the gates."

"No. Something else. A carriage."

Fabrizio took up his telescope. In the mirror-like light that comes just before dawn, he saw a black carriage pulled by four horses as it burst from the dark mouth of a street, racketed into the square and halted. One of the horses shuddered and shook its head.

The lacquer of the carriage was so black it shone, reflecting the astronomical clock on the façade of the tower. As Fabrizio and Omero watched, the door of the carriage swung wide, a round black hat appeared in the opening and down stepped a cleric in a black cassock. The priest stood straight and looked about the piazza, his unhurried stance alone revealing much about the man—his solidity, his pride, his importance. Even at a distance, Fabrizio could see his face with uncanny clarity, the man's penetrating eyes radiating a dark intelligence.

A Jesuit, Fabrizio whispered.

# CHAPTER TWO

The people loved to talk of Fabrizio Cambiati's miracles. It brought brilliance into their lives, ignited their days. They said that his left hand sparkled and gave off rays of light, that the candles in the church lit themselves when he passed. Once, it was said, he was praying in the cathedral and Christ stepped down from the cross and took his hand. It took four strong men to release the Saviour's grip. Believers related dozens of incidents in which they were healed after praying to Cambiati. The city lived in an impossible state of grace: the healings outnumbered the afflictions.

THE DEVIL'S ADVOCATE
EXPLAINS HIS MISSION

*1758 / Cremona*

More than three-quarters of a century after the time of
Fabrizio Cambiati, I, Michele Archenti, the devil's advocate,
approached Cremona with a mission to investigate the life of
this candidate for sainthood. As the black carriage pulled by
four lively horses streaked across the Lombardy plain under
the wide heavens, the sky was clear as water in a mountain
lake, but it wouldn't last. Already, at the margins of the landscape, I could see an impenetrable fog approaching.

I had left Rome—that snake's nest of plots and sub-
plots—under a cloud, and now it seemed that same cloud
was still clinging to me. Something hung in the air of the
Eternal City—I could not put my finger on it—a new and
richer malevolence. It left me with an inescapable taste of
blood in my mouth. My own state of mind began to reflect
that atmosphere. My life had begun to feel empty, to reek
of emptiness. I don't know when it began, but the cloud that
had settled over the Vatican affected me, seemed to penetrate
my mind and heart and weigh me down. I felt disturbed and
ill at ease, as if a foreign contagion had entered my blood.
Everyone either despises or fears a devil's advocate, and
I was growing tired of it. Even before Cardinal Cozio's
comment in front of the assembled Curia that I was looking

exhausted. But as devil's advocate I had my duty to perform, and perform it I would. I began to wonder if I was clinging to my duty as the proverbial drowning man clings to a piece of driftwood.

The common people expect me, as the devil's advocate, to be not only intelligent but wise, with the ability to see into souls and minds, no matter how shadowed. But I have learned that there is much I do not understand, and will never understand. Why is it, for example, that strange weather often accompanies inexplicable events? I do not speak of the rain of toads or the green tongues of fire or the black snow that those ancient weak-lipped failures, the alchemists, whisper about, but weather that is odd enough, in its own way. Weather, you see, is a kind of music that accompanies all our interactions, all our glories, failures, unspeakable dreams and endless hidden passions.

As long as we are here on this earth, we have the constancy of weather to sing for us: the contralto sigh of the wind, the running scales of rain, the whispering song of snow sifting down.

The tale, as I recall it to the best of my ability, arose in a mist, dwelt for a time in that mist and dissolved. The sun broke through on occasion, if I am remembering correctly. And near the end we had several bright sunny days, in stark contrast to the dark events of that time. You see, I am trying to tell the truth as I recall it, but that will be a more difficult task than anyone could imagine. The problem is not the poverty or porosity of my memory, but the mist that enveloped us, that enveloped me, penetrating clothing and skin and sinking into the very matter of the brain, there to cloud and distort all perception and memory.

The general of the Society of Jesus—the head of all the Jesuits—sent me to Cremona as the devil's advocate, a shatterer of saints, besmircher of the holy, lawyer for demons.

Oh, I found the holy there, alive and radiant as the most sublime music. And I found evil as well—a stench that afflicts me still, causing my nostrils to slam shut, along with my eyes and ears and, most tellingly, my heart.

Father, forgive me, for I have indeed sinned, *we* have sinned, *they* have sinned, perhaps even the eminent cardinals—forgive my impertinence—have sinned.

And still, there was the holy through it all, shimmering like music that forever graces and blesses the silence whence it comes.


My story pertains to deeply hidden truths that can burst forth, without warning, on a grey spring morning when the fields are heavy with fog.

It was just such a morning when I arrived in the town of Cremona. Almost two weeks in that noisy, bone-stiffening carriage to travel the nearly three hundred miles from Rome—up the ancient Roman road, Via Flaminia, to connect with Via Aemilia at Rimini, and thence to Bologna. After a pleasant night's stay in that fair town we travelled on to Piacenza, on the River Po, whence we joined the Via Postumia, and finally to Cremona.

It is no easy task being charged with the role of devil's advocate. The name alone frightens some, but I believed in the importance of my responsibilities and was determined to carry them out fully, as I had in twelve previous cases. I took my duty seriously. The devil's advocate is a canon lawyer of the Church, appointed by the head of the Jesuits. My official title was Promoter of the Faith. The Promotor Fidei is commonly known as the devil's advocate because it is his responsibility to search out the moral flaws of any candidate for sainthood.

In each of those earlier cases I was able to ferret out the failings in the life of one proposed as a saint. In Florence the supposed saint was a murderer; it had been a discreet and ingenious murder, by means of poison, but a murder nonetheless. In another case, in a village near Palermo, I revealed that the supposed saint had been a sodomite. In Naples, a thief. In Venice, one candidate for sainthood kept a convent full of nuns as his private bordello—what else would one expect in that haven of lust and debauchery? But please understand, it is not lust I truly despise, but hypocrisy. (Excuse my frankness, but I have grown used to telling difficult truths. An occupational hazard.)

On another occasion I journeyed to Arles, in France, and exposed a heretic there: a saint, perhaps, but in some other Heaven. In Spain, in the city of Pamplona, I unveiled a cleric addicted to bestiality. My most recent case revealed a liar. A mere liar, but such lies—the entire population of Brindisi was convinced of his sainthood, but I did not have to dig too deeply to find that he lied like a Greek. Yes, eighty years after his death and it was clear that he had authored a series of manuscripts whose sole purpose was to have himself elected as a holy one. It took me four months in that sombre town to find the truth but, in the end, find it I did.

In each case the sinner had a champion. Usually a cardinal or a bishop from the candidate's own region or town, who had proposed the individual for sainthood, citing acts of holiness and exceeding generosity, as well as miracles and observed penitential actions of such severity as to make a surgeon-barber blanch. The citations, always well reasoned and seductive, were, every one, based on hallucination, hysteria, exaggeration and outright falsehood. None of the twelve was a saint, despite the howling from the faithful of their villages and cities, despite protestations from cardinals and archbishops.

I answer to no one, you see, but God, Mother Church and the Society of Jesus. And the Devil too, if necessary.

In each case, it was my decision. I took responsibility, played the role of Satan's henchman. In each case, it was the vehemence of my report to the College that quashed the submission for sainthood. I am no cynic, however. In fact, I remain convinced that cynicism is the great sin of our age. But as the dog grips his bone, I am dedicated to Truth. Truth, in the end, and naught but Truth.

I believed that it was my calling to reveal a great saint. Perhaps there was a touch of madness in this, I admit. The true saints have often proven to teeter on the edge of madness. If I was to recognize this madness I must experience it myself, to know it in my heart, the better to acknowledge its true manifestation when I beheld it. Little did I expect that it would come cloaked in a ferocious and dangerous beauty.

As I said, after travelling all night, I arrived in Cremona at break of day. The foolish driver had become lost and, unable to find the inn along the road, we had continued, stopping at times to rest the horses. A grey pall of fog hung low over the countryside by then, and drifted ghostlike down the streets of the city as we drove in.

I had the impression that the fog was causing the magnification of sounds—the clatter of the carriage and the horses' hooves as we rattled across the cobbles echoed off the surrounding walls of the square. As I stepped down from the carriage and turned to close the door—the huge clock on the tower reflecting in the carriage door's shiny black lacquer—I felt someone watching me.

Turning again, I looked about the piazza. A few early workmen pulled carts, one stacked with boards, the other piled with rounds of cheese. The square had the look of a prosperous provincial town in farming country, which is exactly what it was.

I noted that the most striking element on the square was the massive redbrick tower, impossibly tall, heaving into the heavens. Next to it stood a cathedral, its marble façade the colour of mother-of-pearl, from which a crowd of stone saints gazed down, their faces locked in a paralysis more severe than serene. The cathedral was graced with a delicate rose window, and innumerable small, pointed, Byzantine-influenced towers that reminded me of Venice. Across from the duomo stood the town hall, dark and forbidding, with a deep, shadowed portico beneath and a castellated battlement along the roofline. At the far end of the square, at a right angle to the cathedral, an eight-sided baptistery awaited newborns, while at the other end stood a row of shops which, at this early hour, showed no signs of activity.

On the surface it appeared peaceful enough, but I could not help but wonder what lay beneath, for I had discovered again and again that wherever there exist great saints, there also one will find great temptation and great evil, for sainthood must meet and defeat powerful demons to prove itself.

The red-faced coachman called to me from his perch, asking where I would like my trunks taken.

I settled into my rooms—a convenient suite at the rectory, which stood next to the cathedral at the far corner of the main piazza. I had been given a trio of inner chambers for my living quarters, and a parlatory, a large outer office panelled in dark wood, where I could conduct my interviews. The trunks had been placed in the bedroom, against the back wall. One contained my personal effects, while the other held papers and manuscripts, the *positiones* and *vita* pertinent to the case of Fabrizio Cambiati.

While still in Rome, meeting with the Sacred Congregation for Rites concerning Don Fabrizio, I had read the *vita,* the accounts of the candidate's life, virtues, death and attributed miracles. At that time I had also read the *positiones.* There were a number of reports from Padre Merisi of Cremona, whom I was sure to soon meet. Also earlier documents and affidavits from the monsignor's three predecessors, including eyewitness accounts of Padre Fabrizio Cambiati's miracles. In addition, I had brought along my well-thumbed volume of Pope Benedict XIV's *On the Beatification of Servants of God and the Canonization of Blesseds.* Like any good advocate, I wanted to be as prepared as possible for the eventual trial concerning the life of Cambiati. I had examined all the documents once again on the long carriage ride from Rome, to ensure that I was thoroughly acquainted with the case.

The facts are as follows. Fabrizio Cambiati was born in the village of Crema, on the road between Cremona and Milano, a nowhere, out-of-the-way place in the middle of the Lombardy plain. Quite early on, it was claimed, he had shown signs of the stigmata, but with more evidence, and more frequency, in the left hand. *A mano sinistra.* I made special note of this.

The documents mentioned a few of the hundreds of miracles that were attributed to the candidate, each uniquely questionable.

The first supposed miracle occurred when little Fabrizio was six years of age and was having lunch with his younger sister of four. The girl began to choke on a piece of meat. The father was next door, in a hut, tending to his silkworms. The mother, unable to dislodge the obstruction, ran there to fetch him. When they returned, they found that the girl had been saved. Apparently, the boy had grabbed the ewer on the table and poured olive oil down the girl's throat. He showed how he had gently stroked her neck, causing her to swallow the piece of meat.

The candidate performed another supposed miracle some years after his ordination, by which time he had moved from Crema to Cremona. An old man in the city, blind since birth, had come to the candidate to request an unguent for a sore foot, since Cambiati had gained something of a reputation for his salves and cures—medicinal cures of the ordinary, non-miraculous variety. After treating the foot, Cambiati also rubbed a salve on the man's eyelids. In moments the man had regained his sight and went stumbling through the town singing Cambiati's praises. It must be noted that the foot was never cured.

The final miracle happened well after the candidate's death. When it came to the attention of the local bishop that the candidate could well be considered for sainthood, he had the body exhumed to protect it from thieves and relic hunters. When the tombstone was lifted, the attending officials reported a delicious and inebriating scent emanating from the casket and the white cerement that wrapped the skeleton.

These supposed miracles, attested to by the local populace, had been noted in the official documents, as well as numerous other claims by the townspeople that their prayers to Cambiati had been answered by miracles performed by the long-deceased candidate. These types of claims are always suspect, of course.

The noted miracles can all be fairly easily dismissed. The first, possibly the result of fortune favouring a child. The next, the curing of blindness, somewhat more intriguing. The third, the scent from the grave, again not truly a miracle. I suspected that once the hearings began, there would arise a multitude of other dubious claims from the local peasants. All peasants so badly want a saint to call their own.

On retiring to my rooms, I carefully withdrew from my trunk the burial cloth that had wrapped Cambiati's corpse. The cloth had been sent to Rome and handed over to me there. Now I held it in my hand and sniffed it. It gave off the mingled scents of honeysuckle and lemon flowers, smelling not unlike the coat of a hound after it has run through early summer fields thick with wildflowers. The cerement, of worn cotton, was an unstained white. Again I placed it under my nose and smelled it. I had a compulsion to smell it all afternoon. In fact, I realized that the odour was inducing in me a delicious languor. I was drunk on it, pleasantly so. The sun above the low-lying mist shone in the window onto the papers on my desk. Running my fingers over the place where the light touched the desk, I felt the warmth. I was awake, but exceedingly peaceful and calm. The world seemed to have been brought to a standstill.

The housekeeper knocked on my door. Looking up as she announced the evening meal, I realized that hours had passed. I stared at the cerement still in my hand, rerolled it and placed it in my desk. Though I am a priest of the Church, and sincerely believe in the possibility of sainthood, I, for one, do not believe in miracles.

THE   LIBRARY
OF   AN   ALCHEMIST

"My good padre, what are you gaping at?"

"I, I did not expect the devil's advocate to be one so young." Padre Merisi had a confused look on his face, his nearly bald head showing pearls of sweat. He was continuously wringing his hands.

"I am far from young, and yet I suppose I am considered young for an advocate, it is true."

The older priest could barely look at the Jesuit. "Excuse me, Your Excellency. It is, it is just that I have never met a devil's advocate before."

"What did you expect—Satan himself?" The Jesuit smiled, but with a shrewdness that he didn't bother hiding. He also did not bother to correct the priest's mistake in calling him "Your Excellency." The previous devil's advocate had been an archbishop and had certainly deserved the exalted title, while Archenti did not. Taking their lead from Padre Merisi, the Cremonesi adopted the same form of address. The advocate rather enjoyed his new-found status.

"I am a humble servant of Christ." He bowed slightly. "You have nothing to fear. I am only here to accomplish one simple task." Despite his soft words, he had a look about him—black eyes that seemed to penetrate the speaker, seeing into the core, behind the surface. Always seeking out hidden intents, secret purposes behind what people said.

"Your Excellency. I beg your forgiveness. Though we have many towers here in Cremona, a sign of our good fortune, we are a small city, far from Rome. One can walk from the east gate to the west in a mere twenty minutes." The priest bowed his head, and twisted his hands together.

"Well, that's neither here nor there. Now, I would like you to take me to the former dwelling of this Fabrizio Cambiati. I understand his house has been preserved."

The priest grew excited. "Yes, yes, this way, Your Excellency. Come, come."

They had been standing in front of the cathedral on the main square, near a pair of recumbent stone lions guarding the duomo's entrance. Padre Merisi led the devil's advocate along the edge of the piazza, under the great clock on the tower. As they passed under it, the Jesuit looked up. "Tell me, Don Merisi, why does this clock have four hands?"

The enormous astronomical clock on the façade of the *torrazzo* indeed had four hands on its face. Don Merisi explained: "The hand with the sun affixed to it marks the hours of the day and night; the one with the moon, the moon's phases; the other two, as I understand it, Your Excellency, mark the days and months of the year, and the constellations and signs of the zodiac."

The background of the clock was elegantly painted with these latter signs, from the ram of Aries all the way round to the fish of Pisces.

The local priest explained further. "When the zodiac hand aligns with the sun and moon hands, it indicates an eclipse. That is my understanding, Your Excellency."

"I see," said the advocate as they turned right from the square onto Via Santa Maria. They descended together, following the cobbled street as it curved behind the cathedral into a warren of dwellings. A woman threw a bucket of water into the gutter before them, looked up and smiled at the local priest. When she noticed the Jesuit beside him watching her with a penetrating intensity, the smile vanished. She hurried back into her house. Two children ran past, a dog barking and bounding along with them. The smell of baking bread was in the air, as well as the reek of rotting garbage and sewage rising from the street.

Although the day had started with a spring rain and a heavy mist, the sun was shining high above, not exactly lifting the grey but infusing it with an opalescent glow and turning the air clammy.

"Do you think we will have our own saint, Your Excellency? Is it possible?"

"It is much too early to tell." The Jesuit did not wish to explain further. He knew Merisi's type. The questions would never end. He chose to change the subject. "This dwelling, why has it been kept all these years?"

"My predecessor told me that the responsibility had been handed to him and he was passing it to me. It was always believed that this day would come—that the good

Cambiati would be declared a saint, and his house and library should be saved."

"A library? There is a library as well?"

He shrugged. "Yes."

"What is in it?"

"Books. Many books. And manuscripts, I believe."

"Books, of course. It's a library. What kind of books?"

"I know not."

"You've never looked." It wasn't a question.

They walked along the street, turning several times, nearing the wall of the town. "Tell me, padre, have you come up with a list for the interviews, as I requested?"

"Oh yes, Your Excellency. It is in the rectory. When we return, I will give it to Your Excellency."

"Of course." Archenti did not thank him. He believed it was essential that a devil's advocate keep a respectable distance from those who favoured sainthood for their local candidate. It was the only way he had any hope of maintaining objectivity.

"Here is the house, Your Excellency."

The advocate noted that Don Merisi appeared to enjoy saying the words "Your Excellency" as often as possible, as if he could not believe he was in the presence of one so exalted and had to keep reminding himself. The local priest took an iron key from his cassock and unlocked the door, pushing it open, allowing the advocate to go first. They entered a small dwelling with a table and sleeping quarters in the front room, but the advocate showed little interest in this first chamber. To the rear, another door opened onto a long, narrow workshop with a high wooden table running along one side. At the back wall of this room, he noted, a fireplace had been converted into a brick furnace. *Hmm. A kiln might be needed for distilling and separating elements, the work of alchemists.* On the long table, three different sizes of mortar and pestle, two crucibles and several pots and flasks stood coated in dust. Above the table, ranked on the wall almost up to the ceiling, simple shelves held labelled sachets of dried herbs and small containers of wood and glass. The advocate began to inspect these with close attention.

"He was an herbalist, Your Excellency, as you can see. He used them for his poultices and unguents." Padre Merisi followed along, looking over the advocate's shoulder. Monsignor Archenti ignored him. He held a vial up, trying to determine its contents. "Move please, you are blocking the light from the window." The padre moved back and watched from several steps away.

"Hmm."

"What is it, Your Excellency?"

Archenti ignored him again. He continued inspecting the herbs and vials. "There is more here than is required by an herbalist," he said to no one in particular.

"How so?" Don Merisi hurried back to his side.

The advocate pointed at a line of vials. "Mercury, sulphur, copper, mica, cinnabar. These quite clearly suggest an interest in alchemy. Was there ever any mention that he was an alchemist?"

"I heard no such thing, Your Excellency. Never."

"Where is that library you mentioned?"

Another room led off to the left from the rear of the workroom—a small cubicle, about three yards by four. Shelves ran from floor to ceiling on every wall in the windowless room. The advocate stepped into the library, removed a book, held it in the light entering through the doorway and looked at it. He nodded. Merisi crowded him again, peeking over his shoulder, rubbing his hands together. Monsignor Archenti returned the book to the shelf and read the other titles quickly, scanning the rows of books.

Finally he stopped and turned to face Merisi. "All these are religious tomes, as one would expect. Tell me, padre, why is it that only little more than half the shelves are filled with books, and the rest stand empty?"

"I, I don't know. It's a mystery. Could it merely be that he did not have enough books to fill them?"

"This I doubt." He glanced about. "Is there another room? A room above? A cellar perhaps?"

"No, not that I know of. This is the last room. I know of no cellar."

The advocate was only half listening. Already he was searching the floor, shifting a pile of old firewood scraps at the rear of the workroom, looking underneath. He found nothing. Several empty wooden crates and dusty baskets were stored under the long table. "Pull those out," he said to Merisi, and the padre did as instructed.

"As I thought." Beneath one of the crates was a trap door with an inset iron handle. "We will have to move the work table. Give me a hand."

One at each end, they lifted the table to the middle of the room. The advocate pulled on the iron ring and the trap door opened, revealing a black, dank-smelling cellar and a set of stone steps. On the advocate's instruction, Merisi hurried to a neighbouring house for a lamp. While he waited, Archenti stared into the darkness, felt the heavy cool air emanating from the cellar. He had always believed that one could see into the soul of a man by examining the contents of his library. What a man read revealed who he truly was, much more so than the face he presented to the world.

When Padre Merisi returned, the advocate took the already lit lamp and began his descent into the dark. Don Merisi followed hesitantly.

Once below, the advocate turned about in the middle of the tiny cellar, the lamp held above his head. On a low stone shelf were stacked numerous instruments common to the practice of the alchemical arts: an alembic, retorts, crucibles, an airtight vessel or kerotakis, a small alchemical furnace in the shape of a tower. Everything was coated in white mould. The advocate smiled wryly and poked around among the instruments. *This will be easier than I thought. His sanctity should be readily disproved. The man cannot be a practitioner of the black arts and a saint at the same time. And yet the case appears almost too obvious, too easy.*

He turned again. On the wall opposite were two stone shelves filled with old books and manuscripts. Two steps brought him across the room, where he plucked a book off a shelf. These too were coated in white mould. Handing the lamp to Merisi, he wiped the spine to read the title. Again Padre Merisi stood behind him, holding the lamp aloft, watching, examining, trying to determine what he was thinking.

"Ahah!"

"What is it, Your Excellency?"

He held the book out and Merisi read the title: "*Secret of Secrets*. What is it?"

"A famous book of alchemy by the one called al-Razi. This does not bode well for your candidate, I am afraid. But we will see. Have the entire contents of this cellar brought upstairs and cleaned. I would like to inspect everything, beginning tomorrow afternoon."

A DISCUSSION CONCERNING
IATROCHEMISTS, OVER
CAPON WITH PRUNES

A few days later, the advocate was dining at the table of Duke Pietro and his wife, the Duchess Francesca, and their daughter, Elettra. The advocate was comfortable spending time with people of a certain class and status. As a high-ranking member of the clergy, he considered himself the equal of any cultured duke or wealthy merchant in any of the city-states of Italy. He was happy enough to be invited to their well-laid tables and to take part in discussions on the latest developments in the Vatican, what artist was now the pope's favourite or who was increasing trade with the Levant. After discussing a common friend they had in Rome, the bear-like, bearded duke spoke directly to the point as a tempting platter of capon with prunes was being served: "So, how goes the inspection of Cambiati's library, Your Excellency? I hear you have been perusing it these past few days. Is there anything of interest? Was the man a saint?"

Monsignor Archenti lifted his goblet of wine and drank, staring at the duke as he did so. "It is an intriguing case indeed, Your Grace. At first I thought the candidate was easily dismissed as an alchemist, and it is true he possessed many of the implements and manuscripts one would expect to find in one devoted to the alchemical arts, as well as the usual volumes on religion and theology. He apparently travelled throughout Europe for a year or so—in England and France and Germany, collecting books and such. And I believe he was able to purchase others from the traders coming up the Po on their barges. As I'm sure you know, books from the East are always a rarity, and of extreme interest among certain individuals."

As the devil's advocate spoke to the duke, he noted that the girl—aged about sixteen—followed the conversation closely, her gaze fixed upon each speaker in turn. She seemed to focus on her father and then the advocate with inordinate intensity, as if she were not merely listening but looking into the true heart of the speaker. Instantly, without her having said anything, he was convinced of her intelligence. It was apparent in the vitality and avid curiosity of her silence.

"In any case, I believe a portion of the library was hidden after his death, by local clerics who feared it would doom his candidacy. I believe also, based on the volumes in his collection, that he must have had a grasp of the world's many languages almost equal to my own. Whether he was versed in a full dozen tongues, as I am, I remain unsure. This is most unusual for a simple priest living in a provincial town. His intelligence is beyond doubt. The veracity and depth of his holiness, however, are another issue entirely. Suffice to say, I am not completely convinced of the danger of his studies in the alchemical arts, nor am I convinced of his holiness."

The duchess spoke up. She was a woman not yet out of her prime, her jet-black hair showing a single streak of grey. The advocate thought she appeared to be a woman who knew her own mind, as she spoke forthrightly. "I sense you were prepared to dismiss our dear Cambiati. Have you changed your mind on seeing his books?"

"Not entirely, but there is an intriguing pattern to the collection. The majority of the works are by known iatrochemists."

"Iatrochemists?" The duke sounded out the unfamiliar word. "I do not recognize this term." He motioned to the servant to pour more wine. Meanwhile, the advocate noted that the eyes of the girl widened slightly, and she licked her lips as her intense gaze bored into him.

"They were medical chemists. Alchemists who attempted most wholeheartedly, yet mistakenly, to bring together alchemy and medicine. People such as Paracelsus, Avicenna, al-Razi, Roger Bacon, Arnold of Villanova and others. I am convinced that it was their studies of tinctures, essences, salves and extracts of plants that influenced the candidate's interest in similar subjects, for many of the books were well worn, and had numerous dried leaves of various sorts stuck among the pages throughout."

"So he was a physician and herbalist, nothing more?" Elettra spoke for the first time. The devil's advocate stared at her. She had spoken up with a confidence that he found intriguing. And still those dark, penetrating eyes searched him for an answer. For her, he sensed, it wasn't just a conversation but much more.

"No, I don't believe he limited himself to being a physician alone, but it appears to have been his primary interest. He also had many books and manuscripts on astronomy, automata, clocks and other machines, the casting of bells, and so on. A man with many and varied interests."

The duke eyed the advocate. "It may be of interest to you that my grandmother knew him. Personally. She always spoke highly of Don Fabrizio."

"She is still alive?"

"Yes. My mother is gone but my grandmother lives on. She is quite elderly but remains lucid."

"Is she on the interview list?"

"Yes. Elettra was helping her look at your request yesterday."

"Good, good. I look forward to meeting with her."

"Were there any other books of interest?" the girl asked.

"Yes. As I said, his interests were wide-ranging. Of course, he had a copy of the classical *Historia naturalis,* by Pliny the Elder, quite popular. Pliny, as I am sure you know"—he glanced about the table, addressing everyone "was from Como and is a local hero here in Lombardy. Another book the candidate possessed is by the great mathematician Fibonacci of Pisa, which I have yet to explore. Another in the collection, which I found equally intriguing, is by one Francesco Stelluti. This work, *Descrizione dell'Ape,* consists of large detailed drawings of a honeybee, and was one of the first I opened when I set to work exploring the library. I am of the opinion that its peculiar vision of the world of nature is a satanic one. When I first opened it, I was horrified to see that this Stelluti had turned the common insect into a monster of demonic proportions. Its terrible eyes and dangling limbs, its malformed body, when seen close up, are reminiscent of beings from the realms of hell, at least as I have seen those demons represented in paintings. To see the world in such detail is certainly to be reserved for God and His angels alone."

"Indeed," the duchess agreed, and the duke nodded. The girl showed no reaction, seemed neutral to the suggestion.

"But more important, tucked into the pages of this book I found a sheaf of drawings—all depicting the face of a young woman." The advocate saw the girl's eyes flicker at this comment. It was almost unnoticeable but he was sure of it.

"Perhaps they were studies for his painting of the Virgin which hangs in the cathedral," the girl suggested.

"Yes, perhaps," the advocate said without conviction, and took a sip of wine. A moment later, he continued. "Another book that drew my interest was called *The Sceptical Chymist: or Chymico-Physical Doubts & Paradoxes, touching the Spagyrist's Principles commonly call'd Hypostatical, as they are wont to be Propos'd and Defended by the Generality of Alchymists,* by an Englishman named Robert Boyle. A work whose title alone proves how inescapably ridiculous the English can be."

*How like a Jesuit,* the girl thought, *that he would remember the entire title.*

The advocate added, "Although I make light of it, I believe this Boyle is quite possibly more dangerous than all the other alchemists combined, for although he believes in the ultimately fraudulent dogmas of alchemy, he believes further that the study of chemicals and elements and other suchlike is worthy *in its own right.* At least many alchemists have their eye on a transcendent purpose for their work, but Boyle, in his arrogance and his pride, ignores a greater purpose altogether.

"Speaking of the English," he went on, "as I was about to leave the Vatican on my journey here, I heard there was an English scientist who predicted some years ago that a great comet is due to arrive in our skies shortly, if it has not already done so."

The duchess complained, "We would never know. We have had much fog and rain of late, cloudy days and nights for weeks on end. The spring has been exceedingly damp, and warm as well."

"Who is this Englishman?" the duke asked.

"A scientist of the heavens. Dead now. He predicted that a comet that came seventy-six years ago would return this year. There was much talk of it in Rome. I believe his name was Holley, Edmund Holley."

"Halley," the girl said. "Halley, not Holley."

After a momentary silence, the advocate nodded. "Perhaps you are correct."

The duke shrugged. "The girl spends all her time in our library. You must forgive her impertinence, Your Excellency. The library, assembled by my father, is vast, and I believe she has read through a good two-thirds of it."

"You exaggerate, Father."

"No," agreed the advocate, "I'm sure she is correct. Halley, not Holley."

The duke sounded him out again, probing. "So, getting back to Cambiati—on balance, you are opposed to the candidacy?"

The advocate paused and smiled. Before he answered, he noticed that the girl reached for her wine and drank, her dark, round eyes watching him over the rim of her glass. "Your Grace, one might think, on the basis of what I have revealed, that the case could be concluded clearly in the negative. But I believe acting in such haste would be a mistake. There are numerous other factors to consider in this complex person, factors that I must explore thoroughly if I am to fulfill my duty. I must admit, of the many cases that I have investigated, this is indeed the most intriguing, and perplexing. Tomorrow I begin the interviews—perhaps, when those are finished, we will know more."

Although the duke and the duchess had many more questions concerning Fabrizio Cambiati, Monsignor Archenti cut them short, saying that he preferred to wait until he was further into his investigations.

## STAR CHARTS IN AN EIGHT-SIDED LIBRARY

Elettra sat in the library reading. The heavy oak table before her was strewn with leather-bound books, one of which was open wide to an illustration, a star chart of the heavens. As she read from the book she held in her hands, she kept referring to the illustration, and occasionally referred to other books on the table. Outside the single window that revealed the abundant gardens, the mid-afternoon light was pale and grey, though the green of the pine trees, palms and other plants was luscious and rich, gold-tinged, as if saturated with the moisture that appeared, not to be falling from the cloud-choked sky, but to be congealing out of the thickened air itself.

The library was a small eight-sided room crammed chockablock with books on shelves of dark wood towering to the high ceiling. Narrow wrought-iron stairs led to a second level, where a walkway, also of wrought iron, circled the room. The silence was deep, the only sounds being that of Elettra turning the thick pages of her book, and the sigh of her breath, steady and calm.

She looked up. The door to the library opened with a wheeze and in stepped her mother. She looked at Elettra seriously but said nothing until she had taken a chair across the table from her. "Elettra, we must talk."

"One moment." Elettra held up her hand as she finished the paragraph she was reading. When she raised her head, before her mother could speak, she said, in a rush, "I was interested in the conversation we had last night with the advocate about the comet that's coming and I decided to look into it. Father has a number of books on it. It's fascinating. Did you know . . ."

"Elettra, I said we must talk. Are you not listening? Close your book. Please."

Reluctantly, her eyes downcast, the girl shut the book she was reading.

"We must begin planning. The betrothal ceremony is not far off and then comes the wedding, and we have done little to prepare. Your father is worried. So . . ."

"There will be no wedding."

"Elettra. Do not say that. If your father hears that, there will be no controlling him. You know his temper."

"And you know my feelings about the matter, Mother. I will run away to the university at Bologna, or perhaps I will go to Spain, to Salamanca—there is an ancient and wonderful university there."

"Stop. You are going nowhere. You are still a girl and the wedding is set. Forget these silly dreams. Your father has given his bond to Gennaro's father. You know what that means. He cannot go back on his word."

Elettra did not respond but sat in hardened silence. She had secretly kept her finger in the book, and reopened it now to the page she had been reading. "We will talk about it later, Mother. I'm busy."

"Elettra, you cannot keep ignoring your responsibility. Time is passing. I will not continue to argue with you now but soon we must talk. Your father is very worried. Please, be reasonable and come talk to me when you are finished here. This wedding will be a great joy, for your father, for you and for me. Our only child, our daughter, given away in marriage—what could be more wonderful? So, you will come?"

Already back into her reading, the girl nodded without even hearing the last few urgings from her mother. Later, when she had tired of reading, she decided to go for a walk with her great-grandmother, and once again the plans for the wedding remained undiscussed.

# *THE PLAY—ACT ONE*

## THE PLAYERS ARRIVE IN CREMONA

The family of *commedia dell'arte* players known as Ingegni, the Talented, came once a year to the city. No one cared whether the travelling company was really a family or not, or even whether they were truly talented, just so long as they put on an entertaining show.

At first light on Saturday, the town awoke to the sound of creaking carts, farmers and their families heading towards the main square for the busiest vegetable market of the week. Groggy and thick-headed, the farmers drove from dark, sleeping fields to the streets that radiated into Piazza del

Comune, dragging the light of dawn with them to the heart of the city, yellow melons piled high on their carts. At the same time they unknowingly drew behind them, from fields along the shores of the Po, rags and tatters of early-morning fog that drifted through the square.

The farmers set up their stalls, working in near silence. From their carts they heaved out baskets brimming with red, yellow and green vegetables, waxy smooth peppers, zucchinis like dark green clubs, radiant tomatoes. Woven baskets filled with peaches, pears, apples, and swollen clusters of Nebbiolo grapes coated with a white bloom and sparkling with dew. Other baskets filled with almonds shaped like Arab eyes, and knobby walnuts. Already the old ladies in black, who can never sleep, and the overexcited children were arriving at the square, the former to be the first to clamp their wrinkled hands on the plumpest produce and the latter to run from stall to stall to see all there was to see.

In front of the Palazzo Comunale, the town hall with its sombre arcades, the actors busily set up their raised stage of wide planks, with two wooden ramps at the rear. Above the stage they hung worn tapestries that wavered in the faint breeze. Standing in the shadow of a column by the front of the cathedral, Fabrizio watched the actors at work.

In a leather mask that was lumpy with warts and covered the top half of his face, a player stood on the newly assembled stage, thumped his drum three times and announced in a stentorian voice that the play would take place later that morning.

"Magic and wonders as you have never before seen," the mountebank boomed. "The renowned Ingegni, marvellous players famous throughout the Italian peninsula. They have entertained the kings of Naples and Sicily, have appeared before emperors and empresses, dukes and duchesses, as well as countless counts and countesses. As seen and lauded in Roma, Palermo, Firenze, Venezia, even in Parigi. You will be amazed at their skills, amused at their talents, entertained by their adventures." He was warming to his theme, his litany of half-baked exaggerations and outright lies listened to by a few dozen goggle-eyed children. Fabrizio, half-hidden behind his column, watched in silence. The townspeople were busy filling handbaskets and cloth sacks with purchases for the week, moving among the stalls, displaying interest in everything, despite the fact that they knew most of the farmers already and always bought from their favourites, usually their own distant cousins. The air was filled with chatter, conversations flying back and forth as coins changed hands.

From the raised stage, the player had a clear view of the enclosed piazza. The square was less than half the size of Piazza San Marco in Venice, an eighth the size of St. Peter's Square in Rome. Across from the stage stood the cathedral, and to its left the great bell tower rising into blue heaven. The first glimmer of the sun shone high on the tower.

"Magic and wonders as you have never before imagined," the player shouted, repeating himself, more or less, to a gathering crowd. "A time for magic and wonders without cease."

Fabrizio melted deeper into the shadows among the cathedral's columns and statues, and seemed almost to disappear as the devil's advocate, a man from another time and place, swept down into the piazza from his well-appointed rooms. Rags of mist, like ghosts risen from the Po, floated about the square, their sinuous motion suggesting seaweed undulating underwater. As the devil's advocate passed not three feet from Fabrizio, a banner of fog slid between them, curling about the shoulders and heads of the two priests, joining them in an invisible embrace.

Every townsman in Cremona could hear the cry of the barker on the piazza. Costumed in the garish colours of a tropical bird, the player pattered on ceaselessly, gathering a crowd from all quarters. They came, oblivious of time, crowding into the square, longing to be entranced by the arabesques and arpeggios of his voice.

And such a voice it was—the boom of a peddler, the smooth seduction of an itinerant preacher who could reach right into the chest and grab the heart, a voice that bubbled silver like a river, crackled with lightning and shook the earth with its quaking. It was animal and mineral and human, your lover whispering in your ear, crying out under you. He was a magician who, with the judicious beat of his drum and the slippery cadence of his tongue, could put the crowd into a trance—a magician, an alchemist of song.

Other players mounted the stage, dressed as masked acrobats, ready to tumble into the crowd at a moment's notice.

The mountebank swept his eyes over the assembly. "Elixirs, aphrodisiacs, balms, potions and compounds, my friends. We have remedies of all kinds—specifics, restoratives, salves, antidotes, cataplasms and carminatives. Every physic available from the pharmacy of Mithridates. We bring every concoction to ease your lives and cure your ills. To begin, I have here in my hand, good people of Cremona, a vial whose potency is an antidote to all the poisons of Venice, can you believe it?"

"No, we cannot," a young blade shouted, but was ignored by the player.

"An antidote guaranteed to work. If it does not work, bring it back and we'll exchange it without charge, no questions asked."

"If it doesn't work, won't the purchaser be dead?" heckled the young blade.

The crowd laughed; the mountebank ignored him again and thumped his drum once, tossing the stoppered, waxed vial towards the crowd. At that moment one of the acrobats leapt from the stage, somersaulted in the air, caught the vial and walked through the crowd looking for someone who might be interested in purchasing it.

Already the barker was on to the next vial. "I am sure, good Christian people of Cremona, you have heard the term 'cure-all.' This vial and this one alone straightens aching spines, relaxes the feet and legs, smooths the skin, stops the itch and soothes the cough, calms the heart, quiets the liver and delights the bowels. The truth is, my friends, I myself was incapacitated with fever in Naples, had the shakes, and a single draft of this very elixir had me back on stage in hours. As God is my witness." He held his palm out and looked at the heavens. He flipped the vial over to another acrobat, who caught it as he was leaping from the stage.

"And this one, lucky people, was carried back from fabled Cathay by Marco Polo himself, Marco 'Milione' of Venice. He brought six vials, and only this precious one remains."

"What's it do?" a stocky bearded man in the crowd shouted.

"Let me tell you what it does. This elixir is destined to make the poor man rich, the rich man richer, it does not come cheap, no, no, but what wonders will fall from heaven on the user of this guaranteed potion, what fabulous dreams of wealth will visit you at night"—the acrobat to his left shook a tambourine—"and in the morning you will see what golden fruit has been born of your wise decision to purchase this ancient and magical elixir." He flicked it into the air as an acrobat leapt above the crowd, caught the vial in his teeth by its cork stopper and proceeded among the entranced on-lookers, dangling it from his fingers. Fabrizio, from his place in the shadows, took a half-step into the light, but halted and moved back on hearing the player describing the next potion.

"And now, gentlemen, ladies, cover your little ones' ears, for this next and last compound, this intoxicatingly sweet-smelling elixir, of which I have only several dozen vials remaining, is not for children at all, not at all.

"You will not believe such potency was ever possible. It will give men the strength of a bull, six, seven, eight times in a single night. It will make the ladies melt and run like the Po in springtime. It will make the skin and eyes glow, turn lips into rose petals and tongues into lightning. Nothing like this has been seen since the days of Cleopatra. It is today secretly used in the finest brothels of Venice, where both men and women swear to its efficacy. Yes, it's true. It works on the signorinas as well." He took a breath. "And now, ladies and gentlemen"—he flung a worn leather bag to the last of the leaping acrobats—"we must sell every last vial before the play can begin."

A crowd of men of all ages, including Duke Agostino, instantly surrounded the acrobat, clamouring for the vials and holding out coins. Moments later, as the player waded through the crowd dangling the last vial for sale, he passed near Fabrizio. The priest drew him into the shadows and offered him a coin of silver.

Fabrizio merely wanted to learn the true nature of the vial's contents. He thought it might help him discover new and effective remedies for his patients, who came to him with a dizzying array of maladies. The acrobat, with a puzzled tilt to his head, sold the old priest the last vial of elixir.

# CHAPTER THREE

*The miracles attributed to Fabrizio Cambiati were legion. They multiplied with the telling, and time embroidered them. A fetus was heard singing inside its mother's womb. The region's fruit trees blossomed in midwinter. The Po ran backwards on his feast day to protect the city from enemy ships. In my role as the devil's advocate I have heard accounts of miracles beyond belief, but never before have I heard such a flowering of the human imagi-nation. The people of Cremona tell them to me constantly. They have prayed to him, they have seen him mounting the steps of the tower, walking the transept of the cathedral. Their prayers have been*

*answered in a thousand different ways. Healings
without number. The people believe they are being
healed by him before they become sick. How am I to
separate proof from hopes and dreams?*


## IN A CREMONESE LABORATORY

*1682 / Cremona*

"If you cannot abide the smell, Omero, I will be forced to find
myself another assistant."

On the workbench, the pot over the flame continued to
steam and vomit up a froth that stank like a recently disturbed
grave. Don Fabrizio stirred the contents with a wooden
paddle and stared fixedly into the pot. The stirring action
brought clouds of new steam and, with it, malodorous airs
beyond belief.

"I think you enjoy the stench. You don't suffer as I do."
Omero grimaced.

"Yes, long ago I trained myself to unravel scents and
smells without passing judgment as to whether they were
pleasant or vile. It is all the same to me." The priest laughed
and stirred the pot. Omero looked at him. His master's eyes
were watering again, as they always did, inside the laboratory
and out.

"What is it you are trying to do?" Omero, standing on
his tiptoes, peered into the pot and held his nose. "Why do

you waste your time with these vile concoctions? You will create gold, yes?" His eyes widened.

While he continued stirring, Fabrizio answered, "Do you know the ancient alchemical saying? 'Stone which is not stone, a precious thing which has no value, a thing of many shapes which has no shape, this unknown thing which is known of all.' Do you know it?"

"No. It sounds like a riddle. What does it have to do with making gold?"

"Nothing. Nothing at all. Gold is simply a by-product. Something that arises while I search for the answer to the riddle."

"No gold?"

"No. I seek not gold but what is called the Philosopher's Stone—that which can cure mankind of its suffering and perhaps lead to immortality."

"But will we not have gold in the end? What is the point if we don't have gold . . . in the end?"

"You see no value in curing humanity of its suffering?"

"Oh, I suppose . . ."

Cambiati sensed someone at the open door, where afternoon sunlight attempted to penetrate the gloom of the workshop. A young boy of about seven years stood in the doorway, shaking.

"My momma, my momma said . . ."

"Yes? Out with it, child."

"Please come," was all the boy could say, as he pulled Padre Cambiati by the hand.

The priest gave orders to the servant. "Keep stirring the pot. I will return shortly."

Two hours later Omero's arm felt heavy as marble. He continuing stirring as he had been instructed, holding his right arm up with his left, the paddle feeling heavy as a tree trunk, the compound thickening to a rubbery slub. Finally he gave up. "God forgive me, but this is impossible." He blew out the flame, sat in a corner on a pile of straw and fell asleep.

Meanwhile, Don Fabrizio had followed the boy to his home, where he met the mother, who informed him that her husband, that very afternoon, had broken out in boils. "Is it a punishment from God, padre?"

"I don't know. Has he sinned?"

"He must have." She gazed at the man lying on his stomach on the rough bed, moaning, his back a raw slab of suppurating boils.

Just then, Duchess Maria Andrea, young wife of Duke Agostino of Cremona, and one of her maidservants appeared at the door. The duchess lifted her skirts and stepped over the worn sill and into the rundown house.

"Don Fabrizio, I am glad you have come. I was told that one of our guards was sick, and I wanted to check on him and the family. Can you help him?" She glanced at the man and smiled.

"I believe so, my lady. I do not believe it is serious, though one never knows in such cases."

Fabrizio was struck as always by her youth and vitality— a woman at the peak of her beauty—and when the duchess turned to the wife and asked, "Is there anything I can do, anything you need?" he was touched by the genuineness of her concern.

The mother shook her head. The duchess placed her hand tenderly on Fabrizio's arm. "Send for me if there is anything I can do. He is a good servant, a good man, and I consider his entire family my charges. If there is any cost, any cost at all, let me know. I must hurry back, but thank you so much, Don Fabrizio, you are most kind."

Before the duchess left, she took the hand of the woman, held it a moment in silence as she looked into her eyes and smiled. "All will be well," she said, turned away, lifted her skirts and exited.

Don Fabrizio watched through the doorway as if in a trance as the duchess and the maidservant faded down the alley.

"Padre?" the wife said, but he didn't hear her, lost as he was in his reverie. "Padre?" she said more loudly.

The priest shook his head and turned from the doorway. Reaching inside the basket he had over his arm, he withdrew a stoppered jar and sat in a chair next to the bed. "How are you, my good man?" he said rather too loudly, as if the man were asleep. "Not so well, Don Fabrizio," the man replied.

"I see. I have here a medicine, a cataplasm that I have never before used." He held it before the man's eyes. "It is no catholicon, but I am sure it will be helpful in your case." At the sound of the strange words, the wife gave the priest a blank look.

"It is a powerful vulnerary that I have just recently discovered. It worked on a horse last week. It was a beautiful horse, you should have seen it, black with a white spot . . ."

"Padre, please." The wife nodded at the afflicted back.

"Ah, yes, of course." He spoke again to the man. "The salve may burn when applied. It *will* burn when applied. Shall I proceed, then?"

The patient mumbled something that sounded like assent and wrapped his arms around his head, his entire body going rigid. Padre Fabrizio began to apply the salve, to the terrified screams and lamentations and curses of the victim, who was kicking his legs in the air and flopping about on the bed. The wife retreated and stood at the door, biting her hands, six children of various ages gathered like windblown rags about her legs and feet.

Several hours later, Don Fabrizio walked home singing in a light rain, his belly filled to the brim with the wife's good meat and wine. His thoughts were on the duchess and the place where she had touched his arm. He still felt her hand there, its softness against his skin. And he could still picture the smile she had given him like a gift as she left—a smile shy but intrigued, a smile that said much through its silence. "Pah, no value in these thoughts," he said to himself. "No cursed end to them either. Amen to all that." He reached his house and pushed open the door.

When he entered the laboratory, he saw Omero asleep on the hay, noticed the flame extinguished under his experiment and saw that the pot held nothing but black gunk that resembled muck from a swamp.

"Once again, Omero, you have ruined my efforts," he mumbled. "I know you are only here to test my patience, and for that I am grateful." He looked upon Omero resignedly at first, and then his face softened with a trace of fondness. The manservant appeared to be grinning in his sleep.

## HOW TO BRING A BODY BACK FROM THE EDGE OF DEATH

A little over a year earlier, on a quiet night in the city of Cremona, Padre Fabrizio had lain in bed listening to the rain streaming down outside. Across the room, a steady stream of rumbling snores emanated from Omero. The damp of an early spring penetrated the room. Don Fabrizio wondered how long it would rain, if it could rain forever. He was thinking about Noah and the Ark, pictured his own house floating away. He was pondering this when he heard a timid knock at the door. He thought perhaps he was dreaming, but a moment later it came again. Timid but insistent.

Rousing himself, he went to the smouldering fireplace, ignited a spill and lit a lamp. The knock came again. Fabrizio shuffled to the door and opened it on the damp night, the flame wavering. Holding the lamp up and away from his eyes, he peered into the black. An old woman inched forward into the constricted circle of light, her scarfed head bowed. "Don Fabrizio?"

It was difficult to coax the woman to speak, but Cambiati was able to learn that she lived alone in a hut near the river. That very night, she explained, she had heard a cart approaching along the road. Expecting it to pass, she had grown curious when it stopped nearby. From her doorway she had heard someone dragging something into the reeds by the water. She could see nothing in the dark but, after the cart left, she had wandered out to look. It was then she had found them.

She looked into the priest's eyes and then quickly back to the sodden ground. "The bodies of two men."

"Alive?"

She shrugged. "Come. I will show you where."

He dressed and followed her into the night.

A half-hour later, the priest and the old woman approached the place near the river. For a moment the woman became disoriented, but then she spotted the location where the reeds had been flattened and pointed at them.

"There," she whispered.

Cambiati approached. Sinking up to his ankles in cold water, he stared at two forms that had been tossed on the soggy ground. He went to the first man and lifted his head, which had been thrown back and immersed in a pool of brackish water. Bringing his face close to the man's, he noted pustules marking the skin. He determined that the man was old and quite dead.

Cambiati turned to the second man. Younger, but the same pustules marred his face. He could not determine if the man was breathing. He shook him. Nothing. The old woman stood a few steps away, watching. He forced the eyes open. No sign of life. Nothing. He hesitated. The other man was obviously dead, but this one—he wasn't sure. With a gesture to the peasant woman to look away, he pulled the man's trousers down and moved his testicles and member out of the way. With his hardened fist, he struck with all his strength at the perineum. "Whoo!" the man grunted, and his eyes shot wide open.

Lifting the man onto his shoulder, the padre thanked the old woman and headed back to the city, his lips mumbling prayers for the dead man left behind and the one he now carried like a sack of peas over his shoulder, the one who had already placed one foot in the land of the dead.

Back home, he laid the young man in his own bed. Although the man had awakened momentarily, he had passed out again and remained sleeping. With the help of a groggy Omero, he removed the man's clothes and inspected him. Weeping sores covered his body from head to toe. Cambiati knew it was not the plague but he did not recognize the disease. He washed him thoroughly. After applying an unguent that he hoped would be helpful, he slept on the stone floor next to the bed.

For two weeks Fabrizio administered a variety of herbs, applied both internally and externally. He spooned thin soup into the patient, kept him cool when he was hot and warmed him when he was cold. He watched over him day and night, and he also prayed for him.

One morning the stranger awoke, his eyes wide and clear. "I believe you have saved me, padre. Brought me back from that place where they were already making preparations to welcome me. I must thank you."

"It's nothing," said the priest. "What is your name?"

"I am called Rodolfo."

"Tell me what happened. Who left you to die in the reeds, and why?"

Rodolfo turned his pockmarked face to the window. "My brother. For years he has longed to keep our father's farm for himself. I am the eldest and would have had it soon, since our father is ancient. I told my brother he could have the land himself—I am no farmer. I long to wander. But he would not believe me, always saying that I would come back and claim what was mine. He feared that greatly. When we took ill, my father and I, I believe he secretly rejoiced. I was too weak to resist when he dragged us to the cart, and my father . . . my father, where is he?"

"Gone to God, my son. He died in the reeds where you were left."

Again he gazed out the window into the radiant April sunshine. "I see."

"Rest now. Rest. I will get you some soup."

A day later, Rodolfo stood at the door, ready to leave.

"Where will you go?"

"I will begin by avenging the death of my father."

"No. You must not."

"I will."

"I have not cured you for this." Fabrizio stood and shook his head, a severe and pained expression on his face. "No. I have not cured you for this. You must not kill. I have not cured you so you can take another's life."

Rodolfo spoke calmly. "Padre, the cure is a gift—once given, it no longer belongs to you."

## THE CANDIDATE SEEKS A CURE FOR INFERTILITY

Soon after the incident with Rodolfo, ever after known as the Man of the Reeds, the duchess came to Don Fabrizio to discuss her problem for the first time. Accompanied by an old maidservant with round cheeks who kept her head bowed, she appeared at the priest's door late one cool night in spring. She wore a long cape, the hood pulled over her head. At first Fabrizio didn't know who it could be at such an hour, but when she stepped into his rooms and pulled back the hood, it was as if the powerful spring sun had just burst over the horizon.

"Duchess? What are you doing out at this late hour?" He pulled out a chair at his rough table. "Sit. Please."

The duchess sat down. Her eyes were sad and glowing. Hesitating, she bit her lip before she spoke. "This is difficult. As you know, Don Fabrizio, I was married three years ago."

"Yes?" He was listening, but another part of his mind

was already drawing her face, sketching light lines in charcoal on a sheet of cream paper.

"But . . . all the girls who were married in the same year have already presented their husbands with children. All but me."

"Ah."

"I fear my husband will lose patience with me. He wants a son. I want a son."

"Would a daughter do?"

"Yes, of course." Her eyes moistened. "Don Fabrizio, I know you make mixtures and compounds for many afflictions. Could you perhaps help me?"

"I can try." He smiled. "But what if the problem is not with you but with your husband?"

The maidservant's hand flew to her mouth as a gasp escaped.

"No. I think not," said the duchess. "His . . . apparatus . . . functions well. We have been doing our duty as good Christians in trying to make a child."

"It is a difficult problem. I have not had much success in this area in the past but, as I said, I will try."

"Thank you, Don Fabrizio. I am forever in your debt. I will send my maidservant to collect the concoction when it is ready."

"Tomorrow, by late afternoon."

Over the next year, Fabrizio mixed four compounds for the duchess, changing the mixture with each season. Each was more vile-tasting than the last. Each failure made the duchess sadder and, strangely, more beautiful. But her womb remained unmoved.

He would see her walking about the square in the evening with the duke, or entering the cathedral on Sunday, where Don Fabrizio would stand by the doors greeting the parishioners as they entered. Whenever she could catch his eye the duchess would give the slightest shake of her head, to signal that the latest mixture had not worked.

She came again to his house. "Don Fabrizio, is there nothing we can do?"

"We can only keep trying, my dear."

She shook her head. "Is there any way I can repay you? I know we have failed thus far, but I believe that is more my fault than yours."

"No, do not blame yourself." He paused, reflecting. "There is something that could stand, in a way, as repayment. I would like to paint you. I have been requested to paint a figure of a saint at the Convent of Santa Lucia. I would like to use you as the model. I would have to begin with a number of sketches of your face. Would it be possible?"

"Yes, of course, Don Fabrizio. My husband, I am sure, would have no objection. He is so fond of you, and has mentioned more than once how much he admires your painting of the Virgin in the duomo."

Fabrizio already had a charcoal in hand, and was sketching her face as she sat before him, her eyes sad and luminous, his own heart fluttering madly, like a finch caught in the cage of his ribs.

## A  REFLECTION  IN  A  PUDDLE

*As above, so below,* the ancient stargazers say.

High in the heavens, the comet turned in its arc, and from that great distance, its power was felt on earth in the subtlest ways, in the most secret corners of the heart. Not that the comet alone precipitated the events of this tale, for the shifting of the heavens are never the drivers of fate but merely the perfect reflection of earthly happenstance.

The comet influenced the people of Cremona and their deeds in the way that a star chart, on an exceedingly clear night, can be read by the light of the stars.

It was an ordinary moment, but by the time Fabrizio Cambiati's foot reached the far side of the puddle, everything had changed.

He was crossing the main piazza after a sudden rain-shower, heading for the cathedral. The rain had passed as quickly as it had appeared, and now the sun popped out. Fabrizio glanced up at the clock and noted that it was three in the afternoon.

As he neared the cathedral, he went to step over a puddle. In the middle of taking the long step, he looked down and saw the rose window of the cathedral reflected there as in a mirror. A flash of sunlight bounced off the window and entered his eye in a reflection from the puddle. Everything seemed to slow down then, and take on a distinct, unusual quality. Although these ordinary events seemed to happen one after the other, they also appeared to happen all at once.

As he saw the rose window and the light, he also noticed his own face in the puddle as it moved over the reflection of the window—and then he and the reflection and the entire world around him were filled with a flood of light, a luminous presence, a light that was charged and awake and like nothing he had ever experienced. And yet he felt he was finally recognizing something that he had always known. It was as if he himself had expanded into the world, in the sense that he was no longer the centre but the centre was everywhere. And yet he remained acutely aware of colours and sounds around him. The clip-clop of a horse's hooves on the cobbles as it was led across the square rumbled magnificently; the creak of a cart was the thunder of a hundred carts; the eye of a swallow arcing halfway up the tower met his eye in mutual recognition; the infinitesimal scarlet dot on the back of an insect spinning in the air became a swirling thread of light. Every detail was significant, not because of anything outside itself, but in its own right.

Later, when he thought about it, he pictured what he had seen in layers. The first layer at the bottom of the puddle was the sun-filled sky, the next layer up was the reflection of the rose window, and on top of that the reflection of his own face. Then came the surface of the puddle, a mirror of water. The next layer, in the world above the puddle, was his own face again, then the actual rose window, then the sun-filled sky.

In fact, his foot never came down on the far side of the puddle, but he instantly felt as if he were floating five inches above the cobbles of the piazza. He had passed over the puddle; all his senses were clear and open as if he were an infant just born to the world, and now he stood five inches in the air. He glanced around the square. The few people about—a pair of merchants in conversation, an old lady going about her business, three children playing tag—didn't notice him. Nevertheless he felt extremely uncomfortable. He was able to step forward, just as he would have if he had been on solid earth, but he was also beginning to rise uncontrollably. Finding his way to the narrow alley between the cathedral and baptistery, he held onto the stone wall and headed back to his small dwelling, keeping as much as possible to the shadows, inching his way along so he would not rise any farther.

Back in his house, he greeted Omero.

"You're glowing. Why are you glowing?" Omero asked, on seeing him. "And you seem exceedingly tall. Perhaps after poking about in one of your alchemical concoctions you carelessly licked your finger?"

"No, not that I recall. I'm not sure what happened. A flash of light while I stepped across a puddle, that's all, then this." He indicated the fact that he was still floating five inches above the floor, holding onto a table at the same time to keep himself from going higher.

"Saint Paul on the road to Damascus. Flash of light and all that. It happens." Omero shrugged his shoulders.

"I wonder how long it will last, if it will pass?"

"No doubt. In the meantime, I'll tie a rope around your ankle when we go out so you don't float away into the heavens."

"But people will wonder . . ."

"At first, most won't notice. When they do, it will only enhance your reputation. They already think you're a saint. This should bring the blind and feeble flocking to the door. At all times of the day and night, I might add."

"Yes, and when I try to sleep, how will I keep from rising to the ceiling?"

Omero thought a moment, then said, "I'll stack books from your library on your chest to hold you down. Put them to some good use at last."

"And if I'm not able to sleep, I can at least have something to read. I'll give you a list of which books I want. Definitely include that volume by the Arab, al-Razi, *Secret of Secrets,* because my alchemical experiments are going extremely well, and I feel I draw near to finding the Philosopher's Stone. Perhaps the Arab will have some helpful suggestions. Oh yes, also include the *Epistles* of Filelfo, and the *Lives of the Philosophers,* and the Bible, of course, and the *Epistles* of Filelfo . . ."

"You just said that. You said *Epistles* of Filelfo twice."

"I did? Perhaps I have two volumes of it? Do I have two volumes of it? I wonder . . ."

Omero shook his head in disbelief.

It lasted a week and then Don Fabrizio returned to earth. "I'm not a saint, you know," he tried to explain to Omero, "not about to float off and become an archangel or even an angel. I had to come back to earth to become entirely human, completely human. It's the only way."

Before he came back down a few people had noticed his hovering, and word had soon spread. Children had kept coming to the door that week, to Omero's dismay, and singing: "Come out, Don Fabrizio, come out in the crowd. Fly like a swallow and float like a cloud."

Once in a while, when the crowd of children became insistent and tired of waiting, Omero tied his rope around Don Fabrizio's ankle and they walked together down the street and back. The children ran and skipped behind, laughing and clapping their hands, while Omero paced with a scowl on his face.

"That's enough now, run along home," he'd say to the children when he and Fabrizio returned to the door of their house. "What do you think this is, a circus, a theatre? He's not a saint, you know, he beats me!"

Then he'd stick his tongue out at the children, and they'd stick their tongues out back at him and run off.

## A RED TINCTURE,
## CONTENTS UNKNOWN

One day, some time after the players had arrived on the square and shortly after these recent strange events, the priest looked up from his workbench, where he had just added a quantity of powdered glasswort plant measured out in half a goldfinch eggshell to an iron cauldron in his never-ending search for the Philosopher's Stone. Omero stood at the door to the laboratory, a tall figure behind him. "Your Excellency," Omero mocked, "you have a visitor."

Fabrizio tossed Omero a withering glance before noticing that the visitor was his friend the violinmaker. "Niccolò, come in, come in."

After greetings, Niccolò came to the point. "Ten years ago, I came upon a lovely slab of excellent-quality spruce from the valley of Brembana, which I have been aging all this time. It has a faint reddish hue that I would like to bring out more fully. Could you recommend a tincture of some sort that I might add to the varnish?"

Fabrizio thought a moment. He scanned the jars and bottles on the shelves before him. Reaching out, he plucked up a glass vial. "This one I obtained a short time ago from the mountebank on the square. An aphrodisiac, apparently. As you can see, its hue is a deep red. I have not yet had the time to determine its contents." He handed it to Niccolò.

Niccolò held it up against the light coming from the window and nodded.

"Is it the correct colour for your needs?"

"Indeed. Perfection itself."

"Begin by adding a single drop to your varnish—I suspect the concoction will spread into it with ease."

"I see."

"I will give you a small amount." The priest reached for an empty vial on his shelf and opened it.

Omero, who had been listening to the conversation, attempted to take a closer look at the compound. He sniffed in its direction.

"Omero, I believe there is some wood to be stacked outside, is there not? It is the same wood I asked you to stack yesterday, and the day before that. Now would be a good time to accomplish that one simple task. I do not ask much of you. It would please me greatly. As you know, I am a very patient man, but when my patience has run out . . ."

Omero fled for the door.

Don Fabrizio stoppered the small vial with a cork and handed it to Niccolò, who slipped it into his pocket. His "thank you" trailed behind him as he hurried out the door.

## THE PAINTER'S FLOWER

A few weeks later, the warm sun leaking into the laboratory, Fabrizio puttered about at his workbench. "Omero, run to

Niccolò's workshop and the house of the duchess—ask them to meet me at the Convent of Santa Lucia. It is an uncommonly fine day. We can work on my painting of Saint Agata. Tell Niccolò to bring a violin, as the duchess is in need of entertainment. I will require his services for the entire afternoon."

Fabrizio stood pondering the collection of vials and brushes before him. Holding a wooden bucket, he dropped a handful of brushes into it. "Now, the pigments. Ah, here it is, the lapis lazuli, *azzurro transmarino,* the painter's flower— I'm surprised Omero hasn't sold it behind my back."

He placed it and the other pigments in the bucket and hurried off to the convent. As he walked, the face of the duchess drifted before him. He had been staring at it for days while working on the painting, and now that delightful visage came to him often. He knew the young woman had a will to match her husband's. The duke was feared about the city for his temper, but Fabrizio had no doubt the duchess could hold her own with him. She came from a distinguished family that included six brothers. As the only daughter, she had learned at a young age to stand up for herself. He rounded a corner and neared the convent. *More than four years of marriage without a child. People are beginning to talk, and I have failed utterly. I have only succeeded in giving her false hopes with my concoctions.*

On arrival, an uninterested nun with a straight back escorted him to the courtyard. The duchess and Niccolò were already there, awaiting him. "My greetings to you both. Is it not a lovely day for this, the feast day of Saint Luke?"

"How appropriate," the duchess said. "The patron saint of painters."

"And doctors," the violinmaker added.

"And butchers," Don Fabrizio said. "His emblem is an ox. He is often shown painting the Virgin, did you know? But we must begin."

He turned to the duchess. "Have you explained to Niccolò why I asked him here?"

"No. We have both only just arrived." She lowered herself carefully onto a stool, arranging her skirts, while Niccolò sat on the edge of the stone fountain.

"I see you have brought a violin, my friend. I must explain. You see the portrait I am working on." Fabrizio indicated the half-finished work on the wall of the courtyard. "Our poor lady has been sitting for me five full days. As the time grows long, her face grows sadder and sadder. Of course this won't do. I want her to have a transcendent look—as if lit from within. To raise her spirits, you will please play your violin while she sits."

"I won't sit another day without entertainment," she announced.

"Yes, yes, we understand, my lady, we understand." And to Niccolò: "You will be handsomely reimbursed, my friend, as soon as the convent pays for the work. It will be a pleasant afternoon, don't you think?"

He nodded. "We shall see. I would rather be in my workshop, but I await my next commission in any case." He picked up the violin and tucked it under his chin. "I was looking for an opportunity for you to hear my latest instrument. I believe it is the best work I have ever done—a violin to make one forget time entirely, and fall in love. I reddened the varnish with the tincture you gave me. It worked wonders."

"Lovely indeed." Fabrizio eyed the violin. "Let me see it." With one hand under its neck and the other under the body, Niccolò handed it to him as if passing an infant. Fabrizio took it in the same way. "A lovely colour. And it feels lighter than air."

His friend agreed. "A great violin weighs almost nothing. No more than a handful of rose petals. A badly played piece of music weighs more. When the violin is passed into your hands, it is difficult to feel its presence, to know when you have a grip on it. The ideal violin seems to float on its own in the air and play itself as in a dream. The music pre-exists within the instrument, and its voice speaks to us with the purity and clarity and intimacy of our own thoughts."

"Indeed." Fabrizio returned the violin. Niccolò took it back and for a few moments ran his bow across the strings, as he tuned them. He finished, tucked the violin under his chin and raised the bow. There was a moment of silence before he began.

Fabrizio loved that momentary hesitation, that caesura of silence before the rush and cascade of music. It was the ripe pause before something wonderful, that fulsome emptiness at the edge of a thing unknown, not yet existent but about to exist. The duchess looked beautiful in her stillness, her skin glowing, a peaceful look on her face. He looked at the paints laid out on a board before him, a brush of fine mink hair in his hand. Licking the brush tip, he dipped it into the lapis lazuli and moved through the silence towards the portrait. A dot of paint on the tip of his brush caught the sunlight.

A moment before Fabrizio touched the painting, Niccolò started playing—a plaintive, deeply pleasing adagio. The music poured from the strings like a cool stream in the mountains, like the Po in springtime—utterly smooth and without disturbance. Fabrizio stopped and looked at his friend, who had closed his eyes, listening to his own music as if from a great distance, as if the courtyard had expanded enormously. The duchess, too, stared, unable to hold her pose. Her eyes had filled with tears, and already they were pouring down her cheeks. Fabrizio was stunned. He said nothing, did not paint, but stood staring, stilled by the sounds that seemed to flow in waves from his own heart. Niccolò's words came back to him: *"A violin to make one fall in love." Fall in love with what,* he wondered, *the music itself or something else?*

After a while the duchess regained her pose; Fabrizio let out a sigh and started to paint. Niccolò played on, despite a tiny songbird that kept hopping onto the end of the violin, returning again and again as he tried to chase it away with the tip of the bow. He stopped and laughed. "This little bird believes I am upstaging him."

"It has a beautiful voice, this violin."

"Yes," the duchess agreed, without looking at the violinmaker. "I will ask my husband to buy it from you."

"Tell me about this violin. Why does it sing so sweetly?" Fabrizio stopped painting, holding the brush before him, and waited.

"It must be your elixir in the varnish, the aphrodisiac you obtained from the player on the square."

"I think not—I doubt the elixir has such power. But there is real magic in this violin. Why?"

Niccolò thought a moment. "Yes, it does carry a special sound, unlike any other I have made. I believe there are several reasons for this, some of which I can explain but others about which I remain ignorant. I recall when I found the spruce tree in the Dolomites from which the wood came. It was over ten years ago." The duchess turned in her seat to listen to his story. "It was an ancient tree at the edge of a cliff, and I heard the wind sighing in its branches before I saw it. It was twisted and bent like an old man, not the sort of tree I would normally bother to cut. It was . . . a strange moment . . . the new moon in December, when I always cut my wood. An eclipse of the sun must have been in progress that day, because the air grew still and the light began to fail and, as the light faded, a bird, a nightingale, confused as to the time of day, landed in the tree and began to sing. It was an extraordinary song—clear and crisp in the cold air. And then the sun returned, the bird flew away and I cut down the tree.

"The wood turned out to be so tough and unworkable that I was unable to use most of it. But I managed to secure a single log, which I cured for the usual ten years and which I recently used, at last, to construct this violin."

He held the instrument up. "Would you like to hear more?"

"Please." The duchess nodded.

Niccolò played for another hour—a series of adagios so sweet and sad as to melt the heart of a marble saint—and then he announced that he would return home.

After he left, Fabrizio worked on the painting for a while and then put down his brush.

"Are we finished for today?"

"Done."

The duchess stood up and walked about the courtyard, stretching and rubbing her neck. She came to stand behind him as he sat on his high rush stool and regarded the portrait. He could hear the rustle of her long skirts as she paced behind him, moving away now. She paused.

He kept staring at the painting and listening but did not turn around.

He heard her approach again, the sound of her skirts, the smell of her presence. She placed her left hand on his right shoulder as she stood behind him.

He bowed his head. Still he did not turn around to look at her.

The air was unnaturally quiet, as if something was about to happen. He was only pretending to gaze at the painting. He could hear her breathing near him, could smell her sweetness. She leaned forward and whispered in his ear.

"I think I should go now."

"Yes."

## FABRIZIO CAMBIATI'S
## PERSONAL PHARMACOPOEIA

Fabrizio held the vial he had bought from the player on the square and shook it before his eyes, watching its contents swirl. The tincture had certainly worked beautifully in enriching the colour of Niccolò's violin. Noting its precise tone and viscosity, he tried to recall others he had seen like it. For a long while he considered the contents, trying to let its nature sink into him, to apprehend its essence through sight alone. This was the first step in his study of the elixir.

Don Fabrizio felt at home with his poultices, ointments and unguents. He had spent a lifetime learning and experimenting, for he took great joy in attaining knowledge. At the same time, he sensed that the Philosopher's Stone was within his grasp at last—the cure for all mankind's afflictions, mental, physical and spiritual. He had no real interest in elixirs or potions, except as possible remedies for the astounding array of maladies that visited the people of Cremona and the farmers of the surrounding countryside. Their pain touched him, he couldn't escape it. His eyes watered constantly at the state of the world, and he could barely breathe if he saw someone beating a dog. Once, as a youth, he had seen a man killed on the square in a knife fight, and the look in the dying man's eyes—part fear, part disbelief, part terror—still haunted him.

Hundreds of glass vials and bottles, sachets and small bags, were lined up on the shelves over his laboratory table. He had memorized the smell and contents of every one— each of the thousands of herbs, flowers, oils, vinegars, minerals, greases, waxes and other ingredients that made up his personal pharmacopoeia.

He knew which herbs could be added to calf, goose, pig, goat, slug or snake grease to make foul-smelling, smooth-spreading, palliative ointments. Which could be added to vinegars to treat bites, burns, skin diseases and coughs. Which could be mixed into almond, walnut or laurel oil for a pleasant-smelling unguent. Which could be added to milk or water to brew infusions. Under the table he kept a dozen baskets of dried animal dung—from rabbits and lizards, goats and squirrels. He knew what herbs to mix with white or red wines as an antidote to poisons, for parasites and heart diseases. He had learned how to mix herbs with honey and water to make hydromels to treat fever, and how to use honey, vinegar and sea salt to make oxymels for treating snakebite. He collected rainwater at various seasons, and boiled grape juice for coughs and fevers. He had witch hazel for applying to cuts, and a small amount of the ancient *ma huang* plant from Cathay for treating ailments of the eyes. The varieties of disease and suffering were legion—he felt the only way to counteract such fertile virulence was to meet it with a hundred thousand curatives, his own omnium-gatherum of remedies.

At every opportunity, Fabrizio looked to expand his knowledge of medicinal ingredients—obsessed, as a scholar is obsessed with digging up the long-forgotten etyma of words. He knew that many of his predecessors had, on occasion, failed in their cures. He knew not to use powdered pearls for an affliction of the intestines, for example, as had been done in previous centuries. But in his wisdom he did not pretend he knew everything, as some physicians did. He realized that he would never discover the Philosopher's Stone through arrogance, but through a combination of luck, hard work and humility, with, perhaps, a bit of help from the stars.

Still holding the vial he had bought from the player before his eyes, he realized that his acute vision alone would not be enough. A single sniff or two, however, should tell him its ingredients, unless it held something utterly unforeseen. Occasionally, an unguent or exotic spice arrived from the East by way of Venice or from Africa and proved to contain a secret ester or resin unknown to him.

Before he smelled it, he applied the time-honoured Greek physicians' test. With the ring finger on his left hand, he stirred the contents. The "vein of love" ran from the third finger to the heart. If a concoction was toxic, the doctor would feel it in his heart before administering a dose to the patient. He was mildly surprised to feel a tingling in his chest. But there was nothing unpleasant about it—in fact, it was a delightful feeling, as if he were suddenly overflowing with joy. Removing his ring finger, he was further surprised to feel it throb. Lifting the vial, he sniffed deeply, filling his lungs to their fullest.

At that moment, he thought he heard the nearly imperceptible sound of a bow being drawn across the strings of a violin. He heard it not with his ears but from deep within his chest, a hovering *glissando* vibrating faintly inside him. Then the scents came tumbling through to him in a rush. Many of the usual elements of an everyday aphrodisiac were present, an assemblage of herbs as sweet and bitter as love itself: distinctive caraway, basil, powerful clove, mint, a touch of garlic, nettle, gnarly-rooted ginger, leek (probably for the way the plant looked, rather than for any herbal property), valerian, lovage, mallow, marigold—which also cured bites of all kinds—nutmeg, radish, a touch of rocket, saffron, mustard, sage, summer savory. Perhaps even a bit of dried tiger penis from Cathay. Fabrizio mused that the maker was determined not to miss a single possibility from the entire range of aphrodisiacs. Of course, as an alchemist as well as an herbalist, he knew that much depended on the distillation process. A list of ingredients was simply a list of ingredients.

He paused. *There is something here I do not recognize; some ingredient I have never smelled in all my long days—and it is lovely, head-swimmingly lovely.* He was slightly dizzy from it, and again it afflicted him with a feeling that his heart was overflowing.

He sniffed the elixir again and his head swam. *Absolutely irresistible. What is it? I must know.* Raising the vial to his lips, he took a sip, shuddered and shook his head. *Bitter beyond belief.* He closed his eyes. Again the indescribably faint sound of a violin started up inside his chest. Its source somehow seemed to be not only inside him but high in the heavens as well, as if he were feeling the impossible sound that radiated from the turning of stars and planets and other luminaries, the sound of shooting star, lucida and invisible comet. The music was inconceivably deep inside and inconceivably distant at the same time, and it was moving, turning in an arc, the sound of light moving through space, the sound made by a wind of light, radiant, blazing, luminous, lucific.

## A   DESPERATE   WOMAN

That same night, the duchess lay in bed listening to the rain against the roof of the palace. It was more a dripping than a rainfall—the city was saturated with fog and damp and low-hanging clouds. Next to her, the duke snored from the depths of his sleep. Three times that evening they had made love, partly because they were determined to bring a child into the world and partly because the duke had taken a portion of the aphrodisiac he had bought from the players. Before the third time, he had convinced her to take a taste as well. "Perhaps it will help. In our quest, I mean. Perhaps this small vial has within it a little jinni in the shape of our child. Perhaps it will release something within you that will provide fertile ground for my seed. Let us try."

In any case, the elixir of love had worked its magic. The duke had been insatiable, as had she. But a distinct desperation had entered their lovemaking, and was perhaps even beginning to poison it. Also, she could not help but notice that he had decided, without a doubt, that she was to blame.

And blame herself she did. Her eyes were wet with tears when she thought about her failure to provide the duke with a child despite all the concoctions Don Fabrizio had supplied over the past year. Nothing had worked. All they did was upset her stomach and ruin her appetite. And now there was a hint of madness and frustration in the eyes of the duke when they joined together in their marriage bed.

She listened to the tick of raindrops outside, her eyes wide open, her pillow soaked. It was as if all the sadness of the world and in her heart was in that persistent sound. She ached with sadness and felt that, if she truly let herself go, she could weep a torrent that would rival the River Po. At the same time, the elixir was still working on her. A tingling was radiating out to her limbs from her centre, her heart pounding. Rising from bed, she went to the window, glanced out and decided, despite the weather, that walking was the only way to ward off the power of the drug.

As she threw on a long cape with a hood and headed out the door, past the sleeping guard, she felt the power of the aphrodisiac building again within her. And then she noticed the music. It had been there all along, but so faint that it had gone unremarked. Distant, strange music. Enticing. A music out of heaven. Pulling the hood over her head, she began walking quickly towards the piazza at the heart of Cremona.

## THE CRY OF THE VIOLIN

As Fabrizio trudged along the street, his cowl pulled over his head, it seemed the sky had settled down on the squares and alleys of the city. Moisture penetrated every hidden crevice and corner of Cremona. It was a fog of rain, a rain of fog, a thick mist that darkened the stones of every house and church. It seeped inside the houses, waterlogged the fruits, damped the rice and flour, soddened the tapestries on palace walls, lovers in their beds, the hair and eyelashes of children asleep.

When he halted, he could barely detect that it was raining. He felt a single drop form on the back of his neck under the hairline; it dribbled under his collar and, like a cold finger, slid down his spine to the base, where it was caught by the cloth at his cinctured waist.

He was still hearing the music in his head, the distant sound of a violin, but louder now. Convinced that its source was a workshop or drawing room nearby, and not within himself, he was in search of whoever was playing such indescribable music. The sound, like a drug, captivated him entirely. Like light in water, it passed straight into and through his heart.

He trod on. The fog penetrated his eyes and ears, his thoughts, his dreams. It slicked the ancient violins, well stored in their cases, and the new violins, fresh and green. Penetrated the holy Eucharist and subtly watered down wine in church and tavern. Soaked into history itself, as if it had been raining a thousand years, as if the sun had not appeared since the time of the Etruscans.

Fog coated the marble of the cathedral, moistened the crypts and their skeletons, bathed the heads of the saints on the cathedral's façade and filled up the hollow statue of the prophet Isaiah, trickling out his eyes as if he were weeping for all the lost souls of the world. It dripped inside the Sacred Spine in the cathedral of Cremona, and thinned the Precious Blood of Christ, the relic in the cathedral of nearby Mantua.

Don Fabrizio recalled that his first taste of the elixir had made his head snap back. *Bitter. More bitter than pure extract of almond. More bitter than belladonna.* He had felt his stomach churn instantly with the infinitesimal drop that slipped behind his tongue and down his throat. His head had swirled. He had thought fresh air would help. After ten minutes panting with dizziness by the front door of his house, listening to the indescribably beautiful music, he had returned to the laboratory to take an antidote. He had decided that an antidote was essential, for the music was so enchanting and exquisite that he would have gladly let it take him. *I would willingly die in this music. I would let this music take me to the highest heaven. And something tells me, there I would find also the deepest hell.* He had quickly scanned the hundreds of vials on his shelves. To choose incorrectly could prove fatal, but he felt he must do something or he would fly apart into a million pieces, like the stone sculpture of Saint Michael the Archangel that had fallen from the façade of the cathedral the previous year and shattered on the marble steps.

He had taken a palmful of common rue and hops, washed down with water, but had immediately sensed that they would not be strong enough. In desperation he had tried chervil, which quells bad dreams. Little effect. *Something stronger, something with the kick of a horse. Poisonous henbane. It can lead to hallucinations, sensations of flying.* He had reached for the henbane, hesitated, reached out again.

He had grasped the vial with its bluish-purple contents, uncorked it and taken a healthy swig. In his belly the antidote had swirled in a spiral as if it were searching out the intruder. Sighing, he had relaxed, knowing he would not die. Still the music had come to him, voluptuous, fascinating, light as the sound of an April breeze through lime trees, and yet insistent and inescapable. He had headed out into the grey dusk and fog of the city in search of its source.

Don Fabrizio walked past Niccolò's workshop but it was silent and dark. No one was playing a violin there, or in any of the other workshops or houses he passed. The cathedral and the baptistery too were empty. Still the music ached inside him, ravishing.

Fabrizio halted in the main square and stared at the clock face on the tower next to the cathedral. He rubbed his eyes, shook his head. The four hands of the clock were spinning in circles, turning backwards and forwards through time, clockwise, counterclockwise.

"The music, the music is doing this." Soaked through by the fog, he watched the hands of the painted clock turn forward and back. Somehow the hands of the clock and the music were synchronized.

He looked at his hands. They were the hands of a younger man, not his at all, or his once long ago. The blood surged through him; the music, despite its loveliness, pounded in his head.

At that moment, from high in the heavens, above the clouds, light from the comet fell in long, rainlike strings.

Across the square a woman in a hood, the only other person out in the horrid weather, hurried through the fog and slipped down an alley. He caught her movement out of the corner of his eye and followed. *I am no saint,* he thought, *but this is madness.* His feet moved of their own accord. Ahead of him, she slipped into a narrower, darker alley. He followed. When he was ten steps behind her, she stopped and turned on him. It was the duchess. He thought she looked extraordinarily beautiful. She recognized him, and smiled a smile that seemed to rise out of the depths of her belly. "Oh, Fabrizio, it is you." There was a terrible urgency in her voice. "I . . . I . . . can you help me? Please."

He came closer. "Yes, certainly. What is it?"

"I have done an evil thing. I took a taste of my husband's elixir, the one he bought from the player on the square. I think I am going mad. I have been walking the streets for hours. I am so, so . . ."

"Why did you take it?"

She shook her head. "He asked me to. And I had seen what joy, what pleasure, it gave him in our . . . I need . . ."

Gazing directly into his eyes and taking his arm, she urged him into the deeper shadows under a portico.

At that moment Fabrizio heard the faint music of the violin rising higher and higher. Rain pounded into the abandoned alley as water ran in rivulets between the cracks of paving stones. Fog penetrated everywhere, engulfing the city entirely, the moist air charged and flickering with sparks.

Finally, the cry of the violin broke into pure, blinding light.

## *THE PLAY — ACT TWO*

### THE PLAY BEGINS:
### THE LETTER

On the crowded piazza, the sound of pipes, drums and strings drew the audience closer to the stage, as latecomers, hearing the music, hurried to the square. Those standing at the back raised up on tiptoe and strained to see, while the wealthy, sitting on reed stools near the platform, finished their conversations and looked up in expectation. The musicians concluded and exited the stage.

The audience was on edge, savouring that moment when chattering and fidgeting cease and the play is about to begin. The actors could barely breathe. The packed square was silent; even the youngest child looked on wide-eyed, knowing something was about to happen.

And so it started. Two harlequins in black half-masks edged onto the stage backwards, one from each end. The first carried an umbrella, the other a lantern. They wore long, tight jackets and trousers covered in colourful, odd-shaped patches. Their masks had tiny eyeholes, and a wart on top of the forehead. As they backed up slowly, their behinds touched at centre stage. Both froze and cautiously turned their heads. On seeing each other, they twisted about, stood tall and puffed out their chests.

"I am Arlecchino. My mother had such a lively temperament that she bore me five days after the wedding." He spoke in the dialect of Mantua.

"Five days! What took her so long? My mother bore me a mere three days after her marriage. And listen here, you cannot be Arlecchino. I am."

Arlecchino with the lantern held it close to the other's face. "Why the sunshade?"

"It is a hot day, I like to carry a little shade with me."

"What? Are you a lunatic? It is blackest night, no moon. I am seeking a passing comet—her name is Bella, she has a train two hundred leagues long. Have you seen her?"

The other ignored the question. "Night? It is not— bright as day it is."

"Listen, fool. Look at the clock on the tower." He pointed.

"Clocks. What good are clocks? Repeating the same hours twice a day. One never knows whether it is midnight or noon. Bah, clocks. Look at the sky. Listen to the bells."

"You *are* a lunatic." He raised the lantern. "You look familiar."

"And you."

"Have you ever been to Cremona?"

"We are in Cremona!"

"No, no. This is Mantua."

"If you do not stop disagreeing with me, I'll beat you to within an inch of your life."

"Why stop at an inch? Why not half an inch?" Sunshade Arlecchino pulled a clapper stick from his belt and struck the other on the shoulder. There was a crisp clap as the two halves of the stick smacked together.

They proceeded to club each other a dozen times about the head and shoulders. *Thwack! Thwack!* They went back and forth, each waiting stupidly for the other to have his turn before hitting again.

"Are you dead yet?"

"*Imbecille!* How could I be dead? I'm still standing here like you."

"All right then, we cannot go on like this forever, I might miss supper." At that, swinging the clapper up from below, one whacked the other between the legs, and the crowd groaned in unison with the injured player.

The Arlecchino with the umbrella fell to his knees. Staring down at his crotch, he gasped through gritted teeth,

"Ah, you've scuppered me good this time, you devil." He collapsed, kicked his legs straight out and lay still, continuing to hold the sunshade overhead.

"Hah! No more than half an inch left down there for him, that's the truth. What's this I see?" Bending down, he plucked something out of the other's belt. "A letter?" He peered at it. "Too bad I cannot read. But still, it might prove valuable." Tucking the letter in his belt, he folded it over. The sunshade had tilted. As he exited the stage he straightened it.

Pantalone appeared on stage, an old man scraping at a violin, as the "dead" Arlecchino rolled away. The sound of the instrument squealed and scratched and caused the crowd to cover their ears.

"Ouch, ouch, stop!" shouted the first Arlecchino as he ran back onto stage. "I can't stand the terrible bruising you are giving that instrument. I've heard cats in heat screeching with greater finesse, heard pigs being slaughtered that sang their last tune with greater harmony, heard horses farting more tunefully."

"Enough, enough, I get your point." The old man shrugged. "She loves music. What can I do?"

"Ai-ai-ai. Not that."

Pantalone eyed the letter in the other's waistband. The old man, tall and bent, wore a leather mask with a long hooked nose. He was scrawny, richly dressed in black and red silks, had a thin beard and spoke in a whiny voice. "Arlecchino, where have you been? I have been waiting here an hour. I see you have the letter from Niccolò, the master violinmaker." He pointed to the other's belt. "Give it to me, then. Here's your bezant." He tossed a coin.

The harlequin caught the coin, regarded it with puzzlement and bit it. Pulling the letter from his belt, he stared at that too.

"A single bezant? That's it? For all I went through getting this letter to you? A dozen armed guards waylaid me. I defeated them all, of course, but I was hard put to do it. A second bezant would certainly be fitting, a third most appropriate, a fourth most generous." He bowed.

"Stop your gob or I'll demand you return the first bezant. Master Niccolò's house is not far from here. What are you going on about? There are no blackguards in the streets." He gestured broadly, then poked Arlecchino in the chest. "You are a liar and exceeding slow to boot. I'm surprised I got the letter at all. I would have gone myself but you know I am afraid of missing Aurora's promenade across the square. I never know when she will come, so I must wait here all hours of the night and day. Love makes a man suffer. Indeed, indeed."

Arlecchino handed the letter over. "What's it say?" He leaned closer, looking down at the page open in Pantalone's hands.

"He wants two hundred bezants to make me an instrument guaranteed to win the heart of Aurora. Two hundred bezants! I cannot afford that! I wonder"—he scratched his head—"perhaps he could lend me one."

"Two hundred bezants! I'll get you a suitable violin for far less than that. I know a violinmaker named Ugo in Mantua—I'll get him to do it for you. He's an excellent fellow, highly skilled, if a bit frightening. A hunchbacked dwarf. You should see his dog, a mastiff, huge beyond belief. As big as a horse, bigger than a horse . . ."

"Enough! There are no good violinmakers in Mantua, all the masters are in Cremona."

"Ah, but there you are wrong, old one. Dead wrong. This master can build violins in the dark."

"There's likely to be dog hairs marring the finish."

"You may mock, but you know the Cremona masters will not lend you an instrument, especially not one with such magic. Ugo the Mantuan makes nothing but magic violins, of astonishing power."

"Ugo, you say? If you are lying to me . . ." He shook his scrawny fist.

"No, no, it is the truth, before God. Shall I go to him and make you a deal or not?"

At that moment, a fetching young woman strolled by, ignoring the two men. Pantalone noticed her and with an exaggerated gaze followed the movement of her bum. Adjusting his crotch, he squealed excitably, "Aurora, how lovely to see you on the square this evening. It has been too long, too too long."

"What are you talking about? You were here last night, as you are every night. Have you seen Ottavio? He was to play for me this evening. His music melts my heart."

"No, I have not seen him—I hear he went to Roma, or perhaps Napoli, to look for his brother."

"That is odd. Ottavio has no brother. Ah, there he is . . ."

Ottavio came on stage, an elegant young man of proud bearing, a reddish-gold violin in his hand. He began to play and Aurora swooned, falling backwards into the arms of Pantalone, who turned to Arlecchino: "Get me a violin from that Mantuan. Now!"

The musicians once again took the stage, and a musical interlude ensued to please and relax the crowd. Meanwhile, behind them, Arlecchino passed by on a donkey, its huge ears higher than the harlequin's head. As he rode down the ramp, he shouted to Pantalone, "Wait here, old man! I'm off to Mantua, to Ugo's palace, to seek a violin!"

# CHAPTER FOUR

*His miracles pile up higher and higher, a tower of miracles climbing to heaven. The people believe them, every one. Every miracle is attributed to Fabrizio, their would-be saint. One day every man in the city awoke with the stigmata in his left hand. These signs of Christ's crucifixion had faded by sunset. They said Fabrizio's touch could restore withered plants. He revived a dead goat. He was seen to walk several inches above the ground, and his servant, Omero, would walk next to him holding a rope tied about Cambiati's ankle, to keep him from floating off to the clouds. What am I to make of such levitation, such willingness to believe, such faith?*

## A CHANCE MEETING
## ON THE SQUARE

After another day of steady rain and fog, the skies finally cleared about four-thirty in the afternoon. The sun blazed out and suddenly the main piazza of Cremona filled with housewives heading for bakery and butcher, children chasing each other, young lovers, and older citizens out for a stroll and a conversation, trying to catch the last of the light on this unusually warm spring afternoon.

Across the square, wet patches began to shrink under the late sun, which poured into the end of the piazza by the cathedral and baptistery. The rose window of the duomo, with its eighteen glass petals, glowed as if covered in gold leaf. By five o'clock, it seemed that everyone in the city was in the square, visiting for a few moments before heading home.

A group of young labourers stood about laughing at a crude joke while, nearby, Padre Merisi talked with a trades-man. Elettra and a white-haired woman were wending their way across the square towards the cathedral. As the devil's advocate came down from his rooms for a bit of fresh air, following an afternoon of reading the *positiones* of Fabrizio Cambiati, he saw them.

At first he thought he would approach and say hello, but then he decided to stand and watch from the shadows of the narrow alley between the cathedral and the baptistery. The old lady used a cane and leaned heavily on the arm of the girl.

They seemed to be chatting ceaselessly, leaning their heads close together as they circumambulated the square, interrupting their conversation intermittently to nod to friends and neighbours. The old woman was bent, while Elettra carried herself erect—even from a distance the advocate could sense the girl's elegance, as well as the pride she shared with the old woman. She was young but uncommonly sure of herself.

Finally, as they neared the cathedral steps, inching along, the devil's advocate stepped out of the shadows and Elettra spotted him. She burst into a wide smile that radiated youth and warmth and energy.

"Your Excellency, how delightful to see you."

"Yes, a bit of sun has brought everyone out."

She gazed about. "It's wonderful—and so warm."

"This must be your great-grandmother."

"Yes. May I introduce Maria Andrea, Duchessa di Baldesio."

He nodded.

The old lady looked him up and down. "Your Excellency." He wondered, *Was there a slight mockery in her voice?* Her face was so deeply wrinkled that it appeared as if she had been sliced up with a carving knife but was too dried up and old to bleed. Despite her age and infirmities, she had a patrician way about her.

The *duchessa* gave nothing away with her clouded grey eyes. "Welcome to Cremona. How do you find our fair city?"

"A lovely city indeed. I have not seen much of it, but what I have seen is most pleasing."

"You are being well treated, Your Excellency?" the girl asked.

"Yes, yes. Everyone has been quite helpful. Don Merisi showed me several excellent sculptures and paintings in the cathedral yesterday, including one by the candidate."

"And you have seen the Sacred Spine, our holy relic?" The *duchessa* peered at him.

"Yes. Fascinating." The devil's advocate sensed that they wanted him to be more effusive about their city's famous relic, but his always-present sense of responsibility told him to hold back. Ultimately, he reasoned, he was here in a neutral role, and he insisted on remaining objective, for it was all of a piece: the city's desire for a saint, its civic pride, its belief that its own relic was the most important in Christendom. A typical city in that way, he thought. And even as he hesitated, the girl saw it, saw into and through him.

"Ah, but you must remain objective, yes?" Elettra said. "The making of saints, or perhaps the unmaking of saints, must turn many a friend into an enemy. Do you have many enemies, Your Excellency?"

He looked at the girl. It was a leading, a penetrating, question. One a young woman should not normally be asking a devil's advocate. He looked away, thinking, as she waited for an answer. Before he could reply, the old woman leaned further on the girl and said, "I grow tired, dear. Please, take me home."

They started to leave. Too tired to turn her head and look at him, she gave a weak nod of farewell.

As they moved slowly away, Michele Archenti stared at them. At the edge of the square, the girl tossed a surreptitious look over her shoulder to see if he was still watching. By the look on her face, she seemed both frightened and pleased that he was.

Meanwhile, a Hieronymite priest, in his black hood, stood rigid under the deep portico beneath the town hall and watched. His face was tilted up as if he were taking in the sky and about to venture a prediction on the weather. But a close observer would have seen that his mouth was wide open in a rictus of disgust, his eyes riveted and ablaze, staring not at the heavens but down and across the piazza.

## THE ADVOCATE INTERVIEWS THE OLD DUCHESS

One week after his arrival in the city of Cremona, the advocate began his official interviews with local residents who wished to meet with him concerning the candidacy of Fabrizio Cambiati. One by one the interviewees came to the parlatory, the large outer room of his chambers. The parlatory was at the top of a flight of wide stairs that were entered next to the cathedral, off a corner of the main square. Though panelled in dark wood, the interview room was surprisingly bright, as tall windows overlooking the square let in the sunshine. Or they would have if there had been any sunshine. The first two days of interviews had taken place while clouds again settled low over the city, and a steady drizzle slicked the paving stones of the square.

On the third afternoon, after adding thirteen more interviews to the twenty-one he had conducted in the first two days, the advocate sat next to the hatchet-faced local scribe, named Angelo, and waited. He and the scribe could hear someone scraping up the marble stairs with painful slowness and effort. Just then the sun found a split in the clouds and the room's five tall windows lit up, throwing five parallelograms of light across the floor. The devil's advocate considered the patterns of light, and thought it odd that they changed position with the movement of the sun though no one ever saw them moving. He thought for a moment of Copernicus and wondered. *It seems obvious the sun moves about the earth, does it not? Can we not believe our own eyes?* At that moment the *duchessa* appeared at the door, on the arm of the doorkeeper, and the advocate motioned her in.

The woman was ancient, covered from head to toe in black. She tottered into the interview room, leaning heavily on her pearwood cane. Monsignor Archenti was astounded that she could get about on her own at all.

The Jesuit sat behind a heavy wooden table. Next to him, Angelo waited to record the woman's responses to a list of formal questions the devil's advocate would ask. The list of questions constituted the official interrogatory prepared by specialists in the Holy See, based on written testimony by the local bishop and others who were testifying to the virtues of Fabrizio Cambiati.

Each of the thirty-four witnesses to this point had faced the same questions about the life and possible sanctity of the candidate. Each had praised the man, had spoken of his many miracle cures—which Monsignor Archenti considered mere medical treatments, nothing miraculous about them. Few had experienced these miracles themselves, but quoted family stories passed down over the years. None of these rang true to the advocate's practised ear. Like a well-trained musician, he could tell when a single note was off.

At one point the previous day, after a number of interviews were completed, the scribe had turned to him. "What do you think, Your Excellency? Perhaps it is not my place to ask, but to this point do you believe he was a saint?"

"I have heard nothing to convince me beyond doubt."

Monsignor Archenti nodded now to the old woman as she carefully lowered herself into the seat before him. With one hand placed over the other like a bird-claw on top of the cane, she stared at him, unblinking and unsmiling. She held her chin up and, although seated below, seemed to look down at him with her calm, steady gaze.

"Has it been explained that I will ask a series of formal questions, the official interrogatory from the Sacred Congregation for Rites, about the candidate for sainthood, one Fabrizio Cambiati of Cremona; questions which you will answer to the best of your ability?"

"*Sì.*" She gave a quick nod and seemed prepared.

"What is your name?"

In a voice like the rustle of dry straw, she said, "My name is *la duchessa madre* Maria Andrea di Baldesio."

"What is your age?"

"I am ninety-five. Very old, yes?"

"Yes." Monsignor Archenti smiled. "And how old were you when you first knew the candidate?"

"I was a young child. The holy Fabrizio was always there, as far back as I can remember. But the first time I recall seeing him, I believe I was about five years of age. I was walking with my mother and I asked her why the man ahead of us in the square was glowing. She could not see it but my child's eyes could. Then, as I grew older, I no longer saw the glow about him—I believe his radiance had not faded, but I myself had changed and had lost the ability to see what was there."

"I understand. And the last time you saw the candidate?"

Pausing, she took on the blank look—her eyes like cloudy water—of the old remembering the distant past. "It was at his funeral, a great funeral in the cathedral. The whole city attended. All the bells were ringing. It was not long after the birth of my daughter. No one seemed particularly sad that day. In fact, there was great joy in the air."

"I see. Thank you. Now, have you read the Articles of Testimonial Proof of the Servant of God? The document that was delivered to you several weeks ago?"

"My eyes, Your Excellency, can no longer see to read. I was not able to read it myself."

"Did someone read it to you?"

"Yes, my great-granddaughter, Elettra."

"Good. Then you know what was in the document?"

She shrugged. "It was read to me. Yes."

"Do you have any other information to supply that is not contained in these articles?"

"Oh yes, much."

"Please state clearly what other information you would like to contribute."

"Yes, of course. Let me see—where to begin? I will begin at the end—at his funeral just mentioned, which, as I said, was attended by a great crowd in the duomo. All the citizens of Cremona, and many others besides. After the funeral mass, when I came out into the piazza, I noticed a bird—I believe it was a swallow, the bird with the split tail—hovering just above the roof of the palazzo across the square. It seemed to be staring straight at me, and continued to hover there, not landing, as if it wanted me to notice it. I looked at it and the bird squawked once, then flew towards the sun. The bird was Fabrizio."

"Did anyone else see this?"

"No. I felt the swallow was a private affair, a personal moment between myself and the soul of Fabrizio."

"Let me clarify, please. You thought the bird was the soul of the candidate?"

She nodded.

"I see. Anything else?"

"Oh, there are so many things, but things that perhaps I alone saw and not others, not others. You see, Your Excellency, so much has to do with the looking, what is in the heart of the one looking—that also determines what one will see."

"Yes, yes." He nodded impatiently and motioned for her to continue.

"There was another time, outside the city. I was on my way to Milano in our carriage. I saw Fabrizio walking in a field. I told my driver to halt and I watched him in the distance. He was nearly covered with tiny white butterflies as he walked waist-deep in the high grass. He seemed to be shimmering and floating, like an angel. He looked like an angel."

"Did the driver see this?"

"I do not know. Our old driver has been dead now many years."

"I know not what to make of birds and butterflies, but let us move along. Have you any information concerning the early life of Fabrizio Cambiati, other than that which is supplied in the articles?"

"No. I know nothing of his early life. He was in his middle years when I knew him."

"Do you have any knowledge, personal or otherwise, of evidence of a religious vocation on the part of Fabrizio Cambiati?"

"He was a good priest and a good man. Both—as you know, I am sure, Your Excellency—are as rare as grins from a bull."

The advocate smiled at this. "Ah, but was he a saint? That is the question I am trying to answer."

She shrugged. "He always did for people what they needed, no matter what."

"How often were you in contact personally with Fabrizio Cambiati?"

"We spoke on occasion. He heard my confession many times."

Angelo coughed into a handkerchief. The devil's advocate paused and waited until he was finished. Turning back to the woman, he continued.

"Do you know anything of the relationship that existed between Fabrizio Cambiati and his parents or his siblings?"

"No. I believe both his parents died before I was born. I did not know his brothers and sisters. I believe his father owned a small stand of mulberry trees and a silkworm hut on the outskirts of a nearby village. They were silk-makers. That is the full extent of my knowledge."

"Do you know if Fabrizio Cambiati considered well the virtues of faith, hope and charity? If not, where did he fail in the practice of the virtues?"

The *duchessa* rested both hands on top of her cane, and stared at the stone floor as if transfixed.

"Did you hear the question, *duchessa?*"

She did not look up. "I am thinking on it. I am an old, old woman, Your Excellency, the memories do not come back so quickly. And I do want to put things in the correct manner." She lifted her gaze to a high corner of the room. "I believe he was a lonely man. Like any priest. Like you yourself, perhaps, Your Excellency. I am also sure that he was not found wanting, in any serious way. I believe he had great faith. As for hope, I have no idea what was in his mind on the matter. What does this mean, hope? Do you mean did he dream of entering Paradise? I do not believe that was on his mind. He was a man of this world, *this* world." She pounded her cane once on the floor and the sun, seemingly in response, came out again and lit up the room.

"On the other hand, I believe charity is an easy virtue to measure. In the realm of charity he was most unusual—he gave of his talents, mixing his unguents and liniments for the sickly and helping people in every possible way, with no thought to his own condition or safety."

"Can you recall any of his good works?"

"Oh, they were legion. I am sure others have told you of them. But Fabrizio Cambiati was about more than good works. He embodied goodness. Do you understand? It felt good just to be in his presence. He was not a slave to the mere words of charity. He lived them, Your Excellency. He would even endanger his own life and his own chances for eternal salvation to fulfill the needs of others."

The devil's advocate was well trained to react to the subtlest cues, to see into the heart of his respondents, to glimpse the genuine truth hidden among the desires and longings of the faithful for a saint to call their own. At this last comment from the *duchessa* he leaned forward, sensing a slit, an opening into a region hitherto shrouded in darkness. His eyes seemed to grow blacker. "How so? How precisely did he endanger his chances for eternal salvation?"

The old lady turned to the side, as if gazing into the distance. "Some secrets are best kept."

"Ah, but there you are wrong. We must have no secrets, none at all, when it comes to the trial of a candidate for sainthood."

"Your Excellency"—she gave him an imperious look, a sly half-smile on her face—"without secrets the world would die."

"Doubtful. In any case, I cannot report to my superiors that the testimony surrounding Fabrizio Cambiati was a nest of secrets. It would be unacceptable to the Church authorities and, dear lady, it would be unacceptable to me."

"But you have no choice, Your Excellency. You will never know everything about this man—how could you know all there is to know about any man, especially one who was a priest? Clerics are drawn to be clerics precisely because of their interest in secrets."

"Do you refer to the confidences of the confessional, *duchessa?*"

"That, of course, and other, perhaps more deeply felt secrets that exist only in the mind and heart. Secrets that do not need confessing, that do not need forgiveness, secrets that will remain forever unspoken. Look into yourself, Your Excellency. Do you not have at least one secret inside you?"

Monsignor Archenti worried at the direction the interrogatory was taking—he wished to avoid a long philosophical dialogue with the wily *duchessa,* who, he could clearly discern, would lead him down a thousand different dead ends to avoid divulging a secret which she had as much as told him she was withholding.

"Let us move along then," he said, as authoritatively as he dared. "There are many more questions to pose, and but one short lifetime in which to pose them."

She took the gentle rebuke with a smile. "Yes, of course, let us go on."

By the end of the long day's interrogatory, after the *duchessa* had left, the devil's advocate felt he was no closer to the truth than before. He stood at the window of his room, gazing out over the roofs of the city. Again the sun was hidden above the grey, though the clouds were imbued with a faint golden glow, and the few streaks of falling rain seemed edged in gold. He marvelled at the depth of love people felt for Cambiati, even those who had never met him but knew his good acts only through tales from their older relatives. The stories of his cures were not imaginary, but genuine signs of generosity and profound charity. Many of the Cremonesi already considered him a saint and prayed to him daily. Dozens of the faithful claimed miracles attributed to his intercession, but few if any of these were definitive. The devil's advocate was unsure whether Fabrizio Cambiati should have his own church in every city of Christendom or if he should be burned at the stake *in absentia* for his alchemical delusions. *I know how the cardinals would respond to these thoughts: You must decide. As devil's advocate, it is your duty, your responsibility. Mother Church cannot abide ambiguity. You must decide.*

As grey pearls of rain slid down the window, Michele Archenti was overwhelmed again by the same feelings of doubt he had experienced in the carriage on his way to Cremona. Thinking of the cardinals had reminded him of the terrible state of things in Rome. He knew that Pope Benedict was gravely ill, perhaps dying, in fact. If the pontiff died, everything could change quickly. Even at this distance, he sensed that something ugly was happening there. Something he did not like. Yet he felt no desire to hurry back. *Perhaps I should write to Neri. My old friend will be sure to set my mind at ease.*

The advocate decided to brave the rain. Throwing on his cloak and hat, he descended the stairs. As he entered the piazza and crossed it, he never noticed the girl about to enter the cathedral. Elettra stopped in the darkness just inside the doors and watched Archenti pass, her eyes slipping down his form from head to toe and slowly up again.

## LETTER TO AN OLD FRIEND IN ROME

*Dearest Carlo,*
*God's blessings upon you, my friend. I trust you are healthy and are having less rain in Rome than we are getting here in Lombardy, where the weather has been exceedingly damp. I also fervently hope your work is going well and has progressed beyond your expectations.*

*As you know, for the past month or so, I have been in the city of Cremona, investigating the candidacy of one Fabrizio Cambiati. The case has only begun and yet already I am haunted by it. The candidate appears to have been quite the performer of miracles (if his fellow citizens are to be believed) and yet possibly he was an alchemist as well. But I am not writing to you this morning to burden you with the details of my work.*

*We have had no word here about good Benedict, only that his ill health continues. I trust we will hear quickly if the Lord takes him.*

*I write to you as a friend and confidant. Since starting this case, I must admit to being assailed by doubts. I will continue to do my duty here and yet I feel that there are things afoot in Rome that demand my attention. Is Cozio beginning to position himself to become the next pope? I feel it and I also feel it would be a disaster, for me, for the Jesuits, for the state of the Church. We Jesuits are already under attack in France, Spain and Portugal. My head spins and my stomach churns at the possibility of Cardinal Cozio as our pontiff.*

*After Benedict, it would be a nightmare of immeasurable proportions. Why do I feel suddenly as if the world is flying apart? Am I exaggerating, good friend? I feel there is a sense of apocalypse in the air, of end times, and I am sick at heart.*

*On top of everything else, there is a young woman here, the daughter of the duke, who has made me feel as if I myself have stepped off the edge of the earth.*

*Anything is possible these days, my friend, anything.*
*Please hasten to let me know how things stand there.*
*I thank you for your always sympathetic ear.*

*Blessed Be God Our Lord.*
*Monsignor Michele Archenti, Promotor Fidei*

Before sealing it, the advocate read through the letter again. He thought he must have been mad to include the line about the girl. He didn't even recall writing it, and marvelled that he could have carelessly stated something so bald and damning. He decided to rewrite the letter in its entirety, leaving out the line that referred to Elettra, and he was careful to burn the first version.

## THE ADVOCATE HATCHES A PLAN

As the devil's advocate, Monsignor Archenti was forced to put himself in the position of one who must think as Satan would think—with the slyness and duplicity of Beelzebub. When first appointed to his position, he had been uncomfortable with this, for he knew that it posed a considerable danger. One could mistakenly develop certain black skills, and the temptation to put such skills to use would be great. Nearly overpowering.

Like many an intellectual, however, he had a significant weakness—pride. He was sure he would recognize it if he was drifting into sin, but he did not see that there was no guarantee he would realize the power of temptation before it was too late. Perhaps, among those of great pride, a display of weakness or failure is the saving grace.

In the case of the *duchessa,* he was convinced she was withholding something pertinent to his investigation. He had his suspicions about what it was, but as an advocate he needed definite proof; he could not rely on guesswork, no matter how experienced he was at divining the truth. Nevertheless, he had the wisdom to see that the *duchessa* would take the secret to her grave. *A wily and determined old woman, of a sort I have come across on occasion. She will not bend. But perhaps there is another way to get at the truth.*

Elettra and her great-grandmother were the best of friends—he had seen them walking the streets of Cremona arm in arm, had noticed them on the central piazza watching a *commedia dell'arte* play from rush stools near the stage. He had noted how, when walking together on the piazza or during the play, the *duchessa* would lean over and whisper to the girl, who would nod at these confidences. He wondered if he could not perhaps find a way to convince the girl to divulge the old woman's secrets. He smiled to himself at this possibility.

From high in the heavens, unbeknownst to the advocate, the comet, with infinite subtlety, insinuated its faint light into the heart of Michele Archenti.

### T H E   M A N T U A N ' S   D R E A M

In such a world as this—with comets, miracles and saints all compounding the complex alchemy of the heart—it is clear that the limits of the theatre are inseparable from the limits of the imagination, and that the world of the theatre reaches into every corner of the real world. Thus it was that the audience could see Arlecchino riding for Mantua, his donkey moving along at a steady clip. Arlecchino was excited. He kicked his legs out with excitement. He could smell money, and he sensed that there could be more of it for him before this entire affair was concluded. But he also feared Ugo, the violinmaker of Mantua. Strange Ugo in his vast and empty palace. Mantua loomed in the distance. Arlecchino could see the dark palace, and his heart sank. But he could smell the money. He kicked the donkey's sides and hurried on.

Ugo the Mantuan, thick-lipped, hunchbacked, his mastiff at his side, trudged the rooms of his vast and exfoliating palace. Each time he came to a room where he had previously seen a doorway leading out, he was discouraged to find that his longed-for exit had vanished and in its place had appeared another set of five or eight or possibly even thirteen rooms he did not recognize, which must have been constructed since his dream had begun, numberless years before. He noticed that his thoughts too reflected the complexity of the maze, for he could not form a decent, simple, perfectly understandable sentence in his own head because the words were constructed of fear and sadness and they wouldn't join together like good bricks for building but kept being interrupted and crossed over by other sentences that began in the middle and continued on and on and never seemed to come to an end, or at least an exit, a waking from this lost wandering in a palace without limit and without egress.

Occasionally he would find a way out and, in an act of dark foreboding will, he would tear himself from his palace for a few days—to visit the evil one-eyed bishop in nearby Verona, or to attend a play in the square of Cremona. But then he would always be drawn back to his cocoon, to the heavy atmosphere that repeatedly seduced him.

This was his city. A palace of over five hundred rooms, with endless corridors and courtyards, some views mere *trompe l'oeil* frescoes painted with the most recent discoveries of perspective, and so utterly realistic that he was continually fooled into thinking that he was looking out on the world when, in fact, he was gazing into the imagination of an unknown artist who had wielded his brush with uncanny accuracy. Each of the hundreds of windows offered a limited view of the constricted, geometric gardens, or claustrophobic vantages onto other wings of the palace.

The walls of the rooms were entirely covered with frescoes—in colours fresh or faded, depicting scenes of battle and lovemaking and courtly events. In some rooms the paintings had not yet dried; in others they were already flaking with age.

Newly painted frescoes were drying up and disappearing like a water stain on stone after the sun comes out, while portions of others seemed to have appeared in bands of light even as the Mantuan entered the room with his dog at his side. If he halted, silencing the echo of his footsteps, he could hear other older frescoes peeling off and falling like dry snow onto the marble floors.

He saw no workmen, no painters, no one. Ugo was alone in his palace and his city. A distant relation of the famous horse-loving Gonzagas of Mantua, he had the wary eyes and sensual lips seen in the statues of Francesco Gonzaga, whose family had ruled Mantua for three hundred years, and although this was the palazzo of the Gonzagas he wandered through, it was his own palace and no other—a maze he was dreaming, a dream called Mantua.

The motto of the Gonzagas was "Hostile only to wild beasts," and it was said the family had an unnatural fondness for horses and dogs. Our Mantuan, with his congenital Gonzagan hunchback, was trailed by his huge mastiff through the flaking rooms of the palace, the animal's nails clicking on the marble floors with the authority and persistence of a clock. Although the mud-brown dog with its studded collar was almost the size of a year-old colt, this Gonzaga, this Mantuan, was no lover of horses.

### THE BURDEN OF THE HUMP

Arlecchino stood before Ugo the Mantuan, who sat at a table, his mastiff next to him. Ugo stroked the beast's ears. "Tell me, fool—are you still in the play or are you now in the world?"

"Both."

"How can this be?"

"It is a question of imagination."

"You ask a lot of imagination."

"It is a malleable instrument. It lets us make what we will of the world." A look of doubt crossed Ugo's face. Arlecchino continued. "Let us take the player, for example. While he is a player, does he not remain a man under his mask? And while a man, does not something of the player remain?"

"I suppose. But let us cease these games with words. Why have you come?"

"A fellow named Pantalone seeks a violin—a special violin. One that he can use to counter the power of Ottavio's fine instrument."

"To what purpose?"

"The seduction of Aurora, of course."

"I see. And what will this Pantalone pay for such a violin?"

"A fair and just price, I am sure." Arlecchino nodded several times, and tried to control his excitement at the thought that he could make a small fortune on this exchange.

Ugo stood up from the table and approached a fresco on the wall. He saw a bit of skin from the back of a soldier's hand peel off and drift down. Suddenly he turned. Arlecchino was there, gazing at his hump. "Why do you stare, fool? What do you think is inside this hump?"

The player shrugged. "I know not. Meat? Fat? Gristle?"

"No, no." He shook his head sadly. "I am like a woman big with child. A child not of the future but of the past. I bear the burden of the Gonzagas in this hump—my family, my name."

They stood in a room whose walls depicted scenes of torture. "Look at them." Ugo gestured at the frescoes. "Look."

Arlecchino gaped at a row of men—men of the Bonacolsi family, defeated hundreds of years before by the Gonzagas—hanging in the air, their hands behind them and tied to rings in the ceiling of a columned arcade. Several had their throats slit; one's entrails dangled from his belly, corkscrewing down to the floor. Gonzaga soldiers stood about talking, looking a little bored. Outside the arcade a small white horse could be seen, its nostrils flaring, its eyes wide. It seemed as if the horse longed to run away but was staying out of fascination at the powerful smell of blood. Unused to scenes of violence, Arlecchino shuddered.

"I do not like this room."

"I know. I know." The Mantuan stroked the bone-hard head of the mastiff leaning against him. The dog's pink slab of a tongue lolled out between its teeth as it panted.

Ugo stared at the dog. When he raised his eyes to the scene on the wall, he seemed to be thinking of something else. "That violin, the one Ottavio played—Master Niccolò made it, did he not?"

Arlecchino nodded.

Ugo paused, thinking. "How do you suppose he was able to imbue his violin with such power? It seemed to glow with power."

"You know Master Niccolò?"

"Yes, yes. Everyone knows of him. Tell me about the violin. Tell me, how did he infuse it with such power?"

"The music. The music gave it power. This seems to be true of many of his violins."

"Yes." Ugo looked into the palm of his hand and folded it into a fist. "And yet there was something about that one—so lustrous, a mother-of-pearl radiance to it, like the skin of a young girl. It had an attraction. A powerful attraction."

"That is why they call him the Master."

"The Master," he scoffed. "Like any other simpleton, he must bow to his customers, grovel at the feet of dukes and counts—lesser men and women, fools and hypocrites. A great artist should have great pride—once my work is executed, I never change a thing."

Arlecchino shook his head. "So long as it improves the instrument's voice in the end—that is what they say—the Master only cares about the music."

"Bah! A fool, like so many others. Not a true artist. When I finish an instrument, it stays finished. It is complete, never again in need of change. It is mine, perfection."

"You will make a violin then? For the lovestruck Pantalone? You have decided?"

"Yes, yes I will. A masterpiece to crown an old man's lust. It will produce music to make him dream he is young again." He paced as he looked at the wall. He was staring at the white horse in the fresco, fear stretching its eyes wide. Next to him, the mastiff growled as a string of drool slid from the side of its mouth to the floor.

## THE HIERONYMITE PRIEST
## ATTACKS THE PLAY

Near the stage on the square, the devil's advocate sat on a rush stool next to Duke Pietro. Nearby sat the Duchess Francesca, as well as the elderly *duchessa madre* and Elettra, in an area reserved for the wealthy patrons of Cremona and the local clergy. The players were in the midst of a musical interlude when an outcry came from a man standing at the rear of the crowd.

He shouted each word clearly, his mouth wide, his fist shaking in the air. "Work of the Devil! Good people of Cremona—stop up your ears against this evil! Do not be tempted by Satan's babble. Cease! Cease. This. Infernal. Music!"

The crowd surrounding the man edged away, leaving him alone, still roaring and foaming as spit flew from his mouth. It took the musicians a few moments to realize what was happening, but when they did they stopped scraping their violins and pulled the horns from their mouths and stood gazing out in perplexity.

Monsignor Archenti rose to his feet to gain a better view of the man over the crowd. "He's a priest. Who is it?" he asked the duke, who had remained seated, a peeved look on his face.

The duke flicked his hand at the air as if to dismiss a bothersome trifle. "Padre Attilio Bodini. A Hieronymite priest and fresco painter of the Church of Santo Sigismundo. The order has a small chapter house there. A most troublesome fellow. Always showing up at entertainments such as this, to wreck what little joy people can take from their lives. I will have my men remove him." He stood and signalled to a nearby guard, who started making his way through the crowd towards the priest, his sword swaying at his side. Meanwhile the priest continued with his harangue, turning incoherent.

The duke explained further. "Unfortunately, he has gathered a small following among the simpler peasants and townsfolk. If he weren't a priest I would have him jailed— or perhaps exiled. Excuse me, Your Excellency, but our clerics always seem to be indulging in one extreme or the other. They are either hypocritical libertines or maniacal purists."

"And which do you judge me to be?"

The duke gave him a hard, unwavering glare. "I do not yet know. Our acquaintance has been too short-lived for me to form an opinion. And yet I am a man of the world, Your Excellency, and my experience tells me that one or the other will surface, with time."

"You tread on dangerous ground, Your Grace."

"Forgive me, Your Excellency, this troublemaker of Santo Sigismundo has me in a foul mood. I mean no insult to you, the good order of Jesuits, nor Mother Church." He stood and bowed.

Although the devil's advocate nodded back, suggesting that he was granting forgiveness, he doubted the duke's sincerity. Moreover, he was troubled by the grain of truth in what he had said. The duke interrupted his thoughts. "By the way, Your Excellency, how goes the investigation of the candidate?"

"It goes," the advocate said, without smiling.

The duke turned and, seeing that the Hieronymite priest had been removed, with a gesture ordered the musicians to resume playing.

## EVIL AT THE STABLES

Ugo the Mantuan sat at a long wooden table laden with platters of roast meat and oiled bread, slabs of cheese and goblets of wine. Arlecchino sat across from him, gnawing on a leg of mutton, his chin glistening with grease, his costume stained with red wine and globs of fat. "Tell me, Mantuan. Earlier, why did you stare so fixedly at the horse in the painting?"

"Arlecchino, you are indeed a fool. Yes, I was staring at the horse. I have great need of a young white horse."

The player burped and lost a partially chewed piece of meat. As he attempted to catch it before it disappeared beneath the table, he knocked his plate of food into his lap. He looked up. "Why?"

"I have been thinking about it. This Niccolò is like any other violinmaker—the genuine secrets of his craft will go with him to the grave, so I will never learn how he has made a violin with such power. But I know now how I will treat *my* violin, how I will give it a power dark enough to oppose his."

Arlecchino sat entranced, his mouth hanging open, the half-chewed leg in his hand. "But why do you need a white horse?"

"Not any white horse, fool." Ugo picked up a chop with his fingers and began to chew on it. "There is in Cremona a stable belonging to the duke. In this stable there is a horse, and this horse has a perfect white foal that belongs to his daughter."

"But why this white horse?"

"Because not just any will do. Listen to me—over the years, I have made innumerable violins. And I am a master of the black arts. For this violin, my most perfect, my darkest creation, I must have something taken in revenge from an innocent source. And in this case, it is the eyes of fear I want from that little horse. This violin will be my greatest work—it will have a voice so black it will set even saints and angels to rutting in the streets. Do you understand? Do you?"

"Revenge? Why revenge?"

Ugo turned and considered a *trompe l'oeil* window. "I have a history with that family. Long ago, they wronged me. I, a man from the greatest family of Mantua. They laughed at me. I loved one of their daughters. I gathered the courage to express my love to the paterfamilias."

"The present duke?"

"No, his father. He laughed at my request. 'A hunchback,' he spat. 'With my daughter?' He then offered me a position as official dwarf to entertain the girl. I took it. And I've been planning to exact my revenge ever since."

Arlecchino filled his goblet, spilling wine on the table. "I see."

"At last." Ugo yawned. "Later tonight we will leave for Cremona, and the stables of the duke. It is sometimes difficult for me to leave this palace—but you will help lead me out."

While the city of Cremona and its inhabitants sank into the ink of their dreams, two bent figures hurried from one shadow to another, paused, hurried again. Behind them, one of the duke's guards lay on the ground next to the bloodied club used to knock him senseless.

The pair of silhouettes rounded a corner and entered the courtyard facing the stables of the duke. One carried a wooden bucket with a rope handle. From the deeper shadows ahead, a dog growled. Ugo's mastiff leapt forward silently and a moment later the guard dog lay dead, its neck snapped.

Arlecchino leaned close and whispered, "I won't watch what you are about to do. I cannot."

"Shut up!" hissed Ugo.

He eased open the door to the stables, and several horses shifted in the night at the unusual sounds and smells. The hunchback hurried down the central passageway, opening stall doors and peering in.

"Here. Here!" In the dimness, he motioned broadly to Arlecchino to come. "Bring the bucket."

The white foal stood in the stall, hay gathered about its feet. It turned nervously when Ugo entered. With the faint sound of sifting sand, he drew the long knife from a sheath in his belt. He did not hesitate. Pushing the foal's head up and back, he exposed the long fine neck. The animal's eyes were suddenly large with fear. In a single clean sweep, he slit the little horse's neck clear through.

Arlecchino clapped his hands over his ears at the soft thud of the horse's head falling onto the straw. Blood spurted from the severed neck as the foal collapsed.

Moments later, Ugo knocked his fist on Arlecchino's skull to rouse him. "*Andiamo.*" The hand holding the bucket, his sleeves and shirtfront were soaked in blood. The player's head swam.

"You got what you needed?" Arlecchino asked.

"Yes." He held up the bucket and the fool peered in. With his fist in his mouth, he stifled a scream on seeing, at the bottom of the bucket, the horse's eyes.

Retracing their steps, they dissolved into the shadows, finding their way to the gates of the city and out to the countryside, where Ugo's driver waited with the carriage. They hurried back to Mantua, Ugo urging the driver to whip the horses harder as they sped along the road.

Ugo spent several days in his laboratory, a windowless room in a forgotten wing of his palace.

"I will employ a special solution to draw the fear from the foal's eyes," he had explained. "This I will refine to its purest essence, and will apply, with other mixtures, to my violin. You will see, fool. It will be a violin beyond imagining. A great work. My name will be known in all the capitals of Europe, and this Niccolò, this so-called Master, will be a nobody. A nobody!"

Arlecchino waited outside the door on a stool, the mastiff at his feet. Sometimes he talked to the dog. Sometimes he was silent and waited without thinking. Across the room, a peeling fresco depicted a battle scene from long ago. Staring at it, he saw a single, white, full-grown horse. In a confusion of time, he wondered if this was perhaps the horse the foal would have become. He felt sad and ashamed. *But it is done now—what can I do?* He did not believe that the hunchback was a truly evil man. He had seen what he could do with his hands in shaping a beautiful instrument. He had seen him treat the mastiff with tenderness, stroking its head and whispering endearments to it. He knew it was the hump that made the Mantuan do evil things, the forces of his history and the past that weighed on him and made him believe that nothing could ever change.

The hunchback was driven by fate to play his role, as was Arlecchino.

# CHAPTER FIVE

*The accounts of his miracles grow more and more outrageous, as if the people are competing with each other to tell the most outlandish tales. The stories of Cambiati's doings appear to run through the population like a plague. He was seen in the middle of the night, sitting on the steps of the cathedral, listening to an angel play the violin, and weeping. A silk garment he had worn turned back into silk moths that flew off into the sky. He was said to make huge cathedrals appear in odd places but only for a day: deep among the fields, under the waters of the Po, floating among the clouds. The miracles are so diffuse and persistent, I begin to suspect some of them may actually be true.*

## DEMONS AND DEVILS

"Demons! Devils!" The shriek came from the near-toothless mouth of a servant woman from the household of the duke and duchess. The woman was running across the square, her scarf askew, her face a mask of horror.

*What in the world?* The advocate, hearing her, moved to the window of his room and looked down on the piazza, cross-hatched with early-morning light and shadows. He saw a woman scurrying madly about, screaming as a dozen people, then two dozen, then three, hurried to the square at the sound of the growing tumult. A frenzied outcry was building as more and more of the citizens of Cremona arrived and heard the news.

The advocate resisted rushing down into the crowd, and continued watching. Soon a hundred people had gathered, wailing and gesticulating. From his window he saw the crowd divide to allow the duke passage as he strode out of a narrow street and into the square, followed a few feet behind by Elettra, her head bowed. In his right hand he held out, at shoulder-height, the severed, eyeless head of a small white horse.

*Dio mio!* The devil's advocate hurried down and into the crowd, which was in an uproar, several men shouting that it was the work of devils. "Demons, witches!" screamed the Hieronymite priest, who was already there, whipping the crowd into a froth of anger and hysteria.

As two men placed the body of the dead stable guard on the ground behind him, the duke, grasping the horsehead by its mane, lifted it higher. "Whoever did this will pay with his life!"

The Hieronymite screamed back from the crowd, "This is what comes of your lascivious ways, of a life of wallowing in sin!" No one in the crowd knew if he meant the duke himself or the citizens of Cremona in general. They shifted uneasily.

Just then, a boy of fourteen, with one shrivelled ear and a dirty face, wandered into the piazza, drawn by the commotion. His name was Bruno and he was widely known as an orphan and a thief, living off handouts and garbage left in the streets after market days. Everyone knew he had stolen several candlesticks from the cathedral the previous month. He had been caught by Don Merisi and beaten by the duke's men as punishment.

A stocky, middle-aged groom who worked in the duke's stables saw Bruno and pointed. "Last night—I saw him near the rear of the palace. The wretch must have been plotting to enter the stables."

The crowd quickened into a frenzy, women wailing, men glaring at the boy. A servant woman pushed Bruno, who was shocked to be singled out. The Hieronymite grabbed him and shoved him towards the duke, and the boy fell to his knees. Instantly everyone remembered seeing the boy with a long knife. They had no doubt that he had killed the horse and the guard. The duke, raging, pulled Bruno up by the hair and shook him like a stook of straw. Someone appeared with a rope. "Hang him!" a man shouted. "Hang him, hang the devil!" the crowd shrieked.

"I have done nothing!" The boy quaked, his eyes wide. "Nothing!"

The duke pushed Bruno to two of his men, who gripped his arms while a rope was readied. The duke flung the rope over a flag standard above the entrance to the town hall. "I did nothing!" the boy screamed again. He was shaking uncontrollably, his eyes wild with fear. Just then, the devil's advocate, who had been watching from the back of the crowd but not taking part, saw Elettra step forward.

"Father," she said. "Father," she repeated, gaining his attention. "Stop this, I beg of you. There is no reason to believe Bruno did this evil thing. Please, Father, let him go. The boy is innocent."

The duke looked at her, the rope in his hand. "How do you know this, my daughter? What proof have you?"

"I have looked into my heart. The proof is here in my heart. I know him to be innocent."

The duke's face wrinkled in confusion. Her answer confounded him. He looked away and sighed. Turning back to her, he saw the look on her face—a look of sadness and pleading—and all the anger drained from him. The crowd went silent and the men released the boy, who disappeared down a nearby alley.

Elettra's eyes were wet and dark and she stood alone as the crowd dispersed. Before he headed back to his rooms, the advocate turned and stared at her—she stood, head bowed, perfectly still. Lonely and yet innocently powerful. *Why did she say the proof was in her own heart, and not that of the boy?* The advocate shook his head. *As if she wanted to confuse her father, to cut through his anger, to stop his mind in its tracks with a comment that held no logic.* He saw the girl look up into the blank distance; her face, gentle with sorrow, also displayed a resolve, a hardness, in her eyes and the taut line of her jaw. *She looks like a saint*, he thought, *a sad and beautiful saint.*

## THE DISEASE OF PESTILENTIAL AIRS

A day of interviews, followed by an unsatisfactory meal of overcooked calf liver slathered in butter, and several hours of reading, had fatigued the advocate. Since his eyes kept closing as he reread the same paragraph over and over in the *positiones,* he decided to head down the wide marble stairs and into the piazza for a few breaths of fresh air. The entire city seemed on edge with the recent killings. And he realized that the atmosphere of unease was affecting him as well. It made him think of Rome, and how the cloud from that place seemed to have followed him to this fair city. As he placed the manuscript in his desk, he spotted the cerement cloth of Fabrizio Cambiati and shoved it in his pocket.

Moments later, as he came down into the piazza, his head was spinning with his worries about Rome and what

was happening there without his presence. He sensed something terrible going on, and felt as if his legs had been cut out
from beneath him. He had no ground to stand on.

The round moon's single eye glared down from heaven,
a full complement of stars circling it above the city. Across the
piazza, a hundred puddles from an earlier rain reflected the
moon, and when a humid breeze blew through, it set everything to shimmering. All was flux. Suddenly the stars were
spinning in place as well as arcing across the sky. Everything
was flying apart, moving, above as below. A smoke-coloured
bird the size of a raven landed on the cathedral step a yard in
front of him. It walked back and forth, its beak opening and
closing, but no sounds came forth. With its glossy black eye,
the bird stared at him. It was unnerving. Then another breeze
lifted the bird and it flew away. *Like a puff of dark smoke from
the conclave of cardinals,* he thought. And he knew at that
moment with uncanny sureness: *Benedict is dead. The pope
is dead.*

Archenti felt a quiver of doubt, the first slight shimmer
of the earth before an earthquake hits. He stumbled about the
square, hardly knowing where he was.

He found himself holding onto a column before the
cathedral. His body shook as if the earth had disappeared,
and he recalled that this very cathedral he held to, this
church, this edifice of belief, had collapsed in an earthquake
centuries before, even as it was being built.

*What am I to do? I cannot run back to Rome now. And
yet I am assaulted here by doubts and worries and an inability*

*to decide about the candidate—for the first time in my experience as devil's advocate, I am failing, failing! But I have my duty to perform. I must have the truth, but how am I to know the truth? I despise this ambiguity. Was he a saint or not? Was he or not? Either he was a saint or he was not a saint. There is nothing in between. Or is there?*

Instantly, he reacted; his years of training had prepared him for this moment. A single genuine doubt could be a key brick removed from the tower of belief. He had spent his entire adult life feeding doubt when it came to the lives of supposed saints, but in his own case doubt was to be avoided at all cost. And yet doubt kept forcing its way back, with a power and urgency that terrified him.

*Where has this seed of doubt come from, what has insti-gated it? Is it something that has been working in my belly, a worm in my guts, for years? Or has it been precipitated by this place? That old woman? That young girl? The impossible Cambiati? Or perhaps it is some power in the heavens, a shift in the stars? Or do I sense that the cloud that darkened my days in Rome is now moving quickly this way, has in fact arrived?*

With profound insight and fear he saw a truth, a kind of truth unlike any he had previously engaged. *Either this or that—there is* nothing *in between.* He pushed his palms into his eyes, as if he could block out this vision. *No—I am wrong, have always been wrong—everything* is in between. He bit down on the sound of the word, spitting it out. *Everything . . .*

*How could I not have seen it? All those years, all those years, doing my duty in the face of endless hypocrisy among the cardinals in the Vatican. I sense a disturbance there that will surely end my life. Who moves up? Who moves down? The exigencies and deceits of power are a madness. I sicken of it. I sicken of it all. Why have I not seen it? Something inexorable has shifted in the heavens, I feel it, and here below, here in Cremona and in Rome, a shift begins. Nothing will remain the same, nothing will hold, all will be turned upside down.*

The revelation almost knocked him to his knees, and he opened his eyes to try to clutch at a nearby pillar. His mind was racing, images and figures flickering past with a random-ness that terrified him. *What is happening? I need something to hold to.* He collapsed and sat on the cool stone. He was soaked with sweat.

At that moment he recalled the cerement in his pocket. He pulled it out and, with a deep inbreath, took in its scent, holding it over his mouth and nose. Slowly his mind settled; he breathed in and out and simply sat resting for a long while, eyes closed, thoughtless.

He was unsure how much time had passed—*perhaps I fell asleep*—but hearing a sound of scuffling feet, he looked up. The crisis had passed; he felt calm again and in control. He was relieved no one had seen him in his shaken state. Once again he was the advocate, a man of authority and posi-tion. He got to his feet.

Across the square, a figure, a woman in a white robe, moved stiffly, slowly, through the warm night. She walked in random patterns, stopped, turned, approached a wall and halted. He watched her move in a circle at the square's centre, and then edge towards the doors of the cathedral. She approached the closed doors, veered away and circled the baptistery, continuing down a narrow street. Intrigued, he followed.

As he drew closer he recognized Elettra, and it was clear that she was walking in her sleep. Her eyes were shut and yet she was capable of avoiding obstacles in her way. She glided down the streets, seemingly without purpose—a floating ghost. "Signorina," he said to wake the girl, stepping around from behind to face her.

As she stopped, he stumbled back two steps quite unexpectedly. To look at her was to put his hand into a flame. Her beauty and his attraction to it were both a shock to him. "Signorina," he repeated, softly. Her eyes fluttered wide; she looked at him and burst into tears.

Minutes later she was back in her bed in the family palazzo. The *duchessa madre* stood by the door, glanced nervously at the sleeping girl and whispered. "Every three days she has the fevers—a severe chill followed by a strong fever, then profuse sweating. If I do not watch her every moment, she rises asleep from her bed and wanders the halls, or climbs from a window and disappears. Her nurse fell asleep and she slipped away."

"I understand her mother and father are in Paris—has a message been sent to them?"

"Yes, several days ago, Your Excellency. But it could be a long while before they receive it and are able to return."

"When did this begin?" As he listened to the old woman, he watched Elettra sleep—long, silky black hair thrown across the pillow, a pink flush in her smooth cheeks, the tip of her tongue protruding from between her lips. Again he was struck by her beauty, and had to pry his eyes away from her in order to concentrate on what the old woman was saying.

"It started a little over a week after our return from Mantua. We had gone to see a famous dressmaker there, but the swamps reeked, and the mosquitoes were so thick that we had to leave after a single day."

"*Mal'aria* likely—the evil air. The exhalations of the swamps about Mantua are known to be poisonous. The city is surrounded by stinking, reed-filled swamps, and every year there are outbreaks of this disease. I am sure the foul air is the cause. The fever has been making her delirious, driving her from her bed." He cleared his throat. "What colour, pray tell, is the girl's urine?"

"I handed the pot to the servant yesterday and I recall thinking it odd. It was a pale red colour. It was then I summoned the doctor."

"And?"

"He said it was a female hysteria causing the ague and the sleepwalking. Tomorrow he is coming to bleed her."

"Do not allow it. Ensure she takes as much water as possible." He opened the door and stepped out into the hall, speaking over his shoulder. "There is a treatment—but I must obtain it from Rome. It will take some days. Have you a servant I can send as a messenger?" He was already hurrying down the hallway. "He will need several horses, the duke's best . . ."

A   SERVANT   RIDES   TO   ROME

The servant the *duchessa* sent to Rome was the best rider in the household. Giorzio was a solidly built young man who bore a birthmark on his left cheek, a wine stain the size of a baby's hand. The *duchessa* provided the swiftest horse from the household's stables, the dam of the murdered foal, a magnificent animal that Elettra had named Cruna, as well as a second horse for when the first tired. Giorzio seldom had the opportunity to ride the beautiful white Cruna, but his thighs ached to grip the animal under him and feel its thunderous strength.

Monsignor Archenti came hurrying out to the stables with a letter in his hand, the wax on the envelope sealed with the official ring of the Promotor Fidei. He handed it up to Giorzio as soon as the servant had mounted. "Take this to the general of the Society of Jesus in the Vatican. Await his response and then return here immediately with what he gives you. Do not hesitate. The girl's life depends on you. Ride. Ride now!" He gave the mare a slap on the haunches. The horse and rider, and the second horse on a lead, shot under an archway and were gone.

*Your Excellency Society General Lorenzo Ricci,*
*It is with profound urgency that I address you today.*
*There is here in the town of Cremona a young girl of a*
*good Christian family, who suffers from the ague of* mal'aria.
*I believe this girl's life can be saved if you will send to me a*
*quantity of our Jesuit's bark brought back from the highlands*
*of Peru by Monsignor De Rosa. I realize the cinchona bark*
*is of great value, but I believe her father the duke would be*
*most grateful, and would know how to express his gratitude,*
*if we could save his daughter's life. This letter has been*
*delivered to you by one Giorzio, a servant of the household.*
*I have asked him to await your instructions and return here*
*immediately.*

> *I remain*
> *Your Faithful Servant,*
> *Monsignor Michele Archenti, Promotor Fidei*

## DEATH AT THE DOOR

Monsignor Archenti stood at the window of his parlatory, looking out on the weather. He was thinking about the girl. For two full weeks he had watched over her, awaiting the return of Giorzio. He recalled the previous evening, when he had sat by her bedside until late into the night. The old lady and the servants had retired to their own rooms, figuring the girl was either in good hands with the priest or beyond any help other than prayers. He was happy enough to sit and gaze upon her face for hours.

She had come close to death a number of times, he was sure of it. Each time, he sensed that she would approach death's precipice and then back off. He admired her strength, for he felt it was her character and her will alone that were keeping her alive.

Elettra tossed and turned in the fever's fury, strands of dark hair soaked blacker where it touched her forehead, her lips swollen. Alternately he had prayed and watched her, his breath rising and falling with hers. For a moment he forgot to pray, and drifted. He snapped awake. She was still, her breathing weak and rough. He turned towards the door as he felt the presence of a shadow deeper than the darkness. It was not so much a feeling of malevolence in the air as a curiosity, a raw searching curiosity. *Death,* he thought, *standing in the doorway, trying to decide if it is the girl's time. Death waiting to see who is next.* As Archenti noticed the presence, it instantly fled, slipping into the night, as if the priest's awareness itself could drive death away. The girl moaned and rolled over. Even in this state her skin was refulgent, its glow seeming to come from under layers of creamy flesh.

He had stared at her for a long while, entranced. Sometimes the heart asks a question the mind cannot hear.

Suddenly his reverie was shattered by the sight of a white horse and rider coursing across the piazza through the steady grey rain. *Giorzio returns!* He hurried to the wide staircase, and took the marble steps by twos.

Within a week, it was clear the Jesuit's bark had worked its magic and the girl would recover from her illness. It was then that the *duchessa* asked the monsignor if he would agree to tutor Elettra in Latin during his sojourn in Cremona.

"Of course." He bowed. "It would be my honour."

Normally he would have refused such an assignment during an investigation. But in this case, sensing an opening, he immediately agreed. Perhaps the old lady had indeed confided in the girl, had whispered to her something at some point about Cambiati; perhaps the mind of the girl, in her innocence, would be easier to unveil than that of the *duchessa madre*.

Also, he decided he had no desire to return to Rome, for now. He sensed that events there were not developing in his favour and he felt it would be better to try to wait them out. Spring had passed quickly and summer was coming on. The heat would be intolerable in Rome, worse even than in Cremona.

The next morning began with an unusually vociferous boom of bells from the top of the tower in the square. By the time the advocate reached the bottom of his stairs, he heard the excited citizens announcing and sharing the news—*Pope Benedict XIV is dead.* This statement was always followed by its corollary—*Who will be the next pope?*

*Yes,* the advocate wondered as well, *who will be next?*

The mid-morning sun poured in the window of the girl's room. The fever had abated. Elettra sat up in bed.

Monsignor Archenti, waiting on the chair next to her, noted the thick dark hair, the huge round eyes with an Arabic blackness that was deep, clear, moist.

"Have you heard? *Il Papa* . . ."

"Yes."

"Will you return to Rome now?"

He noted a certain hope, a certain fear, in her voice. "No. It will not be necessary."

"Good. Tell me, what is it like in Rome?"

"What would you like to hear about it?"

"Tell me the truth about it. Do you like it there?"

Turning in his chair, he looked out the window as he spoke. "I will be honest with you. I was happy enough to quit Rome. The city is littered with mouldering pagan ruins crawling with mangy cats. Its old circuses and amphitheatres are soaked in ancient blood that you can smell on hot summer nights; it is a city whose very soul is pagan, bursting with evil thoughts and memories."

There was something about the girl that made him want to tell her the truth of things as they were, or at least as he felt them. He could have covered it over with felicitous words, but the way she looked at him demanded that he peel back the layers of the truth. That look was penetrating, intelligent and innocent all at once, and he felt strangely helpless before it, a feeling that he viewed as seriously out of character for him. *Perhaps I am tired of it all, tired of pretending and hiding and using every conversation as an insidious means to look beneath the veil. And yet perhaps if I share a secret with her, she will share her secret concerning the candidate with me.*

"You may be shocked to hear it, but there is many a robed devil walking the streets of Rome and the halls of the Vatican. Evil incarnate. Ambition beyond belief. Yes, I was glad enough to quit Rome. Lately, especially, there is something brooding about its atmosphere—as if something is about to happen, some evil about to come to the surface. I felt a profound sense of disquiet and unease just previous to leaving Rome to travel here."

"I am surprised a little at what you say." She thought a moment. "And yet, it is as I suspected. My father says that priests are not to be trusted, least of all the priests of Rome."

He was struck again by her willingness to be frank, her natural intelligence and her freshness. "Tell no one what I have said. It will be our secret, yes?"

"Yes." She lowered her gaze and smiled at him, happy to have a secret they could share.

## THE LAST WITNESS

The devil's advocate and his scribe were gathering their papers following the final interview on the last day of the official interrogatory, when Beneficio, a middle-aged, simple-minded servant, came to the door of the high-ceilinged interview room, looking worried, knitting and unknitting his fingers.

"Um, Your Excellency . . ."

Monsignor Archenti looked up and waited. "Out with it."

"A man, a man has come—he wishes to speak with Your Excellency. I did not know if I should let him in?"

"His name?"

"Rodolfo."

Angelo the scribe raised his eyebrows.

Sighing, the devil's advocate motioned tiredly with his hand. "Show him in."

What appeared at the door startled the advocate from his lethargy. He turned to the scribe. "Who is this?"

Under his breath, Angelo replied, "He is a well-known madman who wanders the countryside in these parts. I believe he is harmless."

The advocate considered the man a moment and thought, *We shall see.* "Enter. Sit."

Hair long and straggly, eyes huge and yellowish, face heavily pockmarked, he edged into the room accompanied by a peculiar sound. *What the devil?* As the man took a seat, the advocate realized that the sound came from the clanking of a skeleton he wore on his back, the bones held together with leather thongs that disappeared inside his tatty clothing, strapping the skeleton onto him.

"What is this? Who are you?"

"My name is Rodolfo. I beg leave to speak with Your Excellency."

"First, my good man, explain that grotesquerie on your back."

"Yes, Your Excellency, of course. The people call me the Man of the Reeds. Many years ago, I committed a terrible crime. A murder. The details of that event, that fateful day that is branded on my soul, are now unimportant. Suffice to say I was but a mere youth, quick to anger, and I disregarded fair warning. I have been paying ever since, as justice demands. I was condemned to carry the corpse of the one I murdered roped to my back for the rest of my life. In the early days I nearly went mad—the smell of the rotting flesh with me every moment. The dead man's ghost kept entering me here"—he stuck two fingers in his nostrils—"and tried to take over my soul, to torture me. But I resisted and finally the ghost gave up and left. Since then, he and I"—he motioned with his thumb over his shoulder at the skeleton—"have become the best of friends!"

The devil's advocate said nothing but looked closely at the man. *His eyes glow like the eyes of the mad but I judge he isn't mad. Those eyes remind me of paintings I have seen of mystic saints. Saint Sebastian. Or perhaps Jerome.* Rodolfo stared back at the advocate, hands on knees. When he shifted in his seat, the monsignor could see the skull peeking at him from over the man's right shoulder.

"And?"

"Your Excellency, I realized the obvious. We all have a dead man on our backs. Ourselves in another time. I was forced to confront this truth that most would prefer to ignore. I confronted it. The dead man was my brother."

Monsignor Archenti was unsure if he meant "brother" literally. He decided not to seek clarification.

"I see." The devil's advocate paused. "You have information on the candidate, Fabrizio Cambiati?"

"Yes." Rodolfo nodded. "I will tell you. I knew him."

"That is impossible. I am sure he died long before you were born."

"I knew him in dreams."

"In dreams?"

"Yes, Your Excellency. We would often pass an afternoon, Fabrizio and I, walking in the fields, or sitting under a tree, the last in a long line of poplars."

*Is this final detail important?* the devil's advocate wondered. It was difficult to determine if the man stood with one foot in the madhouse or was perhaps pointing mysteriously at a subtle truth. A silence filled the room, which highlighted the scratching of the scribe's quill, as the advocate turned and glanced out the window at the late afternoon sky, grey-white as the underbelly of a goat and dripping with a steady drizzle. *How am I to determine a man's sanctity in such a place, where mystics and madmen crawl out of every hole? I could end this now. Send him out . . .* He leaned towards Angelo, bent over his work. "Stop." The quill halted in mid-stroke. "I do not want this in the report." He motioned to Rodolfo to continue. *I'll give the man his head, let him spill his guts, see where it goes.*

"Good Fabrizio. He brought me back from the dead. It was in the reeds by the river. That is how I got my name— Man of the Reeds. He warned me not to commit the murder but I ignored his advice. After, when I began wandering the fields with my friend on my back, Fabrizio would join me and we would talk, great conversations that took days, and in which we travelled the world and came to know all there is to know in the heart of man. And then, when he died, we continued our talks, in dreams where he came and sat next to me under the poplars. I would drink wine but he did not, saying the dead cannot drink wine."

"And of what did these conversations consist?"

"Oh, many things, as I mentioned. Fabrizio and I, we would often speak of the city in the sky above Cremona. He knew of it. Like me, he had walked its streets."

"And what is this place, this city in the sky?"

"It is a city exactly like Cremona in every respect. It includes the city of Cremona, but it is more."

"More? How so?"

"With all due respect, Your Excellency, it is difficult to explain. I can only call it a place where time is perfected, or has ripened, or perhaps I should say a place where time is complete."

"I do not understand. Explain yourself."

"It is a city where all the Cremonas *that were* and all the Cremonas *that are to come* are apparent, at once."

The advocate paused. "In the present?"

He nodded vigorously, the skull bobbing behind him and the bones clacking.

"And Fabrizio saw it, as did I."

The Jesuit brought his hands together slowly before him, the tips of his fingers touching, and thought. A devil's advocate, he knew, must be a slave to reason. Even the miracles—unbelievable sightings, risings from the dead, martyrs floating in high cupolas—all of them must ultimately answer to the laws of reason, even if those laws were bent and twisted under the authority of divine intervention. "Anything else?"

Rodolfo went on. "I have met people from a country far to the north who spoke of great cities of ice that grow in the northern seas."

"Yes? Are these cities inhabited?"

"This I do not know, Your Excellency. The stories I heard did not mention inhabitants."

The scribe raised his eyebrows and shook his head.

"But the cities of ice that can be seen above the water are doubled by an even greater city below the water."

"What size are these cities of ice?"

"Greater than the city of Cremona. At times the ice cities roll over, and the city that was on the bottom is now on top and the city that was on top is now on the bottom."

"I see." *And everything in the world upside down,* the advocate pondered, feeling distinctly uncomfortable with the tenor of this conversation.

Rodolfo paused. "I am telling you a story, Your Excellency, about Cremona and the city in the sky. When time has ripened, when the comet returns, Cremona will roll over and the city in the sky will become the city on the earth."

*He's telling me stories now. A parable perhaps? Or a fable.* "I see. And how does this story relate to the candidacy of Fabrizio Cambiati?"

"It is true, a true story—but only those who know of the city in the sky will notice the change."

"Who?"

"Fabrizio Cambiati, me, and now you."

The advocate nodded and thought a moment. "Anything else?"

Rodolfo either did not hear or had nothing else to say. He sat in silence.

"I will take your comments into consideration. *Grazie.*" Rodolfo rose and the priest watched him leave, the skeleton knocking and clacking as he walked from the room.

Monsignor Archenti sat a long while in silence, watching at the doorway where Rodolfo had exited. The scribe waited. After a while Angelo said, "A queer fellow," as if that concluded it. "Your Excellency, is there anything else?"

*Wants his wine, his dinner.* "No. Nothing else."

After the scribe left, Archenti stayed, staring into space. Feeling profoundly troubled, he thought that perhaps there was more to this investigation than he had suspected. If he had been a more subtle man, less addicted to reason and duty, more in tune with the world, he might have felt the earth already beginning to shift, a fault line running straight from Cremona to Rome and beyond. *This Rodolfo. This conversation.* He shook his head as if trying to drive the memories away. *Very strange indeed.* He sat staring out the window, unable to leave the room.

## A DELICIOUS PURGATORY
## IN LATIN TEXTS

Once the bitter bark from the Jesuits had worked its cure completely, Elettra was ready to begin her lessons in Latin, arranged by her great-grandmother and approved by her parents after their return from Paris.

Archenti looked at the girl, who sat across the table from him. They were in her father's library, the table scattered with books and charts she had been consulting in her ongoing interest in stars and comets. She had recovered thoroughly and, if anything, seemed healthier than ever. *Only the young can recover like this,* he thought, *only the young can rebound from death's grasp with such vitality.* She was reading silently from a book of Virgil and eating a peach. He watched as she smiled at something in the text. He was taken with the slight curl of her lip. She looked up and, wiping her mouth with the back of her hand, smiled innocently at him. He smiled back and nodded.

"Have you finished?"

"Yes."

"Do you understand? Can you translate it?"

She shrugged her shoulders. "I will try. There are a few words I do not recognize. You will help?"

"Of course."

She began a halting translation but Archenti was barely listening. Instead he was entirely submerged in her youthful beauty, watching as she spoke. He found himself looking forward to each time she glanced up to check if she was progressing well with the translation. Then he could look directly into her clear moist eyes. He would nod and she would bow again to the text, pleased with herself.

He sighed and shook his head. *No, I mustn't. This is . . . is*—he gave up and admitted the truth to himself—*impossible. I have never taken such delight in a face in my life.* He wiped his brow and once again abandoned himself to gazing at her.

It was then he noticed her hands as she reached to turn the page. They seemed to be her only imperfection, if they could even be called that. Their appearance was unexpected. Rather than slim, pale hands and fingers, she had peasant hands: thick, heavy, strong, somehow experienced. This didn't lessen his desire. In fact, it only added to her attraction.

The advocate wondered if she was aware of the desire that had suddenly, unexpectedly, taken him over, that gripped him each time he was in her presence. He wasn't sure. It was not a thing he could address—the mere mention of the subject could mean his downfall. Years as a priest, years with his head in books, years playing the priestly role, and here was a lovely little demon he was quite willing to surrender his soul to—at a single sign, a single word. But he couldn't discuss it! Nor could he see into her thoughts. He who had ferreted out the secret lives of a dozen pretenders to sainthood could not see into this one shy heart seated before him.

*How had it happened?* He knew it was somehow bound up with his feelings about those recent events in Rome. Since arriving in Cremona, he had felt of two minds. On the one hand, the heavy cloud had followed him. How could it not have? For it was, at least in part, a brooding in his own heart. At the same time, he had begun to see a break in the clouds. There had been moments when he started to feel liberated from that tangle of corruption, to see it for what it truly was, to be free of it all. Here, no one was watching him, and planning and plotting and measuring out words with careful intent. At least, not with the intensity such activities took on in Rome. Here, everyone seemed innocent, playing at games rather than measuring out the days in a desperate grasping at power.

He stared at her again and admitted it to himself. *I am trapped in her beauty. Like one of those wild finches netted by the mountain hunters.*

And yet, like an old habit, his commitment to his duty returned. *I must convince the girl to reveal her secret. It is essential. I have no choice. A devil's advocate is what I am. Without that, all is lost.* He leaned forward. "Tell me, Elettra, do you ever speak with your great-grandmother concerning the candidate?"

"At times."

*She is paying scant attention, perhaps I can catch her unawares.* "And what does she say of Cambiati?"

"Not much."

"How well did the *duchessa* know him?"

"Well enough."

"How so? What do you mean?"

"Are you asking, did she love him?"

He was taken aback. "Well, yes."

"I would say she loved him."

"How so? In what way?"

"From the highest to the lowest, I should think."

"And what exactly does that mean?" He couldn't bear half measures, insinuations, suggestions. He must have the truth. Bald and without doubt.

"What do *you* think it means?"

"It does not matter what I think it means. I need to find the truth."

"The truth. Oh, the truth."

"Yes."

She seemed to be losing interest. "Ask her yourself. I don't know." She smiled at him. "I know nothing of love. Real love."

It dawned on him that they were suddenly speaking of something else.

"But . . ."

"No more questions, please. I grow tired of your interrogations. It is worse than translating Latin." She pouted. She played at pouting, he thought.

A moment later, saying nothing, she stood up and left the room.

The advocate lay in bed and listened. Strings of rain continued to fall from the heavens. Summer had arrived, with its storms and heat. Thunder rumbled down the streets, dark bells echoed off the walls of cramped alleys. He could hear a violin playing not far off. He listened for a long time, letting the music flow into and through him, like light passing through water.

And then the sound ended with a fillip of the string on a shining high note, as thunder drummed above him in the sky, a long cascading rumble across the Lombardy plain, with no mountains or hills to stop or contain it, so that it rolled straight on and on for minutes without end. He listened to it begin again, and roll on, and before it ended he was asleep.

In the middle of the night he shot awake in his bed, astounded by the vividness of the dream.

*A violin rests at the bottom of a vat, held there by two round stones. He looks into the vat and thinks the pale, wavering violin is a drowned infant. Gazing with more intensity, he changes his mind. Not a drowned infant but one as yet unborn. A fetus.*

*Like a wind passing overhead, the dream changes colour. He is reaching for a brush of black wood, its pointed tip smooth as a held note. Holding the brush lightly in his hand, he raises it in the air and eases it down into a pot of liquid, a solferino purple so deeply coloured it appears black along the edges. He pushes the brush through the fluid, soaking the bristles thoroughly, until drops of pigment drain from the tip when he lifts it. The brush is engorged, swollen with the viscous liquid. As he raises it he looks into the sky.*

*On the workbench before him is a pale, unvarnished violin. He slides the brush over the instrument, letting the liquid soak thoroughly into the thirsty yielding spruce. Again and again he returns to the pot, saturates the brush and soaks the instrument, spreading the fluid into every crack and crevice, around every whorl and into every secret place. In the end, the instrument is thoroughly drenched. The violin takes on a glow, a luminosity and a voice—a quivering sigh beyond normal pitch. A pure unadulterated sound, the hush of light streaming down in a forest, or the clear hollow echolalia of sky in late afternoon. In the dream he listens, the resonance shimmering inside him, the sweet weeping elation of strings.*

He awoke to words ringing clearly in his head: *A ferocious and dangerous beauty.*

The next day—with mounting trepidation impossible to resist, as if fascinated by the danger of a precipice—he returned to their study of Latin, his ninety minutes of delicious purgatory.

# CHAPTER SIX

*I begin to feel I am living in a dream—such a surfeit of miracles and astounding stories that my head spins. Fabrizio was seen talking to a swan beside the Po, and the bird appeared to be listening, turning its head first this way, then that. Cremona's most famous gossip was struck dumb for a day after praying to him. A violinmaker and his helpers, returning from the Dolomites after hunting for wood in the forests, sighted a band of brigands and were saved by being turned into deer. It seems the place is pregnant with miracles, about to burst.*

## THE ECSTASY OF
## SAINT AGATA

Fabrizio thought often in the following weeks about the damp evening he had met the duchess on the square, and what had happened between them in the shadows of that nearby alley. He thought long and hard about what exactly could have been the cause of these actions. He didn't believe the elixir itself was strong enough to make him cast aside his moral discipline. He also did not believe the elixir had the power to allay his fears of the duke, and the complications such an act could cause in a number of lives. He admitted to himself his long-time fascination with the young woman, but he had always thought it was an itch of curiosity that he would never have the necessity to scratch. *Perhaps it was Niccolò's violin that moved me to act,* he thought. It had power, of course, but he was sure the music alone was not the cause. *Perhaps it was everything added together, along with an unnamed power in the heavens, like a number of planets in a line.* He was sure that was it—a conjunction of elements, each adding to the other's power: music, elixir, the inescapable attraction he was sure she also felt, and the power of the heavens. And then he realized what had tipped the scales. *She had need of me. She needed my help.* Of course he desired her—he was a man, after all—but none of that would have meant anything to him if the duchess had not longed so deeply, so acutely, for a child. He smiled to himself. *Mysteries beyond mysteries.*

A few nights later, at a taverna on a small irregular piazza facing the back of the cathedral, Niccolò the violin-maker joined Fabrizio and Omero at a table where a pot of wine stood bathed in its own sweat. As they sat, the inn-keeper's wife brought more jugs and cups. The wine from the tavern's deep cellars tasted cool in the warm room, which was filling up with patrons.

As they talked and drank, Fabrizio looked at Niccolò's hands. He knew the violinmaker's hands had once been as delicate as a girl's, but now they were so chipped and gnarled, scuffed, sanded and pitted that it was a wonder their issue could be anything other than rough-hewn boards or slabs of granite. They resembled hunks of dry veal beaten by a thousand blows from a stippled hammer.

Those hands had experienced every possible assault and wound from chisel, knife and saw. Cuts, abrasions, avul-sions. The tip of the index finger on his left hand was gone, the small cavity of the wound the exact arced shape of the chisel that had slipped and passed through unresisting flesh. Several dozen maple and pine slivers floated under the skin of both hands like evergreen needles frozen in a stream. The skin itself was burned and stained with acidic solutions and solvents, and resembled half-decayed pages torn from a water-stained manuscript.

And yet, the priest marvelled, the violins that were the product of those rough hands were more delicate than the infant Jesus held by Boccaccino's Madonna in the church of Santo Sigismundo.

Niccolò leaned across the table towards Fabrizio, motioning with his hand as if it could help him recall something. "I saw your recent painting in the courtyard at the Convent of Santa Lucia. What was the title? *The Ecstasy of Saint Agata?*"

Omero lifted his cup. "Did you notice? She resembles the duchess."

Fabrizio addressed Niccolò, "Indeed. I'm sure you recall I used the duchess as my model."

Omero turned to the priest. "How were you able to portray such a look?"

"What look?"

"I would say . . . a look of sexual abandon."

"Omero, please, have some regard for your master."

Fabrizio smiled. "No, it is quite all right, Niccolò. I know he asks the question in all innocence, never having experienced a woman in his life."

"Unlike you, Don Fabrizio?" Omero leered.

"Omero, that is enough. I will be forced to send you home in a minute." The image of the duchess flashed in his mind. He took a deep draft of wine, both to cool himself off and to celebrate the wonder of such ardent memories.

Omero leaned back and pouted. Suddenly forgetting the exchange, he bent forward again and looked into the large, shallow pocket Fabrizio had sewn to the front of his black cassock, where the priest had his left hand hidden. "What are you doing in there?"

From the pocket Fabrizio pulled a rosary made of small black glass beads. "I've been rubbing my magic talisman." He held up the tiny metallic crucifix at the end of the rosary. "Rubbing the crucifix keeps me calm, assuages my worries," he explained to Niccolò.

The other two looked at the cross. The Christ on it had been rubbed so long and steadily by the priest's thumb that his entire torso had disappeared. It appeared as if the feet, hands and head, with nothing left to connect them, had each been crucified separately. "You've rubbed it to nothing," said Omero. "Truly, what does a priest have to worry about?"

Fabrizio stuck the rosary back in his pocket with a collection of other oddments: two crusted paintbrushes, a half-used spool of black thread with needle, an assortment of coins, a tattered holy card of Saint Michael the Archangel, a small oily rag and a hardened heel of white cheese. He ignored the question. A momentary silence settled on the threesome, and all drank.

"I will tell you a story about that painting," Fabrizio began. "But first, let us order another jug."

After their pots had been refilled and they had taken a first sip from the new batch, and before Fabrizio could start his story, Niccolò asked, "Why Saint Agata?"

"That's the story I wanted to tell you. How I came to choose my subject. It was a difficult decision, let me tell you. At first I thought I might paint Saint Catherine of Alexandria. I have always been taken with the story that describes how milk rather than blood came from her veins when she was beheaded. I rather like that."

"Hmm. Patron saint of young girls."

"Yes. But then I thought perhaps Saint Catherine of Siena would be more appropriate—closer to home, a well-known mystic and all that. I have an interest in mystics, as I'm sure you know. Unfortunately I was disturbed by the fact that her body rests in Rome while her head remains in Siena. That bothered me.

"Then I considered Saint Apollonia, because I was suffering from toothache that week, but it passed. So I turned to Saint Cecilia . . ."

"Patron saint of music," Niccolò interjected.

"And poets," added Omero.

"Yes, but she didn't seem quite right, I don't know why. Anyway, I considered Saint Barbara. Patron saint of almost everything—architects, builders, engineers, miners, artillerymen, firemen. As you know, the people invoke her against sudden death, fire, lightning and impenitence. I was bound to hit upon something that was appropriate."

"Happy death. You told me she's the saint of happy death," Omero added, and the priest nodded in agreement.

"Once again, however, I questioned my motive. I had to find the right saint, the perfectly appropriate saint for my painting. You can't have the patron saint of miners depicted in ecstasy. It doesn't work. At least, not for me. Finally I decided on Saint Agata."

"Why?" Niccolò looked honestly confused.

Fabrizio turned his head to the left and gazed in the direction of the back of the cathedral. "Because I heard the St. Agata bell from the *torrazzo*—D-flat—one afternoon while I painted, and I recalled that she was the patron saint of bell-founders, and that did it."

Omero gave him a sidewise glance, ran his finger around the rim of his cup. "Your reason does not ring true, master, if you will allow me the weak pun. Did you not settle on Agata because she is the saint who cures sterility? Were you not hoping that through some form of magic, by depicting her as Agata, you could stimulate the fertility of our famously infertile duchess?"

"Ah, you are too quick for me, Omero. A mind like the net of the fisherman—capturing only the important facts, and letting the tiny irrelevant details pass through. My hat is off to you. Of course, I wanted to help the poor woman in any way I could. So that is what I did—Saint Agata it was."

## A VISION IN THE COUNTRYSIDE

Three weeks earlier, before their discussion in the taverna, Fabrizio had been walking in the countryside, where the waving grasses rolled before the breeze like an unstable sea. After days of ineffectual and unproductive staring at the painting he had been working on at the Convent of Santa Lucia, he finally had to admit to himself that he was stumped, locked up, unhanded. The brush would not take life. The face of the duchess/Agata was no more than a puddle of pigment. It had no heat, no blood pulsing under the skin's surface, no breath. The sittings in the garden courtyard had finished two weeks ago, and it appeared that, when the duchess had left, she had taken all the life in the painting with her.

That windy afternoon, he had left the convent court-yard and trudged across the city, down Via del Sale and out the gate in the city wall. He had walked until he was in the country, with its green smells and golden light. An unexpected warm breeze flowed across the Lombardy plain. He breathed the air deep into his lungs and, standing in the middle of a field, looked up into a sky of blue. He didn't exactly forget the painting, but his frustration fell away. He gloried in the private joy of walking great distances with nothing to carry and nowhere to get to. The breeze seemed to push him along.

After several hours, Fabrizio came upon a line of eight poplar trees casting a precious ribbon of shade. Under the last poplar in the row sat Rodolfo, drinking from a jug of wine. Rodolfo saw him and waved, a smile on his pock-marked face, the skeleton's skull nodding over his shoulder. Fabrizio approached.

"Sit. Sit, padre. Have a drink."

Fabrizio settled next to Rodolfo. When the jug was passed, he drank. In the distance across the plain they could see the city of Cremona with its churches and towers, a mirage on the horizon. "City of a Hundred Towers, they call it. It hardly looks real."

"No more real than last time," Rodolfo said.

"What do you mean?"

"Cremona turned over last night. The time has come. We are seeing the other side. In any case, we each dream our own city—you of all people know that."

"Yes. It is true. But how can you say it with such non-chalance?"

"When you have seen as much as I have, Don Fabrizio, there is nothing to get excited about. Simply put, it is time. The city has turned over. What was on top is now on the bottom and what was on the bottom is now on top."

"Perhaps something has happened in the heavens to prompt this event?"

"No doubt. Whatever happens on earth is reflected in the heavens, and whatever happens in the heavens is reflected on earth. They are like mirrors. I feel great change coming, an earthquake of change—a time when priests become lovers and lovers are saints. A time of miracles, padre. A time of unending miracles."

The priest nodded in agreement. Rodolfo drank and passed the jug. After Fabrizio took his fill, Rodolfo clanked to his feet. "Come, priest. I want to show you something."

Fabrizio followed. Soon they were walking next to a rivulet that wandered along a deep cut through the fields. After a while they rounded a bend, climbed up and around a hillock and there stood an immense church. At first Fabrizio thought it was in ruins, for light came through the open ceiling, and several walls were in disrepair. But on looking again he saw that the upper reaches of the structure were crawling with workmen in the act of building it. A number of painters were labouring at frescoes that Fabrizio could barely discern from the ground. No one was speaking. All were working in silence. Nearby a few birds chirped, the stream gurgled. These were the only sounds.

He whispered to his companion, "I do not know this church. When was it started?"

Rodolfo shrugged and put his finger over his lips.

The floor, a lake of travertine, stretched into the distance. They walked about, looking at stone columns that went up so high they seemed to disappear in the radiance of the heavens. Fabrizio felt as if his head were filled with sunlight. He saw two men standing on the ground next to a wall, pulling ropes as they hoisted a young boy on a plank into the air. Besides the boy, the plank held two capacious bowls of pasta and several wine jugs, large as wellheads, wrapped in straw. The boy was going up to serve lunch to the painters in the heights, who would waste half the afternoon if they had to come down to eat and then climb back up.

The light that filled the cathedral was radiant with silence, the occasional birdcall or insect, the tapping of a mallet, the only ripples.

As Fabrizio watched the boy nearly dissolve in the distance, he felt he was both inside the church and outside in the fields, as if the church were as spacious as the fields themselves, as if it encompassed so much of the world that it had its own weather and winds. *This must be the most immense church in creation,* he thought. And then it struck him. *This is the place where earth touches Heaven, the place where there is no distinction between the world of the sacred and the world as it is.*

The air was thick with the smells of linseed and walnut oil, while the sky was the colour of lapis lazuli. Gold leaf clung to portions of the walls, which appeared to be covered with *trompe l'oeil* frescoes. He couldn't tell if the scenes depicted there—fields, cows and horses, workers cutting wheat, fortified cities, rock outcroppings—were painted illusions or empty spaces in the walls where he could see through to the surrounding countryside. He was unable to distinguish the painted architecture from the real—the acanthus leaves that flowed out of basket capitals looked alive, and maybe they were. The pointed vaults gave parts of the cathedral the look of a tent, and a feeling of elegant weightlessness. As his eyes played over the scene, he thought that perhaps some of the painters themselves were actually frescoes of painters, and now the boy on his plank high above seemed to have become part of a fresco as well— or perhaps it was the way distance bestowed a stillness on things—he wasn't sure.

He wasn't sure at all. Suddenly it seemed that stone was light and light was stone, that inside was out and outside was in, and all things took on a stillness and silence in the immensity of time. And then it came to him. He had an insight for his painting of the duchess—*I'll place the truth in the pupil of her eye*—and he longed to return to the courtyard of the Convent of Santa Lucia.

"Wait," said Rodolfo. "There is more we need to discuss."

Fabrizio followed the Man of the Reeds back to where they had been before, but he noted that now there were more Lombardy poplars in the row. *It must be a different spot, although it looks the same.* Rodolfo seated himself and invited the priest to join him.

Throwing his head back, Rodolfo took a healthy swig of wine and passed the jug. He wiped his mouth and stared into the distant fields. Fabrizio waited, knowing that Rodolfo was about to speak. "That music you heard the night with the duchess, it came from within you, priest. You could call it the music that moves the sun and the stars."

"How do you know this? How do you know of the duchess, and me, and the music?"

"Some things cannot be explained. I don't even know how I know, I just know. I see the prophetic in the way the wind moves through the grass, in the way light turns through the trees. In any case, it has to do with the alchemy of the heart. I refer to your situation, the music, the woman."

"The alchemy of the heart?"

"Yes. As you and I both know, alchemy has nothing to do with turning base metals into gold."

"This I understand. The Philosopher's Stone is a means to cure illness, to prolong life, to bring about spiritual revitalization. Gold is merely a by-product."

"The Philosopher's Stone can turn death into life. This is true. I have seen it myself. But even that is too limited. Forgive my saying so, but your thinking is too narrow. The elixir of immortality, *al-iksir,* as the Arabs called it, is about more than that." He paused, contemplating the point where field meets sky. The weather was serene, clear, peaceful.

"The true alchemist transmutes nothing but his own heart. Look, priest, if we see the fullness of things, if we can but realize, truly seize and realize, our common humanity, have we not already achieved immortality? The human play, this tragic comedy, this mystery without beginning or end, it goes on and on and on. The great circle of birth and death and birth continues."

The duchess was still on Fabrizio's mind. "If what you say is true, then . . . consummation itself would be a kind of sacrament."

"Of course—in that it allows the continuance of this play we call life."

"And beauty and attraction are then a kind of divine grace."

"Yes, this too is true. In this state of common humanity, the act of consummation becomes the snake Ouroboros biting its own tail. We say 'biting its own tail' but what we really mean is that Ouroboros makes love to itself."

Fabrizio noticed the scent of honeysuckle in the air.

"Do not worry about the woman, priest. She is happy." Rodolfo yawned. "And now I will sleep."

Fabrizio asked Rodolfo to direct him back to Cremona. Rodolfo pointed. As Fabrizio turned to go, Rodolfo said,

"The time has come. This age has reached its fullness and now time will turn. Do you see? You know and I know. That is all."

The priest nodded and hurried back to the city.

A short while later, Fabrizio stood before the painting in the courtyard of the Convent of Santa Lucia. He reflected on the image of the duchess/Agata. Again his heart was fluttering in his chest as the truth was revealed to him. *She is a woman. She perfectly connects Heaven and earth, one life and the next. This is her ecstasy.*

Three weeks later, on the evening at the taverna when the three friends were drinking, Omero would ask Don Fabrizio, "Master, are you about to found a cult of desire? And you a priest."

Niccolò would pipe up: "Let me be the first to join."

## A   C R O W D
### I N   T H E   C O N F E S S I O N A L

A month later, Fabrizio sat in the gloom of a confessional in the *duomo* on the appointed day, doing his priestly duty as confessor. Sliding back the small door, he revealed a wood-latticed window through which he saw Omero kneeling on the other side of the screen.

"Omero?"

"I wish to confess that I blasphemed my master."

"*I* am your master."

"Yes, and I am your servant. Servants should never blaspheme their masters, or so I have been told."

"This is true."

"I wish not to burn in hell for eternity for one small mistake. And yet, someone must keep you down to earth."

"And you have appointed yourself to take on this onerous task?"

"Not so onerous, really."

"Do you regret having sinned thusly?"

"Oh, yes, I suppose."

"Your lack of sincerity is most apparent."

"I would do it again, if necessary."

"That I do not doubt. Go. You are forgiven. Say a prayer . . ." adding, *sotto voce,* "if you can recall any."

Omero exited, another entered the confessional, and when Don Fabrizio looked again, kneeling before him was Duke Agostino.

"Father, I have sinned."

"How so, my son?"

The duke hesitated, then spat out his confession in a single breath. "In an excess of joy at recent good news that has brightened my days and sweetened my nights, I became drunk and under the influence of the drink I had my way with a scullery maid in my wine cellar. From behind."

"You may leave out the details, good duke."

"Sorry, father."

"Do you regret your sins?"

"Yes. Absolutely."

"Say three Our Fathers, and Jesus Christ Our Lord, in his infinite mercy, will forgive you."

"Thank you, father."

The duke exited and another entered. Kneeling before him was the Man of the Reeds.

"Rodolfo? I have never seen you here before."

"It is time."

"How do you fare? Have you recently sinned?"

"As you know, I am truly repentant for murdering my brother so long ago, and long ago I confessed it. But I have sinned more recently in other ways. Although I know and understand much about the world, still I believe I suffer from an excess of imagination."

"That is no sin, my son."

"I believe it is a form of lying."

"I suppose it could be so. In any case, you are forgiven."

"There is something else, Don Fabrizio."

"Yes?"

"When you rescued me in the reeds, I was a dead man. Without fear, you came into that place—the swamp of the dead—and dragged me out. Since then, I have lived an astonishing afterlife."

"I merely applied a bit of practical wisdom I learned from a physician who had travelled much in distant Cathay. That is all."

"In any case, now I believe I can live forever. To think this is great unforgivable pride, is it not?"

"No one lives forever, my son. You will live a long time, a very long time perhaps, but when it is time to die, like any of us, you will choose to die."

"I see."

"Go now. You are forgiven."

Rodolfo rose, the skeleton on his back clacking as he exited. Another entered. Fabrizio smelled her before he saw her face. *Oh, I know that sweet scent: fresh moist grass, faintest honeysuckle, warm honey.* His head swam. Before him sat Duchess Maria Andrea.

"Father, I have sinned greatly but at the same time my heart is overflowing with joy. I am with child. Yours."

"Mine?"

"Yes."

"You are sure?"

"A woman knows such things. You may not believe it, but I felt your seed take root in my womb the instant it entered. You have brought great happiness and joy to my life and that of my husband. You have saved us."

"Will you tell him?" Fabrizio half-hoped that she would reveal the truth to the duke, although he feared it greatly. He decided that he would accept with humility whatever the duchess decided to do.

"Will I tell him that the child is yours?"

"Yes."

"At times, I think I cannot live with this secret, but then I see the delight on his face and I think, why make trouble? Am I living a lie, Don Fabrizio?"

"No, my dear. Your happiness is justified and natural. If you believe it would serve no good purpose to tell him at this point, then that is how you should proceed. You are sure it is mine?"

"Yes. Am I not a sinner, father?"

"Well, let us look at the situation. You have certainly performed an act that is considered a sin, as have I. But I believe we both did it for a good purpose. Have you done good works of late, to help redress the balance?"

"Yes, father. This week, I stayed up two nights watching over the sick child of one of my servants who was too tired after a day of hard work. The little boy had a fever and I kept his forehead cool all night with damp cloths. I was exhausted owing to my condition but I forced myself."

"You are most compassionate."

"Don Fabrizio, I learned it from you. When people are near you, or even think of you, they realize peace of mind, and are happy."

"I am not sure Omero, my manservant, would agree with you. In any case, my dear, we cannot help what we are. I am no saint, as you have seen. But you should go now. The Lord Jesus Christ, in his infinite mercy, will forgive you."

After she left, Fabrizio sat with his eyes closed for a long while, taking great joy in her lingering scent.

# CHAPTER SEVEN

*People are coming to me now with the most common-place events as signs of Cambiati's holiness. "My cow gave two pails of milk instead of the usual one." "I recovered from boils in a week whereas it took my idiotic brother-in-law three weeks. Good Fabrizio answered my prayers." "My back hurt for years and then the pain went away as if by magic, after I believe I stepped precisely in his footsteps as I crossed the square." "I saw a horse coming out of the fog along the road at night. It looked magical. I was thinking of the good Fabrizio at the time." What am I to make of this? How am I to judge? These people have my head aching.*

## TOWER IN THE MIDDLE

Our story returns now to that first night when Don Fabrizio and Omero climbed past the great clock to the peak of the *torrazzo* in the heart of Cremona. Ever since that night they have remained on the tower; they never came down from the tower, will always be on the tower. Time descends from the timeless, the way a comet descends from space.

Fabrizio and his manservant had waited high above the square, had simply waited and watched for the return of the comet, which followed a spiral of time beyond the ken of normal human lives. Occasionally Fabrizio would scan the night sky with his telescope, then the horizon, and finally he would lower the telescope and look down again on the city.

As he contemplated the square below, he mused, "You know, my friend, here we are on this tower in the middle of this city in the middle of our lives in the middle of time. We are always in the middle, on the peak between past and future, between the last moment already disappearing and the next not yet come. Every path we have taken has brought us to this centre point and every path we will take leads from it. There is a kind of magic in that, yes? A kind of miracle?"

Omero poured himself more wine. "If you say so."

"We are always right in the middle of a miracle, stacked on a tower of miracles of past moments under an open sky of future moments." He paused. "Look, Omero, the play in the piazza begins again."

"Could we go down and see it?"

"Not now. We must wait."

"What are we waiting for?"

"The comet, of course. Do you not remember?"

"And what will we do when the comet comes?"

"Watch its passing."

"That's all?"

"Yes. Is that not enough for you?"

Omero shrugged. "By the time the comet comes, the play will be finished and we will have missed it entirely."

"Oh, I wouldn't worry about that. The play goes on and on. I sense that the comet is actually part of the play. Do you not think they can see it from the square, open to the sky as it is? We too are part of the play."

"If that's true, why don't I know my lines?"

"Whatever you say, those are your lines. This play has nothing to do with memorizing lines, or the lines you are fated to deliver. Omero, you must know that in *commedia dell'arte* the players are to come up with spontaneous lines, on the spur of the moment."

"As in life?"

"Yes, as in life. Do you see?"

"I see nothing, or very little. It's dark. I think I see a candle burning in a window across the square. And I see at least a thousand and one stars."

"Everyone is making love, or dying, or rolling over in their sleep, or dreaming of a play on the square, or worried about a child. Someone is trying to solve a mathematical puzzle—*what is thirteen divided by eight?*—another is writing a poem in his head, a third is hating his neighbour or plotting revenge. Each at the centre point of his life."

"And where is the damnable comet?"

"Been and gone and returning again. It will always return, for it follows the ineluctable spiral of time. It comes when it comes. Like a woman shaking the dew of stars from her long hair."

"Why?"

"Why? Now there's a question one does not often hear. *Why?* I have no idea. *Why?* It is a question for which I have no answer, a question that leaves me in wonder."

Omero stared at him. He whispered the words, speaking for once without mockery. "The Patron Saint of Wonder."

## CHAPTER EIGHT

*Another miracle. They say it happened in 1749, on Cambiati's feast day, August 13, the same feast day as that of Saint Hippolytus, the first antipope, and Saint Cassian of Imola, whose cult is confined to local calendars. It is said that the River Po ran with wine—a clear white wine of astounding freshness and brilliance. And that night it flowed with wine that was red, dark and rich. The people said they could drink and drink of it and never become drunk. By morning, the river had returned to normal. What am I to make of these endless outpourings?*

INTERVIEW

WITH THE HIERONYMITE

Padre Attilio Bodini stood at the door in the white habit and black cloak typical of his order. The advocate instantly recognized the troublemaker who had raised a ruckus on the square during the play. Like other long-time fresco painters, those who had been at the work for years upon years, he was burdened with the usual occupational affliction: his head was frozen in an upward-gazing position. Only with great difficulty and pain was he able to look straight ahead, and bending his head down was out of the question.

He was one of a few latecomers who had requested interviews with the advocate after the official interrogatory had been completed. Monsignor Archenti had decided to allow these late interviews because he still felt he was far from making a final decision about Fabrizio Cambiati's qualifications for sainthood. He knew that the candidate and the *duchessa* had had some kind of relationship, but he needed to pin it down, to obtain a statement of fact. He had had no luck ferreting out the admission from young Elettra, who was proving every bit as stubborn as her great-grandmother.

To the advocate's left the scribe scratched away, while Don Attilio sat before them, his head lolling back, his skull threatening to roll clean off, to go bumping down the knots of his spine. His eyes gazed six inches above the top of the advocate's head.

One would think such an attitude, such a posture, would suggest a temperament filled with the radiance and delights of upper worlds, of skies and heavens, a mind uplifted and at ease with contemplation of airy philosophies and celestial luminaries. Not true of Attilio Bodini. In fact, the opposite was the case, perhaps in resistance to what people naturally expected of him from his stance. He was known about the city of Cremona as one who always saw the worst in things, constantly speculating on doom and pleased to pass on rumours of impending armageddons. It was known that he was hard at work on a huge fresco depicting the Apocalypse at the Church of Santo Sigismundo. He was nearly finished—the project had been ongoing for six years— and it was whispered about the city that the results would be shocking. He was a gossipmonger as well, always speaking ill of people, never a good word to say about anyone.

After asking the usual list of official questions and learning little, the advocate said, "Tell me now—why have you really come to speak with me?"

"Your Excellency, I believe he was no saint, that Cambiati, if you ask me."

"And why do you believe that?"

"Often of an evening, my grandfather said, he would see him, the good padre, drinking at a tavern behind the cathedral with his cronies."

"Did he say which cronies?"

"A violinmaker and the priest's helper. Omero, I believe, was his name."

"Do you know if the candidate was seen to drink to excess, to act drunk in any way?"

"My grandfather did not say. But just being with that whoremonger, Omero, was at least a sin of keeping bad company. The little man was an evil creature, stunted as punishment from God. It was said he touched my grandmother in the shadows of the cathedral while she awaited her confessor. My grandfather, when he heard, went to the priest's house to exact his revenge, but Cambiati had a golden tongue and talked him out of it. I believe he also paid my grandfather a goodly bit of silver to keep the knife from his helper's throat. That insolent Omero was known in the brothels of the city as well."

"And how would your grandfather know this?"

"I know not."

"I see."

Padre Bodini fell silent, afraid that his important news was not believed. Angelo the scribe paused and waited, deepening the silence, his quill hovering over the parchment.

The devil's advocate felt he had to rescue the situation somehow. He wanted to keep Attilio talking. He knew he had to squeeze every detail of memory from his interviewees if he was to penetrate the veils that people naturally drew down to protect their ancestors or their immediate family. At times, he knew, people would speak to him in a way that was quite different from the way they would speak to their friends and neighbours. After all, he was a priest from Rome, a Jesuit, an official papal advocate, a stranger among them. He thought a change of subject was in order, perhaps a bit of baiting.

"Did you see the actors on the square this Saturday past?"

"Yes. A reprehensible display. Actors are worse than pigs and donkeys. Such foulness and immorality right before the doors of the cathedral. Shameful. The players should be banned."

"Hmm." Monsignor Archenti tried another tack, playing dumb. "You are a fresco painter, are you not? I have heard that you are working in Santo Sigismundo."

"I am painting a fresco there. Do you know the church?"

"Yes, of course. I have not been inside but I have passed it. And what is the scene you paint?"

"The Last Judgment."

"The Revelation of John?"

"Yes. I have pictured the damned with faces from our own city, their mouths agape, astounded. They don't know yet what hellish plagues will be visited upon them, but they know something of profound terror is coming. They feel that wind moving towards them."

"It is difficult indeed to paint such a scene."

"I have been at it six years. I will soon be done. And I am sure, when I unveil it to the priest of the parish and his congregation of the damned, they will see themselves and insist that I whitewash it immediately."

"It is that horrible?"

"Yes. It is a nightmare of unnamed fear. They will be unable to withstand its bald truths."

"You are a hard man."

"I learned it from my father."

"And you had no mother to soften the blows?"

"My father learned it from my mother."

The advocate nodded. "I suggest we return to the subject at hand. Do you recall your grandfather or any other of your old relatives saying anything at all about Fabrizio Cambiati, other than what you have just related?"

"Only that he had the heart of a fish—too soft and yielding. They said his eyes would water constantly as he walked the streets, so sad was he at the state of the world and men's souls. Unlike Cambiati, I believe that sin is a thing that goes away only when it is crushed and destroyed. Do you not agree, Your Excellency?"

Monsignor Archenti looked into the down-gazing eyes of the up-tilted head. "There are times when hardness is called for, and there are times when softness is the way to penetrate the soul."

"I cannot agree. There are always those who lie in wait to take advantage of softness. Always."

The Jesuit paused and thought a moment, looking at the back of his hand. "Thank you, Padre Bodini. I will send for you if I need to ask any more questions. And certainly, if you remember anything, anything at all, let me know. Thank you again."

The Hieronymite hesitated. "Indeed, there is one other thing. There is in the courtyard of the Convent of Santa Lucia a painting by Cambiati. I believe you should have a close look at it. It will tell you much about the man, if you have the eyes to see."

"Am I being tested as to the acuteness of my perceptions? Why do you not just tell me what in the painting you find intriguing?"

"Certainly a Jesuit, a devil's advocate no less, should have the insight to perceive what is obvious. If you wish to take it as a test, then so be it."

Moments later, as Bodini made his way from the room, the advocate said, "Perhaps I will come to view your work, your Last Judgment."

The Hieronymite did not turn around. "Your Excellency will do what you will do. But you do me no favour by coming to see my work. *Buon giorno.*"


A   BEE   IN   THE   GARDEN

Before their Latin lesson, the devil's advocate and Elettra walked to the central piazza. The monsignor had forgotten a book they required and had decided to fetch it from his office.

"It has been drizzling all day and now the sun is out. I will come with you," the girl had said.

They took their time in the summer heat, talking easily of this and that, enjoying each other's company. Archenti as always took great delight in looking upon the girl, in seeing her lips move and her tongue dart out and her eyes flicker brightly. She laughed often and it lightened his heart to be with her.

Neither of them noticed the Hieronymite priest again watching them from the shadows of the town hall portico.

After their return, they sat in the garden of the duke's villa, Elettra working through Virgil's *Aeneid*. A few bushes and trees were still dripping with the earlier rain, but they sat in a covered gazebo which was comfortable and dry. The lesson wasn't going well. The girl seemed distracted and Archenti, for no good reason, felt fatigued. Elettra was again eating a huge ripe peach, half the size of her head it seemed to Archenti, the juice running down her arm and dripping off her elbow.

"You shouldn't eat while we are working on your Latin."

She stopped and smiled at him. "But I'm hungry and it is so delicious. Would you like a bite?" She offered it.

"No. Thank you."

She was still looking at him as she half-consciously went to take another bite. In that moment he saw the honeybee that had landed on the peach. It appeared to him with an otherworldly strangeness, enormous and distorted, like one of the demonic drawings in the book by Stelluti that he had seen in Cambiati's library. Before he could speak, Elettra was screaming, her mouth wide, the bee stuck by its stinger to the centre of her tongue.

Archenti leapt up, went to the girl and, gripping the tip of her tongue, pulled the bee out. She continued to scream, her eyes wide with fright and pain. Her tongue began to swell, then her cheeks, lips and chin. He could hardly believe the transformation. A maidservant came out of the villa, attracted by the commotion.

"Send for the doctor. Now!"

The maid turned and ran.

Meanwhile, the monsignor got her to lie down on a bench. She kept pointing at her throat and grunting. Her head appeared to have swollen to nearly twice its normal size. The swelling had closed off her throat; she could hardly breathe.

The girl's great-grandmother appeared, looking dumbfounded.

"She was stung by a bee and swelled up like this!"

"*Dio mio!*" She slapped herself in the face, spun about and hurried off.

While Archenti was trying to decide what to do, Elettra grabbed in desperation at her throat; then her grunting stopped and a terrible silence hung in the air as she thrashed. He felt utterly helpless. In his stupefied panic, all he could do was give comfort by offering his hand, which she squeezed with shocking strength. At the same time he felt in the pocket of his cassock for the tiny vial of chrism he always kept with him for the last rites.

The old woman hurried back with a flask of dark green liquid in her hand. She put the unstoppered bottle to the girl's lips and poured the contents down her throat. Elettra convulsed once, twice, then gasped and was up on her elbows, coughing and spitting but taking gulps of air.

The *duchessa* hugged the girl's head to her thin chest. "Thank God! You'll be all right now. All right, all right." Elettra was weeping and shaking with fright.

After a while the rest of the swelling went down, and the girl slept under the watchful eyes of the devil's advocate and the *duchessa*. "What was that medicine?" he asked.

"Something Padre Cambiati gave me years ago. A distillation of many herbs: anise, cypress, marsh mallow, lovage, I believe, and others. He said it was very powerful. Good for insect bites." She added dreamily, as if speaking to herself, "Thank the Lord she will recover in time for the wedding . . ."

Archenti went rigid. This was the first he had heard of the impending event. He was surprised that Elettra had not mentioned it. Silent, he and the old duchess sat side by side in straight-backed chairs. The Jesuit listened to the wind, wondering what fresh catastrophes it might bring.


## THE BETROTHAL CEREMONY


*Gennaro Pasquali.* Elettra tested the name on her tongue, spitting it out, and found its sound distasteful. Fully recovered, resting in the shade of the garden on a hot summer afternoon, she held a letter open in her hand and sighed. She liked nothing about him, not even his name. *Gennaro Pasquali.* She tasted the name again, with a sneer. *Why must I marry him? A young fool who knows nothing.* Biting her lip hard, she bowed her head. She felt trapped in her own life. *No,* she said to herself.

Years before, when she was nine and he was thirteen, Elettra had been promised to Gennaro. This had been decided after long and serious negotiations between the two fathers, mediated by the marriage broker. Through her childhood years she would try to avoid the older Gennaro on the streets, half-sensing that there was something strange and dangerous about him. Or perhaps she merely disliked his squarish head, the way his ears stuck out, and his swaggering, arrogant attitude, so unbecoming in a young man. Because he was the only son and youngest child of Cremona's richest merchant, Elettra's father figured he had made an excellent match for his daughter, though he had to dig deep for the dowry, as he had reminded the girl more than once. She had heard him explain to her mother, as if she, Elettra, weren't present, "You see, my dear, the fact that Gennaro is both the youngest child and the only boy is a boon. In this case, the youngest benefits most from the accumulated wealth of the parents, and he alone stands to inherit the business."

The duke refused to discuss his own money troubles. His wife was well acquainted with the financial problems they faced and he knew discussing them with her again would only stir her anger and worry. The considerable fortune he had inherited from his father had evaporated over the years: in crop failures, in bad investments, in escalating costs. He saw this marriage as his best means of escape from impending penury. Gennaro's father had made his fortune in the manufacture and weaving of fustian cloth, as well as the making of table-cloths and table napkins, long a fruitful industry in the city of

Cremona. Surely the elder Pasquali, if anyone, would be good for the necessary loans to get the duke back on his feet.

Elettra recalled a feast Gennaro's father had put on the month before. His mother was skilled in the tradition of napkin-folding—she was the expert in the whole of Lombardy, knowing all twenty-six of the classic shapes, although Elettra remembered that she had produced only eight shapes the evening of the feast. There were napkins folded in the shape of Noah's Ark for the local priests, a style reserved for the clergy. And of course the hen napkin was given to her great-grandmother, as she was the noblewoman of highest rank at the banquet. The rest of the women were seated before serviettes in the shapes of chicks, the two fathers received bulls, with bears, carps and tortoises for the younger men. She herself, and a few other young women, were honoured with napkins in the shape of rabbits.

Elettra shook the memory from her head and again read the letter from her father's notary. Twenty minutes earlier, a servant had brought it on a salver and placed it on the table. She had already read it five times:

*Praise be to God, from whom all that is good comes! As your family notary, it is my joyful duty to advise you, dearest Elettra, that your father has betrothed you in the Cathedral this day to one Gennaro Pasquali, as arranged so long ago by the marriage broker. Gennaro is a handsome young man, and carried himself well in the presence of a large and most honourable company from Cremona and environs. All the attendees manifested a singular delight at the ceremony, and a spontaneous cheer arose from the assembly when the fathers shook hands, palm in palm, after signing the contract concerning details of the dowry. It is a fitting and most excellent arrangement between two well-favoured families of Cremona. The wedding is set for the twenty-sixth day of August. May God bless you and your father and mother on this great occasion.*

*Signed: Ser Giuseppe Bresciani, Notaro*

Elettra knew it was normal for a girl to be absent from her own betrothal ceremony, but it still rankled. And the letter from the notary was also typical, a kind of legal form and tradition. But she could ride a horse better than Gennaro could, and for her that said everything.

Both families had attended the ceremony in the cathedral. Everyone had been there: her father and mother, Gennaro and his parents, her great-grandmother. Elettra alone had been absent, not allowed to attend. She had been told that there would be about fifty guests from each party, the number being limited by the sumptuary laws. How strange to think that her life was being planned without her presence.

Later, when she was called down to dinner, she feigned illness and stayed in her room, refusing to celebrate with the others, her mood alternating back and forth between depression and rage.

Finally, as she lay back on her pillows, dreaming awake on an empty stomach, she began to picture someone. She smiled to herself and, with determination and confidence born of a volatile mixture of anger and longing, she began to formulate a plan. She daydreamed of folding a napkin this way and that, into various shapes: a tower, a carriage, a house, a boat, and finally, a horse.

## AN ARGUMENT AND A THREAT

The duke's family had finished their meal. A tense silence lingered in the air.

"Bring the girl here," the duke ordered a servant.

His wife placed her hand on his arm. "Dear, please . . . be gentle with her."

He nodded, took a gulp of wine, wiped his mouth with a napkin and waited. Beads of sweat pearled on his forehead. At the far end of the table sat the old *duchessa* in silence, a stoic look on her face. She was doing her best to stay out of the situation.

"Father?"

"Elettra. Sit down, my daughter. We must talk."

"Father, you know my feelings and yet you ignore them. Why?"

Her great-grandmother watched closely, amazed at the girl's will, a little proud of her spirit. She smiled to herself.

"My daughter, you are like a wild horse, untamed and wilful." His hands were open in front of him, palms up.

"Father, please, you know as well as I do that Gennaro Pasquali is an ass. Do you really want your only daughter marrying a fool? I have known donkeys with more intelligence."

If the truth were known, the duke did have his doubts about Gennaro, but it was too late. "Elettra, Elettra. How many times have we had this same discussion? I am your father. You must obey me."

Her mother jumped into the conversation. "Sweetheart, he's not all bad, not as useless as you say. Surely, with time . . . you barely know him."

"What I have seen, I detest. I fear that what I have not seen will be worse."

The duke turned red. He pounded his fist once, hard on the table, causing an empty glass to topple. "I have given my word and my word is my bond! I cannot go back on it! Do you understand?"

The old *duchessa* watched carefully. Any other girl would have burst into tears by this point. Instead, Elettra's eyes turned steely and she whispered, "I cannot marry him."

"You will marry him! I demand it!"

Still the girl did not raise her voice. "I will not. I will jump from the top of the tower before I marry that buffoon."

Her mother gasped, and the duke shook his head and gritted his teeth.

The girl stood, turned her back on them and hurried from the room. The duke's wife took her husband's hands between her own to try to calm him. At the same time she nodded to the girl's great-grandmother to follow Elettra, to try to console her, to perhaps reason with her.

## A CONVERSATION ABOUT
## LOVE AND DANGER
## UNDER THE LIME TREES

The next day, under a sky the grey of serena marble, the old lady and the young girl strolled arm in arm in the gardens beside a row of lime trees and talked. The courtly *duchessa madre* and the other—no longer a girl, not yet a woman—leaned their heads towards each other.

A pale breeze sighed through the limes.

The old lady shook her head. "No priest can be trusted at this. They have been too long in their lonely pursuits, and then, when the spark of romance ignites, as it surely must, it blazes with uncontrollable midsummer intensity." She paused after they took a few more stuttering steps, the *duchessa* resting her weight on Elettra's arm. "And yet he is a fine man, I must admit."

"Yes. Signor Archenti has saved my life more than once and yet he stares at me as if he is the one drowning. As I said, I think I may have 'feelings' for him." Elettra was not letting on just how strong those feelings were.

The *duchessa* noted that the girl had said "signor" instead of "monsignor." "This is a dangerous situation, my dear. Your father is extremely angry and determined. In any case, the advocate will soon be gone, back to Rome. His investigation must be coming to a conclusion. Probably better to end it now, before anything more comes of it. I have warned you of your powers. Have I not said that your beauty would be irresistible to men?"

"But Grandmama, do you not recall? You asked me to try to soften him in regards to the holy Cambiati. To open his mind and heart to our saint. And I believe I have succeeded. That is why you asked him to tutor me in Latin, remember?"

"Yes, yes, I know it. I admit I did not expect him to be so taken with you. When he is in your presence, he is a different kind of man. I have seen him teaching you. He stares so, as you say. And at times I have seen him reach out and touch your arm or your hand as he speaks to you. He loses the hardness of a devil's advocate then and he softens, grows more human. It has gone too far. You must forget him, and focus your mind on your upcoming marriage."

"Is it so important that I make the right kind of marriage? Do I not also have to listen to my heart?"

"Both, I'm afraid, my little one. Your father and mother fully expect you to marry the young man to whom you have been promised since you were a child. He will bring honour to the family, and wealth too, without a doubt. Besides, the betrothal ceremony has already taken place. It cannot be undone. I am sure Gennaro is someone to whom you can open up your heart—if not immediately, then over time."

"Was that true for you?"

"Yes," she lied.

"The advocate is not so old; at least he does not seem so to me." Elettra's eyes were heavy, grew darker with sadness.

"Do you find him at all devious, my dear?"

"No, I don't. It's strange. He is unlike other Jesuits I have met, and not at all what I would expect of a devil's advocate."

"Perhaps you only see what you desire to see." The old lady stopped and sighed. "We should return. I grow tired."

"Yes, of course." They turned and walked back.

"I agree with you. He is a fine man. But still, Elettra, I must counsel you—there is great danger here."

"I am willing to see what will happen. You know I have no sense of danger, in any case."

"Oh, I do not mean danger for you, my dear. The danger is for him."

The comet continued to streak across the heavens, a white burning jewel, the head of a horse falling through space, its mane streaming out behind, the tip of a brush soaked white moving towards a canvas, the head of a child bursting into the world with a white trailing cry, a wind of light, a wind of burning radiant light coursing through blackness, a great idea shooting up a spine and into the heavens high above.

## THE DEVIL'S ADVOCATE INTERVIEWS HIMSELF

*Do you love the girl?*

I . . . I don't know.

*Do you think you would recognize love if you saw it?*

I don't know. I might . . .

*Are all your answers going to be so ambiguous?*

Is that an official question?

*I will ask the questions here.*

Of course, of course, excuse me.

*Do you find her lovely?*

Yes. At times she gives me a look that I find haunting, as if she is seeing through me, into my soul.

*Is there, in fact, such a thing as a soul?*

Let us not stray from the subject.

*Agreed. You do find her beautiful, then?*

Yes. She glows. She has a radiance that shines from under her skin. And her eyes, those huge dark eyes—when I am with her I cannot stop myself gazing into them, they are so clear and soft. It is as if she is brimming with a natural desire, a desire that is not a function of will but that burns innocently within her.

*Will you tell her of your feelings?*

Every time we are to meet, I rehearse my little playlet. "Elettra, there is something I must tell you. Please do not be upset by what I am about to say, I only speak because my heart is overflowing. I have . . . deep feelings for you. Forget for a moment that I am a priest, that I am the devil's advocate. Remember that I am a man, that I was a man before I was ever a priest, that I will always remain a man. I hope that what I am about to say will not offend you." And so on. But then I never say it when we are together. The words will not pass my lips. My heart rises to my throat and stays there.

*Perhaps she merely wants to be your friend. Is that not a possibility—that she has no inkling of your true feelings?*

Yes, it is possible. I know not. I feel as if I am in a dream, a drowning man struggling in a dream.

*Since you are a priest—one of high standing, no less—
do you believe you have turned into something of a hypocrite?*

I suppose one could say that—and yet, I cannot deny
my heart. All men are riven by mixed emotions. I am a priest,
yes, but not a eunuch.

*Well said. Are you driven not only by your heart but by
your loins as well?*

Love, sex, sex, love—they are so beautifully intertwined
in the human beast. They are inextricable, like the bull and
its maze.

*Does she love you?*

I don't know. It seems each time we meet she goes to
great lengths to dress in a manner that I find elegant and
tempting; and she fixes her hair, and seems delighted to see
me, her eyes shining, her mouth in a full open smile. Several
days ago, I came and sat at her side to look at a text. We were
leaning close together. Her skin was luminous, I could feel
her heat next to me. I had but to turn my head and I could
have put my lips to her cheek. She was glowing and so close.
But then a cloud passed before the sun, and I returned to my
seat across the table. The moment had passed. But truly, I
don't know what is in her heart.

*Could it be youthful innocence? Could she be acting out a
role merely to see where it will lead?*

It could be. She has an air of gorgeous innocence that is
part of her charm. She is indeed young, and I, I am no longer
young.

*Do you fear her father, the duke?*

Yes, very much so. He is a man who is afraid of nothing. To dangle a cleric from the end of his sword would not bother him in the least. If he thought for a moment that I would sully the reputation of his daughter, it would be my end. Perhaps I am a great fool. But . . .

*Are you not a nervous bundle of hopes, fears, hesitations, doubts?*

Yes. Perhaps I will go mad—tortured by an inexpressible love.

*I will ask you again—do you love her or not?*

Yes. Yes, I do.

## LIGHTNING AND THUNDER

Archenti found himself standing at his window in the middle of the night, staring out into the darkness, where a summer storm was gathering. He could feel it, the way the wind suddenly died down and the air grew impossibly pregnant with humidity. At that moment—in exact recreation of the Po and its tributaries, and perfectly reflected there—a branch of lightning shot across the sky, and he realized, *The only way I can live now is if I admit the truth: the fierceness of her beauty is echoed by the ferocity of my desire.*

Then came the thunder.

## PAINTING IN A
## HIDDEN COURTYARD

As the devil's advocate walked across the square heading for the Convent of Santa Lucia, he thought about his disturbing interview with the Hieronymite priest and fresco painter, Don Attilio.

The eccentric painter had said there was a work of art by Fabrizio Cambiati that the advocate should see, in a hidden courtyard at the convent. A painting of a woman, he had said. The old *duchessa* in her youth, depicted as Saint Agata. He had suggested the Jesuit ask the Mother Superior to show it to him, hinting that it would be of some interest in the investigation.

What was it Bodini had been alluding to? And then he had started talking about the name. *Cambiati. The name is close to* "cambiare," "*to change*," he had said, as if he was stating something important. *This name is not from* Lombardia. *It comes from elsewhere, maybe from nowhere. His family was not from here.* The Jesuit had not quite understood what the Hieronymite was getting at, but he would look at the painting and find what he could find. What an arrogant and annoying priest . . .

The Mother Superior had several straggly hairs growing from her chin, and grey eyes chipped from granite. She led Monsignor Archenti down a long hallway that ended at a door, their steps echoing as they walked, two metronomes keeping different times. Using a key she kept pinned under her robes, she opened the door to reveal a tiny, lush outdoor courtyard, a bubbling fountain at its centre. Summer flowers were blooming and there was a faint, fresh, sweet scent of honeysuckle in the air. As there were no windows or balconies opening onto the courtyard, it was entirely enclosed and private, though open to the sky.

Near the far corner, on the wall, was the painting, a small wooden awning jutting out above to help protect it from weather. She went directly to it and the advocate followed. The Mother Superior explained: "It is said Padre Cambiati painted it using the *duchessa madre* as a model, when she was a beautiful young woman. I must return, but you may stay as long as you wish, Your Excellency. Send for me if there is anything you require."

Closing the door behind her, she left the monsignor to the quiet of the courtyard. He listened to her footsteps echo in the hallway for a long while, and then he turned his attention to the painting. It was badly faded, weather-worn, small bits of the pigment having fallen off. The predominant colours in the robes of Saint Agata—if it was her, for it was not entirely clear—were dark blue and gold. The woman in the painting had a lovely calm face, too enticingly beautiful for a saint. The devil's advocate had a sudden insight. *Cambiati must have spent hours in here, in utter privacy, alone with his beautiful model. There would have been plenty of time to . . .* Turning, he gazed at the door. *He would have been able to hear the footsteps of anyone approaching long before the door actually opened.*

Stepping closer to the painting, he searched it for clues. He wasn't sure what he was looking for, but Bodini had insisted, *Look closely, look very closely, and you will see,* and the Hieronymite had nodded his tilted-up head on its stiff stalk of a neck, opening his eyes wide.

In the background, Cambiati had illustrated a typical farm landscape of Lombardy: fields of grain, a few horses, cows, a line of poplars, a river twisting in the distance. He found nothing unusual there. Turning his attention to the standing life-sized woman, he regarded her robes, bringing his face inches from the wall, trying to gather in every detail. Nothing. Her hands, delicate, long-fingered. She held a white lily in the right, the faded green stem echoing the curves of the river in the background. Her left arm was raised and the index finger of her left hand pointed straight up, as if indicating something high in the heavens. There was nothing special about her feet, her stance, her torso. He thought he saw something unusual at the base of her throat, but realized it was a bit of leaf that had stuck there.

Stepping back, he took a breath and regarded the painting anew. He was drawn to the face—its ivory glow. The lips slightly parted, the cheeks pink and heated, the lovely nose. Moving close again, he noticed that the figure was exactly his own height. He stood looking directly into the woman's eyes and then he saw it. He gasped. There in the left pupil, a minute design in gold, like a reflected mote of sunlight.

A few minuscule strokes, and yet it brought everything into question.

Hurrying from the courtyard, he was assaulted by his thoughts. *Why would Cambiati paint it? Should he write the general of the Jesuits? The good cardinal would likely leap to conclusions, perhaps the wrong conclusions. Would he not inform Cardinal Cozio, and perhaps others? If I do not reveal it and it comes out later, what then?*

That evening, as he sat trying to unravel the strands of his thoughts, he decided that he would write again to his friend in Rome, Carlo Neri. Since he was a scholar at the Vatican Library, he would have access to these matters.

He thought again about Rome and what he had left behind. *What is happening there, what plots are unfolding in my absence? Cardinal Cozio cannot be trusted. Neri, though, despite our competition, seems to have supported me these past few years. Sometimes I wish he had been chosen as devil's advocate, as he desired. He was perhaps more suited for it. But, to his credit, I noticed no ill will, no jealousy, once the decision was made. I will write him at first light.*

### A LETTER IN STRICTEST CONFIDENCE

Staring out the window of his parlatory at the dawn, fog thick on the piazza but as if lit from within by a mother-of-pearl blush, the advocate thought of the painting in the courtyard, with its tiny golden aleph, first letter of the Hebrew alphabet, hidden in the pupil of the eye, almost invisible in the pupil of the eye. *And what if Cambiati was a secret Jew, a hidden Jew? Or did he merely have the blood of the Jews deep in his past? A saint who was a Jew—this complicates things, immensely. Of course, if he was a true convert there would be no problem. But how often had these conversions been questioned? Especially ones that took place many years ago and were perhaps forced?*

It was not a complication he wanted to consider, especially at this late stage in his investigation. He shook his head, leaned over the desk and began writing.

*Dearest Carlo,*
*God's blessings upon you. I trust you received my last letter in good health. I suspect Rome is in an uproar now that Benedict has gone to the Lord. You must let me know who appears to be his likely successor. He was a good man with a fine wit, and I for one will miss his presence and his leadership. Let us hope the next pontiff is equally skilled at balancing the many forces in his domain.*

*The case here in Lombardy continues to be a complex one. As I have done several times in the past, I would once again like to ask for your assistance in finding certain information for me. It is information that it would be impossible for me to search out in this provincial town. Lovely as it is, the place is certainly not a centre for learning or study. In any case, I must rely on your considerable skills to answer several vexing questions that relate to the Cambiati candidacy, and I trust that my inquiries and your investigations will both be kept in strictest confidence.*

*First, as I recall, the Jews of Spain were exiled from that country in 1492. Is there any indication that any of these Jews came to Lombardy? I would like to know if any Spanish families or individuals came to Lombardy or neighbouring regions at that time.*

*Secondly, I would like as much information as you can gather on the family name Cambiati. Have you come across it in any of your studies? Any information on this name would be helpful. I have found several church records of birth and marriage here that indicate the name, but nothing before Anno Domini 1577.*

*I hope you will be able to gather this information as quickly as possible and send it to me here in Cremona. Again, I trust you will keep everything you learn, and this letter, in strictest confidence.*

*Blessed be God Our Lord.*

*Monsignor Michele Archenti, Promotor Fidei*

## ICARUS AND THE DONKEY STEW

After a heavy lunch of *stracotto di asinello*—donkey-meat stew had never been his preference, but the housekeeper seemed incapable of cooking anything other than donkey and horse stews and a horrifying selection of organ meats— the advocate decided a walk in the countryside would be rather more invigorating than his usual siesta.

Since the heat of recent days had let up, he thought that he might try to find a pleasant view along the Po. The cassocked priest came to the walls of the city, passed out the Po gate and headed in the direction of the river.

It was a sparkling summer day with a gusting breeze, the tall grasses rolling in waves across the flat land, the sun shining on the dusty swells.

He walked for a long way, knowing he should take this opportunity to ponder details concerning the candidate and all he had learned—and yet his thoughts turned inescapably to the girl. *That old woman, almost as if she were inviting me . . . Or am I still trying to convince myself of something that is vague as mist?*

In the distance, he saw a figure walking steadily along at an angle that would intersect with his own path. Before long he realized that it was Rodolfo.

"Greetings, Your Excellency."

The advocate nodded. "Rodolfo. You are well?"

Rodolfo shrugged. The skeleton clacked, the skull bobbed over his left shoulder.

"Rodolfo, I've been thinking—surely you have expiated your sins by this time. Why do you not cut yourself free of that grotesque thing?"

"I have grown used to him. My brother, you see." He smiled and, looking at the palm of his hand, turned it over to reveal the skeleton hand on the back, its small bones strung together with thin cords of leather.

"Suit yourself, then. However, you might consider it. I would freely vouch for you."

Rodolfo looked away, uninterested. He turned back. "What is your destination?"

"I was thinking of taking in a view of the river. Do you know of a fine vista not too far along?"

"Come." Rodolfo turned and headed off.

"Slower, my friend. I had a load of donkey stew for lunch and it weighs heavily on me."

In a while they came to a slight hillock at river's edge, the water sliding below them black and brilliant in the afternoon. They sat in the grass and watched in silence. Rodolfo pointed upriver a ways, at a wide bend. "It was there he fell."

"Who?"

"Ill-fated Icarus."

"But the legends say he fell into the Aegean Sea."

"This is not true. He fell here, in the Po, as *our* legends of Lombardy tell it. I saw him. He was flailing against the air like an injured bird, a gull maddened by the light. You remind me of him."

"Perhaps he too was weighed down with donkey stew. But you are indeed an odd fellow, Rodolfo. I truly do not know what to make of you."

"Make of me what you will. Mad enough to see what is, mad enough." He smiled, revealing a nearly toothless mouth. "I will tell you what else—look there, down the river, near the place where the water is dark and seems to run in two directions at once, upstream and down. It is very deep. That is where the cathedral stands, hidden below."

"What? A cathedral?"

"Yes, it is true. An entire cathedral of solid marble, carved in secret, in one single piece from the mountains. Ages ago. They dragged it here to the river's edge and built a barge around it. They hoped to float it to the Adriatic and thence up to Venice, but the barge sank. There, precisely there."

"Who? Who accomplished this impossible task?"

"Marble cutters and carvers, draymen. There is a second cathedral in the mountains—an empty space the exact shape of the one in the water. The mountain people worship there in secret. Some of them speak the Greek tongue."

"I see."

"You see nothing, priest, if the truth be known. Or very little."

"How so?"

"This, all of it, is dream. Nothing more. A tale we tell ourselves. A story we watch in a mirror, thinking the doubled world we see is real. We believe it is the only story possible. This is not true."

"I don't follow your logic."

"Logic? It has nothing to do with logic."

"I can see that."

"The story resembles a clockwork but it is not a clockwork. But perhaps I am wrong. I am not making a new religion, only looking at what I see; or perhaps actually seeing what I look at. Perhaps it is both real and a story, a dreaming and a waking, a most ordinary wonder."

"An ordinary wonder. Interesting, Rodolfo, but beyond the limits of my imagination."

"You alone determine the limits of your imagination."

Archenti shook his head. "I will return now, Rodolfo. I believe I have had my fill of your whimsical tales. But you are an entertainment, and I thank you for showing me this lovely vista." The advocate stood and turned away, leaving Rodolfo lying half on his side, stretched out on the grass in the skeleton's pale embrace. Moments later, he was already too distant to hear Rodolfo mumble, "Farewell, poor Icarus."

On the long walk back, pushing the girl from his mind, the Jesuit considered Fabrizio Cambiati and the seven deadly sins. He had once read that every man believes he is defined by one of the seven cardinal virtues. Since he was the devil's advocate, his duty led him to consider the same from the opposite view—that every man is in particular peril of one of the seven deadly sins.

One by one, he went through them.

*Pride.* One must begin with pride, of course. Cambiati did not strike him as a man ruled by pride. Quite the opposite—he seemed willing to minister to the poor and unhealthy, and did not appear to take great credit, although his interest in alchemy might betoken a certain arrogance, or at least the willingness to attempt a certain kind of ludicrous creation of something out of nothing, which of course only God Himself could accomplish.

*Sloth.* He didn't believe Cambiati was a lazy man; he had accomplished much, being both a healer and a painter, and had apparently been assiduous in performing his priestly duties as well.

*Anger.* None of the interviewees had mentioned ever seeing him in a state of high choler. No—all indications were that he was indeed a forgiving priest.

*Gluttony.* Every single interviewee had mentioned his thinness. Unless he was one of those priestly gluttons who can hide a sizable belly under a loose cassock—common enough in the streets of Rome—but no, he thought not.

*Covetousness.* Had he been an avaricious man? Not at all, for by all accounts he had lived a life not unlike that of a pauper.

*Envy.* A deep failing, with long roots difficult to extract. It came from a feeling of never having enough, a feeling that there existed an emptiness that could never be filled. Apparently the priest had never hungered for the wealth or fame of others. No, not envy.

That left *lust*—a common enough weakness. The painting of the beautiful young duchess in the courtyard—did it portray lust? Possibly . . .

The advocate walked through the open gate and into the city. A horse passed, smelling of warm hay; he pictured Elettra for a moment, and then her great-grandmother sitting before him at the interview. A light, a sparkle deep in her eyes, had spoken to him of an ancient emotion in regard to Cambiati. It was the fire of desire, he was sure of it—and then he recalled that he had also seen his own image looking back from those old eyes.

The day's persistent drizzle had driven Elettra and the advocate indoors to a small drawing room on the first floor of the ducal palace. The windows were thrown wide open, allowing fresh air, moist and green, to flood the room. It had been a summer damp beyond belief. A tiny spark of a goldfinch kept coming to the sill, its liquid twittering trill filling the room, then flying up into a tall pine tree. Each time it came, Elettra would stop her work and watch the bird twitching on the sill until it flickered off. She was composed and calm and seemed thoroughly happy with life.

"I enjoy being with you," she said.

"Yes." He smiled and was about to say something, but she turned her head as the bird returned to the sill.

As he walked back to his rooms later, Archenti considered his situation. He knew something was happening—the girl was growing accustomed to his presence, their connection was deepening. For the past two weeks he had seen her every day, and when he looked into her eyes he saw that she was falling, as if tumbling through space. He knew what she was experiencing because he was experiencing the same thing. Her open smiles dissolved any defences he might have had.

*Her beauty is all promise,* he thought. *Such intense ferocious beauty in the young sometimes warns that the form cannot be improved upon—from this day forward it will fade after its first efflorescence. In her case, though, I sense that beauty will go on and on, peaking at some unknown moment in the future when its richness and profusion burst forth and flower and run with a flooding, thirst-easing liquescence . . . Sometimes the look in her eyes is feral, rapturous, frenzied . . . dangerous, she is dangerous . . .*

He placed his hand on the door of his room and hesitated. *Perhaps I should go away for a while. I need to clear my head. A short journey.* The idea of leaving her, even for a few days, was painful, but he sensed that it was necessary. Essential. Turning the handle, he stepped through the doorway and into his room.

On his desk was a letter. He snatched it up. Noting that it was from Monsignor Neri, he slit it open, walked to the window and read it in the grey, diffuse light.

*Dearest Michele,*
*I give you greeting and my most fervent blessing. I have indeed received both of your letters but, as you suggested, the situation here is chaotic since the death of good Benedict. The cardinals have been in conclave for six weeks but thus far nothing but black smoke has issued from their chimney. Rumours circulate that they are close to a decision but it is difficult to determine at this point who is the favourite.*
*Yesterday I saw General Ricci, and he was asking after you. I said I had heard recently from you and he was cheered to know you are well. Do not worry, I did not express to him*

*my worries about the tone of your first letter. I hope the case has become less vexing.*

*My own work goes on forever and ever and will never be done. But then what would I do if it were? As you know I am greatly dedicated to this poring over texts—I harbour no greater ambition, for I have truly put behind me all longing for higher office, as God is my witness. For the most part I am left alone to do my work.*

*And now to answer your questions to the best of my ability. I am happy to be of service, as you have been a trusted friend over the years. It is the least I can do in recompense.*

*First, as to the name Cambiati. It is most certainly not an ancient name, and I suspect it was chosen for its closeness to cambiare. I have been able to determine that several Jewish families in Lombardia are known to have chosen this name, simply because they were in the process of "changing" their names on arrival from Spain.*

*Which leads directly to your other request. Yes, many of the Jews driven out of Spain in 1492 came to Italy, although there were already Jews in Italy at that time, of course. You must know that many Jews called the city of Livorno home, and were active there in banking, trade, medicine, sericulture, silk-dyeing and glass-making. And there were Jews in many other cities and towns as well, though not in such great numbers as at Livorno.*

*Thousands of Sephardic Jews were exiled from Spain with nothing, or very little, and went to many places through-out the Mediterranean. While they were chastised almost* universally, they were treated most kindly by the Turks, oddly enough, and did not fare too badly in Naples. Many also came to Genoa, Ferrara, Rome and other places. In some cities, they were welcomed for the simple fact that they held many secrets of silk-weaving, cloth-dyeing and other crafts.

A few of these Jews could easily have wandered from Genoa to the regions around Cremona, especially since the Po valley is particularly benign for the cultivation of mulberry trees, essential for the production of silk, as I am sure you know. I consulted a priest here, from the region, who knows of a place not far from Genoa called Casale Monferrato. At this town there is a road known locally as Mulberry Road, and also called Jews' Alley, for many Jews there are involved in sericulture, and some in silk-dyeing as well.

I was not able to determine if any of the families in the area bear the name Cambiati.

I trust this information will be of some help in your investigation. I will, of course, continue to keep this information and your letter in strictest confidence. Certainly, if you require my services for further research, do not hesitate to call upon me. It is a great joy for me to ferret out such secret and hidden facts from the deep wells of books, manuscripts and records.

May God's will be done.
Blessed be God Our Saviour
Monsignor Carlo Neri

*THE PLAY—ACT FOUR*

After all the time Pantalone had spent waiting for Arlecchino to return from Mantua with the magic violin to help him win the heart of Aurora; after waiting for the object of his dreams to arrive again on the piazza for her evening stroll; after waiting for the silly girl to realize that Ottavio was a young fool; after waiting for her to discover that he alone, Pantalone, was worthy of her affections; as each day and night he paced the cobbles of the square, hardly eating at all, his heart breaking with an old man's last chance at love . . . He ceased his striding back and forth across the stage and turned to the audience. "Patience was never my long suit."

He let the audience glimpse the club he held behind his back. "I can wait no longer. I won't live forever. I must have her. Now!" He hid behind the screen, his scrawny head peering out as the lovers walked onstage. "With Ottavio out of the way, she'll have no choice but to turn to me. There's no better lover than one who is suffering. Aaah . . ."

Pantalone crept out from behind the screen, snuck up behind them and raised the club high in the air. Just as he brought it down to crush Ottavio's head, Aurora leaned over to whisper something in her lover's ear. Pantalone accidentally struck the girl with a glancing blow. She slumped to her knees and fell prone on the floor. Ottavio stared at her in horror—a horror that quickly turned to anger as he saw the club dangling from Pantalone's hand. Snatching it from him, he started beating the old man about the head and shoulders. Pantalone held his hands and arms up and screamed as the blows rained down on him. "*Dio mio,* I didn't mean to hit her! Stop! Ouch! Ouch!"

Ottavio flung the club away and returned to his groaning beloved, kneeling down to cradle her head in his lap, stroking her forehead.

Meanwhile, Pantalone lay on the floor bemoaning his fate. Believing that he was about to die, he recited his last will and testament to the audience. "I'll have you all know I am dying not from Ottavio's blows, but from heartbreak. In these, my last moments, I now state my final bequests: a full nothing for the wife, half of nothing for each of the children, a quarter of nothing for the grandchildren, a club to the hands for my tailor, a good spanking for my confessor, a draught of Mantuan swamp-water for my wine merchant, a cup of poison for my doctor, a cup of sand for my baker, a cup of worms for my butcher, a cup of dust for my banker. There you have it. I can now die in peace."

"Stop your gob, old man." Ottavio stood over him, hands on hips. Behind him, Aurora had sat up and was holding her head with both hands. "Lucky for you she's going to be all right. But you, you're hardly even bruised, you complainer. I ought to tear out your guts and tie them around your neck"— Pantalone winced—"but I won't, because I'm the one who would end up in prison. But be careful, old man, be careful."

Ottavio returned to help Aurora to her feet. She leaned her head on his shoulder as they stumbled off the stage. A few moments later, Pantalone raised his head and stared after them as the sound of sweet violin music drifted to him. Groaning, he flopped his head back and pounded it against the floor. "Where is he? Where is that damned scoundrel with the violin he promised me? Run off with my money, I'm sure of it. Ah, *dio mio*. I'm an old man. I'm in pain. My head hurts and my heart aches. Have pity on me, good people of Cremona, have pity on me. On the inside I am still young. But my body betrays me. My cod still functions with the virility of an eighteen-year-old, leaping from my loins like a fish from the sea. I am sure it will be the last organ to fail. I am a fount of lust. Will I die without one woman knowing my skill at love? What a waste, what a pity. Look on me with sorrow, people of Cremona. I grow old, I grow old. I woke up one morning and I was old, and that was that. Dip the sails, gather in the ropes. No going back now. I'm old."

## PANTALONE TRAVELS
## TO MANTUA ON
## A HESITANT DONKEY

It has always been the custom to place the main altar at the east end of a Christian church, so that a celebrant turning to bless the congregation faces west. When the players arrived on the piazza, they had erected their stage on the square's west side, facing east, so that a play performed in morning or early afternoon would be lit by the sun. In that way the sacred and the secular were kept in balance.

As he prepared to go onstage, the reins of a donkey resting in his hand, Pantalone stood in the arcade backstage, reading short descriptions of scenes that had been carefully printed on a piece of parchment and nailed to a wooden beam next to the ramp leading to the stage.

"Hmm. Pantalone goes to Mantua on a donkey to see what is delaying Arlecchino. All right then, up we go." In trying to mount the donkey, he slipped. The animal clomped up the ramp onto the stage with Pantalone clinging to its neck with his arms, one of his legs over the animal, the other dragging. "Stop! Stop, you idiot beast!"

The crowd laughed as he righted himself on the donkey's back, adjusted his clothing and prepared to ride across the stage. He kicked the animal in the sides with his heels. The donkey took three steps and halted as if it had arrived at its destination, having forgotten how recently it had set out. "Oh, good Lord! *Andiamo! Andiamo!*" He kicked again and the beast took three more steps, and stopped as before. In this way, donkey and rider stuttered across the stage and prepared to descend the ramp on the far side.

A musician ran out, clinging to his lute. "Where are you going?"

"To Mantua. I must find Arlecchino and my magic violin or my heart will wither into dust. Keep the audience entertained until my return."

The musician held onto the donkey's tail. "But how can you leave the play now?"

"I am not leaving the play—the play continues as always. But enough of talk. I go. I will return. *Ciao.*"

"*Ciao.*"

Other musicians mounted the stage and began to play.

Sometime later, Pantalone could be seen—covered in dust, shoulders hunched, head bowed—seated on the donkey as he and the beast made excruciatingly slow progress across the bevelled cobbles of Mantua's Piazza Sordello. As before, the donkey halted after every three steps, and he barely had the strength to keep kicking it to urge it forward. And on and on it went, as they inched their way towards the Palazzo Ducale.

The piazza, and indeed the entire city of Mantua, was deserted. Not a soul breathed on the streets or in the squares. No guards stood at the open gate as Pantalone arrived and dismounted. As soon as he was off, the donkey turned and clattered in high spirits back across the piazza and down a narrow street. Pantalone watched. "Beast from Hell," he shouted weakly after it.

He peered into the courtyard beyond the gate. A small fountain stood at the centre, gushing a plume of water. In dire need of refreshment, he hurried to the fountain and leaned over to drink. At that moment the flow of water ceased, and the last of the water in the pool surrounding the fountain gurgled down a drain. Taking a step back, Pantalone stared at the fountain, waiting for it to come back on. Nothing happened.

Eventually he gave up and made his way into the cool halls of the palace.

In a distant room, the mastiff lay sprawled under a table, licking its genitals with great gusto. The hunchback and Arlecchino were attacking a platter heaped with black rice and eels. The smacking of the dog's tongue ceased as it raised its head, sniffed the air and growled. "Shush," said Ugo. He drew out from the platter a two-foot-long eel and let the mastiff suck it down.

Again the dog raised its head and sniffed the air, as another growl rumbled from deep within its throat. "Someone is coming," the hunchback said.

Meanwhile, Pantalone wandered through room after room where frescoes both demonic and elegiac decorated walls and ceilings. Lost in its maze of corridors and chambers, he felt the menace of the place. "Arlecchino," he called, testing the silence, his hands cupped around his mouth. Nothing but empty echoes came back, fading diminuendos that continued for minutes on end, echoes that seemed to take on their own life.

Pantalone stopped short. *Was that the grunt of a dog? It could be a big dog. It could be a hungry dog, a mean dog.* Should he hurry back the way he had come, give up his quest to find Arlecchino? Summoning the image of Aurora to mind, he gathered the courage to go on. Holding tightly to his codpiece, he stepped into the next room . . . where the mastiff, snarling, leapt upon him, slamming into the middle of his chest, knocking him to the marble floor.

"*Basta!*" a voice shouted. The dog backed off, leaving the supine Pantalone shaking.

Arlecchino and the hunchback stood over the old man. "Get up, you're not hurt. Who are you? What do you want here?" demanded Ugo.

"It's Pantalone. The one who ordered the violin." Arlecchino smiled at the Mantuan, even as a questioning look passed across his face and he turned back to Pantalone. "But what are you doing here? I said I would bring the violin to you when it was ready."

Pantalone stood, the hunchback giving him a hand, the mastiff still rumbling, its teeth bared. The player spoke slowly with his teeth gritted, biting off each word. "I tired of awaiting your return. Where have you been all this time? I send you to perform a simple errand and you take ages getting back to me. And not a word from you in the meantime. I am a patient man but this is too much, Arlecchino, too much. She will be married soon and it will be too late." His long gnarly hand grasped at the air before him. "I need that violin!"

With a gesture, the Mantuan stopped the conversation. "To do what you ask, good sir, takes time. I have created the violin you requested but there was much trouble in the doing of it. A few minor details must still be attended to. Also, the price has doubled."

"Doubled! This is an outrage!" Pantalone sputtered and fumed. In his frustration he turned to Arlecchino and spoke quickly. "I will cut out the middle man! Thank you, Arlecchino, you are dismissed. I will take delivery of the violin myself, no need for you to hang about. Farewell then." He waved his hand as if to brush Arlecchino away.

Arlecchino hung his head. "Life is so unfair—and me thirteen months pregnant. Whatever will I do?"

Ugo glared at Pantalone but spoke to the fool. "Don't worry. I will see that this codger pays you. The order came from him to you to me. The price has tripled. The old skinflint will pay, you'll see."

Pantalone dropped to his knees. "Oh, I'm a poor old man, a wretch, don't break me on the rack like this!"

The hunchback crossed his arms. "Old, yes. Poor, no. Don't fake it with me. The riches you've socked away—

they're legendary. The price will keep going up until you give in. They have now quadrupled."

"Enough! You win, you win." Pantalone stood up again and shrugged. "I must have her—what can I do?"

"I will let you in on a little secret, old one. The violin will not be enough. You will also have to convince the go-between, the matchmaker, to change her mind."

"Arrgh, bad news comes in batches. How am I to do that?"

Ugo rubbed the head of the mastiff as he thought. Pantalone waited. Arlecchino waited too, with avid interest. He knew the ugly spinster who was the matchmaker, and he wondered if he could be the go-between for the go-between, so to speak. He licked his lips at the profit that might entail. The hunchback stopped and looked up. "She can be bought. It is possible. But she will need some . . . persuading. She clings to romantic notions, but I believe she will toss those to the wind for the right price."

"I know the woman you speak of. The three-warted one, yes?" Arlecchino nodded his head vigorously, and turned to Pantalone. "I will be your go-between for the go-between, for a fair and reasonable price."

Pantalone shook his head. "I am doomed. First it takes me four days to cross the dullest, flattest plain in creation, three steps at a time, on the world's stupidest donkey, and now this. I'd be better off dead."

"Come, come now, old Pantalone." The Mantuan dusted off the front of the player's coat. "What about Aurora? It will all be worth it in the end, will it not?"

A sly smile creased Pantalone's face as his eyes slid back into the warm bath of his fantasy.

Ugo bowed. "And now, come join us in our feast. You must be thirsty after your long ride. I have some local *vino nero* you must try."

# CHAPTER NINE

*Still another miracle attributed to Cambiati, this one related by the duke. Fabrizio is said to have cured thirteen residents of a madhouse in the city. On the same day, thirteen priests at the Hieronymite chapter house were seen to begin babbling uncontrollably, running naked about the main square and acting possessed. By the next morning they had been relieved of their affliction, but their shame was such that they would not show their faces in the city for several months.*

## FRUIT FROM THE TREE OF THE KNOWLEDGE OF GOOD AND EVIL

Fabrizio sat at a high desk in his laboratory, reading a tome on the alchemical importance of mercury and how it could be used to "fertilize" a compound. He paused and looked up. Following the duchess's revelation in the confessional, the overjoyed couple had announced to the world that she was with child. The duke was ecstatic. He could be seen about the city with a broad, unending smile. He was especially gentle with his wife that week, and drank a lake of wine with his friends in celebration. Fabrizio was genuinely happy for them. He bowed his head to his task and went back to reading.

Omero stepped into the laboratory. "Ah, here you are. There was just now a messenger from . . . my, you look like an old Jew, sitting up there reading from your book . . ."

"Omero. The messenger—what did he want?"

"He brought a message from the duke. I took the liberty of opening it as it seemed rather urgent." He held the envelope in one hand, the letter itself in the other.

Fabrizio shook his head. "And?"

"He orders you to come to the ducal palace, immediately."

Fabrizio froze. He closed the book and swallowed. "That will be all," he said thickly, for his tongue had gone dry in his mouth. Omero lingered a few moments, playing his usual subtle game of insolence by pretending that he was not being dismissed but could decide on his own when to leave. Finally he exited the room, taking the note with him.

Fabrizio sat and contemplated the hard heart of the duke. With his index finger he nervously tapped the cover of the closed book. *He knows. He knows everything. What am I to say? I cannot deny it. Oh, God!*

The duchess stood behind the servant-girl who had answered Don Fabrizio's knock, wringing her hands, the intensity of her emotions playing over her face.

"Ah, you have come," she said.

"Yes," he answered grimly. "Where is he?"

"Follow me." She turned and headed up the wide marble staircase. Fabrizio trudged behind, heart leaping in his chest.

They came to a door. She knocked lightly and entered. Another servant, this one an older woman, rose from a chair.

Fabrizio was surprised to see the duke lying in bed. As they entered, he turned to look at them. "Don Fabrizio, thank you for coming. But where are your medicaments?"

"My medicaments?"

"Yes, why else would I ask you here?"

Fabrizio blinked. "Of course, of course. I will first determine the affliction and then return for the appropriate medicine."

"That is a waste of time when I am in such pain! You should have brought them with you." The duke's eyes sparked with anger, and the priest was relieved that he did not have to face his true rage, for the moment.

"Yes, yes. Calm yourself. What is it ails you, Your Grace?"

The two women ducked from the room as the duke pulled down the blanket, yanked up his nightshirt and revealed a pair of hugely swollen testes.

The priest bent down to examine them more closely. He was about to place his finger on one, hesitating, afraid it would burst, when the duke hissed, "Do not touch."

"I have an herbal remedy that I am fairly sure will cure this. I will fetch it and return shortly."

"Hurry," moaned the duke as he yanked his nightshirt down and pulled the blanket up.

As Fabrizio swept down the staircase, the duchess followed and accompanied him to the door. Out of view of the trailing maidservant, who had turned aside, Fabrizio's eyes met the eyes of the duchess. She smiled sadly at him and looked away, and he was out the door and hurrying down the street.

THE PHILOSOPHER'S STONE
FOUND, AND LOST AGAIN

The day after curing the duke, Fabrizio was working in his laboratory, his mind at ease as it had not been in months.

The windows of the laboratory *cum* studio were covered with heavy paper soaked in olive oil. In this way, a soft, diffused light perfect for painting was admitted into the room. However, a half-finished portrait sat untouched on the easel. For the past fortnight Fabrizio had been more interested in alchemy than painting. Intricate new ideas had bubbled up, inspired by an ancient book that had come to him from a friend in Mainz. Fabrizio had been working hard—driven by he knew not what demon, but driven he was. He was obsessed with finding the great secret that had inspired every alchemist since the beginning of time—the Philosopher's Stone. The ultimate answer to the enigma that was life and death. The jewel of Ouroboros. The ancient words came to him again: "Stone which is not stone, a precious thing which has no value, a thing of many shapes which has no shape, this unknown thing which is known of all." He didn't want immortality, like many alchemists—that was foolish—but he did want to cure the world of its suffering. That was all that mattered to him. Many had come close to the truth without grasping the fundamental verity, and yet here he was at the very edge of the great discovery, and yet, and yet . . .

He stirred the large crucible over the flame. Consulting the open book, he flicked the page, reached up to his shelf for a jar and sprinkled the contents into the crucible, turned the page again. He straightened. "Half a turnip? There must be some vital essence within the root." He left the laboratory and returned a moment later with a turnip in hand. Placing it on the high table, he sliced half of it into small pieces and threw them into the crucible, leaving the other half on the table. After a few moments the solution, which had previously been dark grey, turned a radiant gold colour. He watched, astounded, and consulted the ancient tome again. "One more ingredient . . . a handful of good black earth." He hurried out to the small herb garden behind the laboratory.

While he was out, Omero wandered into the room where the crucible bubbled. He noted the pleasant smell in the air and saw the half-turnip remaining on the table. "Oh? Turnip soup? Odd colour." Taking a spoon, he scooped up a bit of soup and tasted it. "Needs salt, badly." High on the shelf was a saltcellar. Snatching it down, he sprinkled the soup liberally. The solution lost its rich gold hue and returned to grey. He was tasting it again as Fabrizio came in from the garden, the soil in his palm.

"Is that for the soup?"

"Soup? What soup?"

Omero glanced at the crucible. "It needed salt. It's just right now."

"Salt? You added salt to my solution!" Fabrizio looked into the crucible and his heart sank. He flopped onto a stool. "I don't know whether to kill you or cry."

"I saw the turnip . . . I thought . . ." He paused. "You could do it again. Repeat the same ingredients, that's all."

Fabrizio waved his free hand. "These things must be so utterly precise, one must be lucky to get it right—the stars and planets must be in their most auspicious positions and phases, in perfect alignment. Everything changes in a moment. It is impossible, impossible . . ." He leaned forward, took a deep whiff of the soil in his hand and sighed. "What do you think it could mean, Omero? 'Stone which is not stone, a precious thing which has no value, a thing of many shapes which has no shape, this unknown thing which is known of all.' The fabled riddle of the Philosopher's Stone. What do you think? What could it be?"

Omero shrugged. "A mystery surely."

Fabrizio suddenly thought better of discussing such deep matters with his manservant. "Of course it's a mystery. I have no idea why I even asked you. It must have something to do with this sudden despair I feel—that I will never attain it, never find the Philosopher's Stone."

Omero didn't hear these last words. He was busy rooting about under the worktable, searching for a flask of wine he had stored there the previous week.

# *THE PLAY—ACT FIVE*

## THE BEAUTIFUL
## DESICCATED GIRL

Ahead of Pantalone and Arlecchino walked Ugo the Mantuan and his mastiff, leading the two players along halls and through rooms of his palace that had been seldom entered for dozens of years. Their steps raised feeble clouds of dust as they tramped.

"Where are we going?" Pantalone whispered.

"He said he has something to show us. It seemed important to him." Arlecchino watched the glistening testicles of the dog as its long tail swept from side to side ahead of them.

Pantalone belched loudly and recalled the garlicky sausage they had just finished gorging on, tasting it again, while Arlecchino waved at the air. The Mantuan ignored them.

For almost an hour they walked along passages that seemed to twist back on themselves like viscera, through darkening rooms and past windows filling with an overripe peach-coloured dusk. Out one window, Arlecchino took in a view of swamps stretching for several miles into the distance, fetid lakes of stagnant water interspersed with tightly bunched beds of reeds. Out another he spied a courtyard overcrowded with twisted barley-sugar columns spiralling up into nothingness. The trio walked on through the increasing gloom.

"I don't like this," said Pantalone.

Arlecchino nodded in agreement.

Eventually they came to a room whose entranceway was bricked up to waist level.

Ugo halted and turned to them. His eyes appeared moist and sad, as if something inside him were melting. He lifted his hand, gesturing. "Behold, Pantalone. And you too, fool. This is love."

Inside the room, on an ornate wooden chair with a worn purple velvet seat, sat a woman, or rather a girl, or rather a being that had been a girl a long time ago. The figure was desiccated beyond belief, almost mummified.

"Ooof." Pantalone turned away.

"Look at her," Ugo insisted. A transcendent rapture lit his face. Arlecchino could tell he was pining for the girl, watching her intently and dreaming about the distant past, the look on his face equal parts pleasure and pain.

The two players turned back to the girl. She wore a zibeline stole of silky fur around her shoulders, walnut-brown with silver tips, the head of the dead sable still attached, biting its own tail. In her hands she held a book of vellum, the leather as dry and wrinkled as her own hands and face. She appeared to be staring at it.

Her lips were moving ever so slightly.

"She's alive!" Pantalone stumbled backwards. "*Dio mio,* she's alive!"

Arlecchino stared in amazement, his mouth a hollow cavern.

Ugo shrugged. "Alive. Yes, in a manner of speaking. She reads from the poem in her hands, and that gives her immortality. The poet had a profound power—he told her she would never die as long as she was reading his poem."

"But she ages?" Arlecchino noted.

"Yes." Ugo said dryly, and gazed with uncontrived sadness. "She ages."

Arlecchino leaned forward. "I can't hear the poem. I would like to hear it."

Ugo grabbed the fool's shoulder and pulled him back roughly. "No! If you hear the poem, its sounds, its irresistible rhythms, will capture you—forever. You will never be able to pull yourself away."

The room was stuffed with priceless objects covered in a heavy patina of dust: faded paintings of gods and goddesses in their swollen paradises; a pair of lutes with mother-of-pearl inlay depicting scenes of the grape harvest; three violins and a cello, seemingly in whispered conversation with each other; little bell-towers of latched books stacked on table and floor; jewelled necklaces and bracelets piled on a platter of dull gold; bronze sculptures, some quite fine, others of incomparable ugliness. The walls were stained with frescoes of peach and pear orchards the colour of warm sand; the ceiling gilded and carved with stuffed cherubim and angels looking as if they were returning from an all-night tryst in a graveyard. In cabinets of black exotic wood were piles of coins, medals, gems, ancient manuscripts, goblets of gold and silver, crucifixes, and a skull with onyx eyes, Arabic text written in an elegant script upon its forehead.

Arlecchino asked, "You loved her?"

Ugo offered no reply but continued staring at the girl.

"Describe how she looked, before." Pantalone suggested. "*Per favore.*"

Ugo glared at the old scoundrel, trying to determine what was behind his request. He then turned and regarded the girl as he spoke. "She had the clearest blue eyes, like melted sky. And a husky way of speaking that used to break me open inside, so unexpected in one so young. It hinted of deeper rivers flowing through her, rivers I wanted to wallow in, to drink to the full, until I was drowned in their smooth darkness.

"She always dressed in cloth of watered silk, her curves liquid, her skin cool. If she walked through an orchard, the apricots and plums, incited by her presence, would split open and drip with sweet juices. If she walked beneath the lime trees, the songbirds would sing in warbling arpeggios to try to impress her. If she entered a room filled with girls just ripening to their fullness and young men with fresh hard eyes, she would attract everyone's gaze instantly, without trying in the least."

He paused and Arlecchino asked, "Why did you not marry her, then?"

"Idiot. I was her official dwarf. I was a Gonzaga—that used to mean something, but it meant nothing to her father. At the time, I was simply an object of ridicule, doomed to entertain her, to draw her out of her profound despair. I alone could make her laugh. And such a laugh it was—unreserved, black and rich as soil, deep and round as the moon.

"But I was merely her dwarf, her little plaything, her charming hunchback; she was as aware of my love as a leopard is aware of the pain it causes when it crushes the bones of some small soft beast. She would have laughed had I spoken of it, would have split me in two with her astounded look. I kept my silence, and waited."

"Waited? For what?" Arlecchino asked.

"I didn't know. I waited for something to happen, something to change, something to arrive out of heaven to make it all right. But it never came. Then I discovered the mad poet with his immortal poem. He sold it to me for three gold coins and a barrel of black wine. I continued waiting, but a plan was forming at the back of my mind. Over the years, as her beauty ripened more and more, my bitterness grew. I would never have her, could never have her—what kind of cruel God would throw such a delight in front of a man deformed like me? A temptation beyond all resistance. She was swarmed by suitors, a flood of young men knocked on the palace doors. But I was in a unique position. The suitors had to come through me first. They were forced, each one, to wait alone in an anteroom where I was the only other person. The girl thought that I, her official dwarf, would keep them entertained as they waited to see her. I used my time well—a perfectly placed word of doubt for one; for another, a whisper that her family riches were soon to be replaced by mountainous debts; a lie about her intimate smell being inconceivably horrible. In truth, it was quite the opposite. To one shocked suitor I blathered about her infertility; another I told of her anger, that had resulted in the death of an infant she had borne, adding that it had had incipient horns and cloven hooves. The young men were no match for me—every one, smitten at first, was driven away, tortured by fear and doubt. She was never wed."

"You are a cruel man." Arlecchino looked sadly at the girl.

"I have my good side." The Mantuan patted the head of the mastiff standing next to him.

Pantalone spoke. "And the poem?"

"I eventually gave it to her, without telling her of its magic power when read aloud. She has been reading it ever since. Over and over. It is a black art of the highest order. No one will have her. No one will ever have her. Not even Death."

An hour later, Pantalone and Arlecchino were on their way back to Cremona. Ugo had given them the use of his carriage and driver for the return trip. "We must hurry—the play awaits us," Arlecchino shouted. As they entered the carriage, Ugo said, "Soon I will have your violin ready, old one. And what a violin it will be. The girl will be yours—have no doubt!"

## PANTALONE AND THE
## PERSISTENCE OF PASSION

As if waking from a dream, the audience watching the play in the square of Cremona realized that Pantalone and Arlecchino had returned to the stage. The play was beginning again.

On stage, a table was set for dinner: three plates, four empty platters, three cups and a pale blue earthenware jug of wine.

Aurora and Ottavio approached the table; he bowed, she curtsied, he helped her into her chair and took his seat next to her.

Ottavio wore a red-lined cape draped over his shoulders, a large white ruff of a collar, knee breeches and leather shoes. On removing his wide-brimmed felt hat, he shook out his shoulder-length black hair.

Aurora had a stiff lace frill in her hair, and her long scarlet skirt touched the floor. Her eyes and skin glowed, and her dress presented considerable cleavage.

A towel draped over his arm, Arlecchino approached their table and bowed. "*Buona sera.* The signora looks ravishing tonight, and you, good sir, a real gentleman. What shall it be? We have wonderful capon, recently roasted."

"Not pigeon?"

"No, no. Genuine capon, sir."

"Let us have it, then."

Arlecchino reached into his capacious pantaloons, pulled out the juicy roast capon by a leg and plopped it onto a platter on the table.

"Blackbird pie?"

"Oh yes, I love that," said Aurora, beaming.

Again Arlecchino dug about in his pants, and removed a large pie, still steaming.

From inside his boots he snatched a half-dozen buns which he also placed on a platter, then added a bulging cluster of purple grapes from inside his shirt. From the jug on the table he filled the cups with wine, and he took his leave, bowing out. "Enjoy, enjoy," he said.

As the loving couple touched cups and gazed into each other's eyes, Pantalone sidled onto the stage. His codpiece rampant, he leered at Aurora but edged towards the table, afraid of attracting Ottavio's ire.

"Might I join you?"

Ottavio looked up. After a moment's hesitation he smiled. "Ah, Pantalone. Yes, yes, of course. All is forgiven. I know, and she knows, and everyone else knows"—in a sweeping gesture he included the crowd—"that you are nothing more than an old dog in heat. The only one who does not seem to know it is you."

Pantalone shrugged. "I can't help myself. In the presence of a lovely woman, I am utterly helpless. A young woman makes me feel young again." He bowed his head. "I, I am afraid of growing old."

"Yes, I understand."

"Desire never dies, don't you see?"

"In your case, old dog, it never even gets sick."

Pantalone sat and the trio commenced eating and drinking. At one point, Aurora reached across the table for the jug of wine. When Pantalone saw her hand moving towards the wine, he slyly pushed the jug out of reach. She stretched again, bending over the table. He slid it farther away. Ottavio, busy chewing on a leg of the capon, saw nothing. Aurora reached again, still unable to fasten her hand around the neck of the jug. Each time she stretched, she bent over farther. Pantalone's eyes grew wider and wider at her blossoming cleavage; she was practically falling out of her dress. He licked his lips, and finally she gained the jug and sat back down.

"Ass," she hissed at him.

Going back to his meal, Pantalone, in a spasm of overexcited nerves and shaking hands, was having difficulty ripping a wing off the fowl. He yanked hard and a glob of fat flew through the air, landing in the tender hollow at the base of Aurora's throat. Gnawing on a bone, she was blissfully unaware. Pantalone stared as the knuckle of glistening fat slid down her upper chest.

"Let me get that for you." He moved his scrawny hand towards her bosom.

Ottavio bolted to his feet and drew his short sword. "Let it be, you old dog, or you'll leave this table one paw short."

Meanwhile, the knuckle of fat disappeared in the cleavage.

"Leave it, old man," Ottavio warned. "After it slides over her belly and comes to rest between her thighs, I'll have it for my midnight snack."

Pantalone bowed his head low, pushed his plate away and wept, gritting his teeth and mumbling to himself, "Where is that damned violin?"

Aurora turned to observe him. "I do believe he has had too much wine."

Ottavio nodded. "His blood has turned to vinegar. It's pickled his heart. Leave him be."

# CHAPTER TEN

*It is said that Cambiati was seen standing atop the torrazzo one morning, glowing with an indescribable radiance. They say he leapt from the tower and fell like a normal man at first, but then appeared to float down to the piazza with the lightness of a leaf. All that was found on the square where he landed was an empty cassock, nothing more.*

A   DIFFICULT
CONVERSATION

Michele Archenti turned down a narrow street on his way to give Elettra another lesson in Latin. The heat was already rising from the cobbles. Latin, he realized, was the last thing on his mind, and he suspected it was the last thing on hers as well. He felt confused, for many reasons. A priest in love. With a young woman, already betrothed, her wedding date set. He was in turmoil, also, because he was not being honest with her. About his feelings for her; and because he was using her to try to reveal the *duchessa*'s secret about Cambiati. At the same time, he began to suspect that the old lady and the girl were using him to ensure the success of Cambiati's candidacy. *But the girl is irresistible, irresistible . . .* He stopped, realizing that he had given voice to this last thought. He looked about to ensure that no one had heard him, and then hurried on, came to the heavy doors of the ducal palace and knocked.

"We will not be able to meet over our Latin for the next while, as I must make a short journey to the town of Casale Monferrato."

Elettra shoved the book aside, tired of the slow translation work. Reaching into a bowl on the table, she took up a large purple grape almost the size of an apricot. She bit into it with sharp white teeth. Archenti watched closely as she closed her eyes, savouring the juice. With the back of her hand, her eyes still closed, she wiped at the corner of her mouth. "Why? What's there?"

"Something has come up having to do with my investigation of the candidate."

She waited. "You aren't going to tell me what?" Her eyes were open wide now, staring at him.

Archenti hesitated. "I really mustn't."

Her shoulders slumped. "Oh, you priests and your secrets! Tell me, or I will tell my father that I have learned nothing in twenty sessions of Latin with you."

"It's not true. You have learned well. Truly, it is astonishing how quickly you have learned."

She spoke without looking at him. "Why do you stare so at me? Each time we are together, you stare and stare at me. I would say you are trying to look into my soul, but it appears it is more the surface that interests you, yes?" Turning, she confronted him, a hard and beautiful look on her face, her dark eyes burning.

His mouth suddenly went dry. *I am being interrogated by a mere girl.* He licked his lips. "I stare because, if I may be so bold as to admit the truth, I find it impossible not to."

"You find me beautiful?"

He nodded slowly.

"You won't tell me why you are going to Casale Monferrato because you think I am too ignorant to understand your investigation."

"No, that is not true."

"Then tell me. You must tell me."

"You are a persistent young woman." He paused, thinking. "If I tell you, it must remain between us, you understand?" *If I let her think I am confiding in her, perhaps she will naturally confide in me.*

"Agreed."

"I am going there to search out any families with the name of Cambiati. It is possible that Fabrizio's family came from that area and that they were silk-growers. There is a place there called Mulberry Road, also known as Jews' Alley."

"I see. Were his family Jews then? Could our beloved local saint have Jewish blood?"

He knew without a doubt that she would understand the implications. "It is . . . possible."

"And would that be a problem? For you?"

"Not for me personally."

"What do you mean?"

"I mean nothing. I have nothing against the Jews, though others seem to blame them for every ill under the sun. It would likely not help his candidacy, unless he was a genuine convert, a fact almost impossible to prove after the passage of so much time."

"Jesus was a Jew."

"Of course. But many Christians blame the Jews for killing him."

"He was not killed by Jews. He was killed by Romans."

Again, he enjoyed her simple clarity. "Nevertheless, many, even at the heart of the Church, blame the Jews."

"They are afraid of being blamed themselves. The Romans killed our Saviour, not the Jews. Romans like you."

She said it with such finality that he knew their conversation had come to an end. He reflected again that she had the strong, unyielding opinions of the wealthy, and the air—a natural pride that bordered on arrogance—of those who were born to rule.

As he walked back across Cremona, he realized that he, a powerful man in the Church, had been dismissed by this . . . this . . . girl. But from another view, he didn't mind at all. In fact, he marvelled at it. How sublime beauty and great natural power, in combination, were an irresistible aphrodisiac. He dwelled on the thought of her cheeks flushed with anger, the blood rising to the surface, her eyes shining bright. The Romans . . . Yes, of course, it was the ancient Romans who had brought all the most beautiful women in the known world back to Italy for their pleasure and for breeding. She was part of that bloodline. Without a doubt.

A  S H O R T  J O U R N E Y
T O  C A S A L E  M O N F E R R A T O

For the entire seventy-mile journey from Cremona to Casale Monferrato, north of the city of Allessandria in Piedmont, the rain fell slanting into the earth. The devil's advocate watched it stipple the surface of the Po as the carriage inched through the mud, heading along the river. Numerous times the carriage sank in the slick, softened roadway and the advocate had to join the driver in working it free. Three days it took, with nightly stopovers in damp roadhouses. Monsignor Archenti ached with the journey, and was glad to see the sun greet his arrival at the gates of the town.

"To the priest's residence near the church," he instructed the driver, leaning out the window. They could see the church bell-tower not far off, in the heart of Casale Monferrato.

The priest, Padre Grasselli, was wide-bottomed and took tiny steps, perhaps in fear of falling and not being able to rise again. His round, smiling face showed that he was honoured to put up such an important and dignified guest.

That evening, feasting on eel and tench as well as polenta and the local Barbera wine, the two priests came to know one another. The devil's advocate told Padre Grasselli why he had journeyed to Casale Monferrato.

"Why is it you want to talk to Jews?" the padre asked, a distasteful look on his face. "Nothing but moneylenders. They are not to be trusted."

"That I doubt—if they are all pawnbrokers and money-lenders, how is it that some know how to cultivate silk, while others know the secrets of dyeing and glass-making?"

The priest shrugged.

"I need to find a place called Mulberry Road."

"Jews' Alley," the priest said. "I know it, but you must go with someone who understands these people. They do not trust us Christian men. If you insist, tomorrow I will take you to a synagogue the Jews here claim is the most beautiful in the world. Perhaps the rabbi there will have the information you seek."

In the morning, under a strong sun that was quickly drying out the town, the priest led Monsignor Archenti to the synagogue.

Hung with chandeliers and glittering with gold, the synagogue was indeed the richest, most beautiful one the devil's advocate had seen. The painted ceiling was dominated by a phrase in Hebrew, which read, "This is the door to the Heavens." On one wall was a bas-relief of Jerusalem; another city, unidentified, was opposite it. All along the walls were plaques with Hebrew inscriptions. Monsignor Archenti walked about reading them as Padre Grasselli, unable to read Hebrew, shuffled along nervously behind him.

After a while, the advocate asked, "Where is he? The rabbi?"

"He must be in his room in the back."

They knocked on a door at the back of the synagogue and, hearing a voice, they entered a room where a man sat on a tall chair, leaning over a book and mumbling. By the only window was mounted a mirror that directed sunlight onto the book. The thin-faced rabbi, a black skullcap clinging to the back of his head, looked up as they came in but did not smile, and did not cease saying his prayers. *How strange,* thought the advocate, *he bears a slight resemblance to my own father.* After a moment the rabbi finished, closed the book with care and reverence, turned to them and smiled, climbing down from his seat.

"Padre Grasselli, to what do I owe the favour of this visit?"

"We have an important guest in our town." He indicated Monsignor Archenti. "All the way from the Vatican in Rome. He would like to ask you a few questions."

As the advocate asked his questions about the Cambiati name and family, the rabbi listened with his hands folded together before him, a patient look on his long, narrow face.

"Yes, I know this place. Mulberry Road, where the silk-growers live. Yes, many of them are Jews, it is true. There is one family with the name Cambiati—an old man who lives alone, and his son, who lives with his own family nearby. Perhaps we can go see them. It is not far."

An hour later, the rabbi and the advocate stood at the door of a hut surrounded by mulberry trees. A bent old man with a scrunched-up face and rheumy colourless eyes opened the door and nodded happily at the rabbi, while he eyed the priest with suspicion. They entered and sat at a rough wooden table in the kitchen that held a brass lamp for burning the dregs of olive oil. The floor was spread with dried reeds. In the next room, Archenti could see stacks of what he took to be shallow wooden trays for holding silk cocoons.

"Yes, we Cambiatis are originally Sephardim from Spain, it is true. Long ago, long before my time, Jews came here—not many, five or six families, I believe. Now there is just me—and my son's family over that hill." He pointed out the window. "But I do not know if any of these Cambiatis moved to Cremona. It is possible. I heard some travelled east from here, many many years ago. I do not know why."

Just then the door swung open and a tall, broad man entered. "My son." The younger man nodded at the rabbi and scowled at the one in priest's robes. He had the glistening black hair of a Spaniard and sharp black eyes. The old man introduced the advocate and repeated the questions he had just attempted to answer. The son had nothing new to add. When he saw that his father and the rabbi treated the advocate with respect, he changed his mood. "I fear I cannot be of much help."

The advocate and the rabbi rose to leave. As they stood at the door, the old man gasped, bringing his index finger to his temple. "Oh, wait, wait, I remember now. I knew that town sounded familiar but not quite. It was not Cremona they went to long ago but a place called Crema, I believe, a village."

"Yes, I know it." The advocate nodded. "It is close by Cremona, on the River Serio, on the road between Cremona and Milano."

"I believe my grandfather said it was in the time of his grandfather, or perhaps even his grandfather's grandfather. And he mentioned that an awful thing happened there, a terrible thing." He glanced at the rabbi, who nodded for him to have the courage to go on. He whispered it as a blank look came to his eyes: "They became Christians."

"Father," the son spoke up, "the priest here is a Christian; there is no need to insult our guest."

"No, no; no insult." The old man waved his hands and tried to explain. "This priest from Rome has always been a Christian; but it is those Jews who change, who deny their own people, who err greatly. But he, he is a Christian man, a Roman Christian, this is fine."

The advocate spoke: "Perhaps they were forced to convert."

"Terrible. Terrible." The old man shook his head.

The advocate and the rabbi left and the son came out with them.

"Come." The son stood taller and puffed out his chest. "I will show you our silkworm house."

The advocate nodded and he and the rabbi followed the son into a nearby grove of mulberry trees, where a stone hut stood.

Inside the hut, the son showed the advocate a silkworm cocoon. He held it before his eyes, the delicate object in contrast to his rough fingers. "As you know, the silkworm wraps itself in its cocoon by spewing silk filament from its mouth. Unfortunately, we must kill most of them before they can hatch, for hatching breaks the silk threads of the cocoon and ruins it. Of course, we let some stay alive and hatch so they can lay more eggs on the mulberry leaves." He went on to explain other operations in the making of silk. After listening for a while, the advocate and the rabbi took their leave.

As they started down the hill, the son hurried out with a handful of cocoons. He handed them shyly to the advocate, who understood clearly, from the look in the man's eyes, that this was a gift, all the poor family had to offer a guest. The advocate slipped them into the pocket of his cassock. The son nodded and bowed and went back into the hut.


OMNIA   VINCIT   AMOR

On his return to Cremona from Casale Monferrato, the devil's advocate once again went to the ducal palace to give the girl a lesson in Latin. They sat in the dappled light of the garden as Elettra translated Virgil.

"Did you know that Virgil was born near Mantua, and that he was educated in his youth here in Cremona?" he asked.

"I had no idea." Elettra looked blank, not uninterested exactly, but with her mind on other things.

"And that in the time of the Romans, the farms around Cremona were taken away from their owners and given to the troops of Antony? Your father could easily be a descendant of one of those soldiers."

"Hmm." She appeared bored but had a sweet smile on her face.

"You seem to be lacking interest this afternoon. We shall only do a bit more."

Elettra took a while completing translation of a short but difficult passage. When finished, she stopped to look up at a finch singing in a nearby tree. "He sings happily today." She smiled again. Archenti watched her closely as she looked at the bird. She sighed and returned to the book in her hands.

"*Omnia vincit Amor: et nos cedamus Amori.*" She paused and bit her lower lip. "Love . . . conquers everything: let us, too . . . yield to love."

He tilted his head, listening. "Again?"

"Love conquers everything: let us, too, yield to love." She said it quickly, as if she had just discovered the truth of the words. "I like that. I like that very much."

She seemed amenable today: soft, open and friendly. A little bored, but perhaps more interested in talking than translating. The devil's advocate thought it might be an opportunity to draw out the information he had been seeking for weeks. He knew already, beyond mere suspicion, that the *duchessa* and the candidate had been involved in an amorous relationship, but he wanted certainty. *And why is it I seek certainty? So I can spend more time with this little temptress before me? So I can justify my own weakness by seeing it in another, in Cambiati, a supposed saint?*

"Elettra, I know we have discussed this before, but I must ask again. It is extremely important and my duty demands I find an answer to this question before I can complete my investigation."

She didn't smile when she spoke, but looked straight into his eyes: "And what if I don't want you to finish your investigation?"

"What do you mean?"

"When you have finished, you will return to Rome— and I will learn no more Latin!" She was happy to be able to tease him. "You looked so serious," she laughed.

"No, truly, Elettra, I must have an answer. Put the book down a moment and listen. Has your great-grandmother mentioned many details concerning the life of Fabrizio Cambiati?"

"Yes, of course."

"What did she tell you about him?"

"That he was a good man, very kind."

"Nothing surprising or unusual there. That's what all the townspeople claim. Anything else?"

She thought a moment. Archenti wondered if perhaps she was trying to decide whether or not she should reveal the *duchessa*'s secret at last. But the moment passed and she shook her head. "No, nothing else, or nothing that I recall."

"Think hard. It is very important for my investigation of Padre Cambiati."

Her eyes were suddenly angry. "We have discussed this before and now you ask again. Always prying, prying, prying. Why do you insist there must be something hidden about him? Everyone says he was a saint, a kindly man, and yet you are always digging for the worst, like a pig nosing up something rotten from the mud. You already talked to my great-grandmother. She has told me nothing, nothing that she wouldn't have told you."

The girl was as hard-headed and intractable as the rest of her family, if not more so. Her eyes went dark, her body tensed and she appeared about to explode.

While Archenti experienced deep frustration at his continued difficulty with the case, he also realized that, at times, he hardly cared whether he found the truth about Cambiati. *Why?* he wondered. When he tried to approach the subject of Cambiati's candidacy with the logic for which he was renowned, his mind drifted and the girl kept appearing before him. It was both wonderful and terrible, what was happening to him. As if he were being torn in two—one foot in an old life, one foot in a new one. But he couldn't pull himself wholly into one or the other. His duty forever dragged him back. Finally, he acknowledged that he wanted the girl to admit to the secret. *Even if I have the truth from the old woman, that won't be enough. It must be the girl. I must get her to see the overwhelming power of desire? Why?* And even though he asked, he already knew why, and knew that it had nothing to do with the candidate or the investigation.

### DREAM OF THE RIVER PO

Pale brown edged by enamelled silver, the River Po under cloud cover appeared slick, with long, supple, rippling tendons that pulsed endlessly in a display that was energetic and vital, as if the river were a living animal, a liquid muscle that twitched in broad bends and curves through the flat landscape. The layer of cloud above was thin enough for the sun to shine weakly through, appearing occasionally behind the fleeting grey like a dull gold coin.

Rodolfo and the devil's advocate had discussed many things as they walked on a well-worn path beside the river.

Eventually they had fallen into an easy silence. Rodolfo found a comfortable spot overlooking the river and sat down in the summer grass. The advocate joined him.

They sat watching the water flowing past. Always changing, always the same. They sat a long while as the advocate's mind drifted back to the girl, like a boat caught at first in the reeds and then slipping inexorably into the current.

"Look at this red flower." Rodolfo lifted a blossom growing among the grasses, cupping it in his palm at the end of its long green stem. "Beauty alone has always been enough for men. Beauty alone caused the Greeks to leave for Troy. Paris was faced with three choices: worldly power, military glory or feminine beauty. He chose the last. Homer never spoke of Helen's great intelligence, never mentioned her abilities at child-rearing or poeticizing. Beauty alone was enough to set men marching. Never forget that, of all the gods, Aphrodite alone had the power to prevail over Zeus."

The advocate glanced at Rodolfo sitting next to him. *He knows what I'm thinking, reveals my deepest thoughts.* "Tell me, Rodolfo, is it enough, this beauty?"

"You mean to ask, priest, is it everything? No. It has the power to move the world but no, it is not everything. Beauty fades, sometimes with the haste of a passing cloud. We try to catch it in its moment and it ages in our hands. But that will never stop men from trying to hold to it. Beauty flows through the world constantly. It's like the river. The water flows on but there is always more beauty, more river, sluicing down from the mountains. The only problem with you, priest, is that your idea of beauty is so narrow. There is much more beauty than you can imagine, much, much more."

The priest turned and watched the river, wondering.

"Let us walk." Rodolfo stood and headed off.

The advocate followed, watching the pale bones riding the other's back, and as they walked farther along the river the clouds thickened and darkened. Raindrops spotted the river's surface and disappeared, water joining water—like a comet dissolving in the light of dawn.

That night Archenti slept fitfully in the humid heat, as images of the girl's face overlapped with images of the *duchessa*, while the faces of Cardinal Cozio and Neri and others flowed into and out of one another. He tossed and turned in a fever of indecision. Finally, towards dawn, he fell deep asleep and a dream streamed down into him.

*A book appears floating down the River Po, inches below the surface—a luminous book filled with graceful and elegant words. The water of the river dissolves the glue that binds the pages together, and the book separates into sheets floating just below the surface. Slowly the water also dissolves the ink, and the words melt into the flow, becoming themselves water. Finally, with time, the blank pages dissolve into fragments, and fragments of fragments, until they as well are indistinguishable from the river.*

## A FRESCO OF
## THE APOCALYPSE

The next day, the devil's advocate decided he must go to see the painting of the Apocalypse that had been revealed the week before at the church of Santo Sigismundo. The entire town was talking about it. As the Hieronymite, Attilio Bodini, had predicted, the faithful, many of whom recognized their own faces among the tortured visages of the damned, were enraged and demanded that the fresco be whitewashed, destroyed, removed.

Entering the spacious church, Archenti felt the damp air on his skin and smelled the heavy scent of must and incense. He saw Bodini, with his distinctive up-tilted head, speaking with another priest in the nave of the church, both clothed in their white habits and black cloaks. On the left he saw the fresco in question running halfway along the wall of the church.

It was an enormous work, in both size and concept, attempting to capture the story of the Apocalypse in its entirety. In style, the advocate noted, it was anti-classical, executed in a feverish and tormented hand. It was disconcerting that none of the hundreds of figures had pupils in their eyes.

The entire story of Revelations was depicted without mercy. Archenti picked out a number of quotes on banners flying over the scene: "The time is at hand," "I am Alpha and Omega," "I have the keys of Hell and Death," "I will write upon him my new name," "And in those days shall men seek death and shall not find it," "Time no longer," "The Great Whore which did corrupt the earth with her fornication."

The overall effect of the painting was horrific. Where were the mercy and love so characteristic of the New Testament? Revelations, he mused, seemed born of the Old Testament, a throwback at the very end of the Bible. He shuddered at the utter bleakness and terror before him: hundreds of avenging angels; God Himself with hair of white and eyes of fire, His tongue protruding, a sword with two edges. There was a host of beasts: full of eyes front and back and eyes within, each beast with six wings.

Archenti saw the opening of the book of seven seals, with its four horses, their riders terrible to behold, carrying bows, swords, a pair of balances. Swirls of frenetic, malignant energy and chaos made it impossible to tell the angels from the damned. A moon of blood shone down as earthquakes swallowed the good and evil alike. The trumpets of seven angels incited hail and fire that rained on everyone. The seas and rivers turned to blood, the bottomless pit vomited up scorpion-tailed monsters on horses, and a third of the stars fell from heaven on the heads of all.

And there was John himself eating the book of prophecy, as the winepress squeezed the harvest of the earth and blood poured out, and seven vials spilled forth seven plagues and "they gnawed their tongues for pain." And the advocate was astounded and overwhelmed, for he saw that the Hieronymite had blamed the Great Whore for all of it, the Mother of Harlots and Abominations—one could read it clearly in the painting—there she was, drunk on the blood of saints, in purple and scarlet, with gold and jewels and pearls . . . Staring in disbelief, Archenti suddenly gasped and stumbled backwards. He stood with his mouth gaping open. There was no doubt. Bodini had depicted the Great Whore of Babylon with the face of Elettra.

"So, what do you think of my painting, Your Excellency?" Bodini appeared next to him but the advocate, who was reeling, turned and almost stumbled again. "You hear the people are calling for its destruction, as I predicted. They cannot face the truth, the fools. Look hard, Your Excellency, the time will soon be at hand."

"Why? Why did you use the face of the girl? This is an abomination. The duke will have your head."

"Oh, I think not. He will soon be more interested in your head, I believe. I have seen the way you look at the girl. You think I am blind?"

"What have you seen? You have seen nothing!"

"I see everything, my friend. I see all, and I know what you are up to but I do not blame you—it is the girl I blame, she has power over you. In her womb she bears the seed of evil." A strange, knowing look on his face, he turned and regarded the Whore of Babylon in the painting.

The advocate shook his head in anger, and began to leave. "Wait!"

Archenti halted. "What is it?"

"You saw the priest I was talking to when you entered?"

"Yes?"

"Padre Ghislina. A Hieronymite, like me. He is from near Livorno. I was asking him about you. He said he knew a family there with the name Archenti. Glass-makers, Your Excellency, glass-makers." Bodini grinned at the advocate, who turned and hurried out.

## APPROACHING THE
## FINAL CIRCLE OF PARADISE

The maid led the devil's advocate to the library in the ducal palace, where Elettra awaited him. The door swung wide and there she was, sitting on a straight-backed chair at the table, absorbed in a book.

"Elettra?" He thought perhaps she had not heard him enter.

"One moment." She kept reading. "Let me finish this canto." He took a seat and stared unabashedly at the girl as her eyes skimmed the page, her hair hanging partly across her face. When she finished, she looked up at the ceiling and sighed. "I love the music of Dante—'the beauty I saw there transcends all measure of mortal minds' and 'I bent down to drink in Paradise of the sweet stream that flows its grace to us.'"

"Yes, I recognize it," said the advocate. "Canto XXX— a vision of the River of Light as revealed by Beatrice."

"Must we translate more boring old Romans today? Could we not do something else?"

The advocate glanced out the window. "It looks like rain—a walk is out of the question."

She put her elbows on the table, her face in her hands, and questioned him. "Have you been to Santo Sigismundo? Have you seen the painting they are all talking about? Have you seen me in it?"

"Yes. He is a powerful painter, but a madman."

"And a fool. I believe my father will make him pay for his insolence. At the very least, he will have the painting whitewashed. My father refuses to let me see it. I wonder if perhaps the Hieronymite is the one who killed my foal?"

"That I doubt."

She paused, tilted her head. "Is it a good likeness of me? Did you enjoy it?"

"An excellent likeness, yes, but enjoy it? No."

"Oh! I forgot. This is for you. My father says you have refused payment of any kind for my Latin lessons, so I convinced him that you should have this."

To his surprise, she held forth the copy of Dante's *Divina commedia* she had been reading.

He took the thick volume, its leather wraparound cover fastened with a small wooden toggle.

"It's lovely." He opened it at random.

"It is one of the oldest books my father owns."

He slammed it shut. "No, I cannot accept it." He handed it back.

"You don't like it?"

"No, it's not that. The book is beautiful."

"I want you to have it."

"I had a dream . . ."

"Yes," she interrupted, "it's all about Dante's dream."

"You don't understand."

In her excitement at giving the gift, she ignored him. "Read the inscription. I wrote it myself. A quote from the 'Paradiso.'"

He opened it again. " 'But already I could feel my being turned . . . by the Love that moves the Sun and the other stars.' From the final poem, the highest circle of paradise," he mused.

"Yes. Do you not find the story full of 'turnings'?"

"How so?"

"Love turns the sun and the other stars. Comets too, of course. Especially a comet that always returns, yes?" She was delighting in her own understanding.

"Yes?" He nodded.

"It's the same love that turns Dante towards Beatrice. Their love is a lesser expression of the same love that sets the universe in motion. Don't you see? And the planets, and stars and comets too." She was dancing, turning, spinning around the room. "Don't you see?"

"Yes. Yes, I see. I do."

She stopped. "You will keep the book, then?"

"Yes, I will keep the book." He smiled at her, his heart lighter than it had been in years.

# THE PLAY—ACT SIX

## A SLINGING OF INSULTS
## FOLLOWED BY AN ARGUMENT

Arlecchino and Pantalone stood on stage shaking hands. On a table beneath their handshake was a large piece of vellum, the dowry contract, curled at the corners. At the edge of the table, a pot of ink holding a quill. For this scene Pantalone stood in as the father of Ottavio, while Arlecchino played the role of Aurora's father. Both players had removed their regular masks and wore leather half-masks with piglike snouts.

"What can we do? We are a tiny troupe of poor players," a musician had explained to the audience. "Each of us, as you can see, must play many roles. Just as in life. The father is a son and the son a father. The mother is an aunt, a grand-mother, a great-grandmother and forever yet a daughter. And so it goes."

The hands of the two fathers were gripped tightly together.

"My son will make a fine husband for your daughter," Pantalone announced.

"My daughter is an excellent catch for your boy." Arlecchino grinned.

"And I . . . I mean he . . . will be happy to have access to such a munificent dowry."

"First work out the details of the contract; then the betrothal; then the wedding. One step at a time."

"Indeed. Well, we've signed it. No going back now. Although I hear you are renowned for slipping out of contracts."

"Not true, not true. They say the fruit never falls far from the tree, but I hope they're wrong in your case."

"What do you mean by that, you dull-eyed carp?"

"I just hope and pray that your boy is different from his ancestors, who, I have been told, were rubes living in the mountains, eating goat dung and mating with wild beasts."

They still had their hands joined, but each was squeez-ing harder, fingers growing red, their faces too.

"At any rate, my daughter is a stunningly beautiful young woman."

"And my Ottavio a handsome and virile young man."

"Is he well-hung?"

"Of course, just like his father. Your daughter, I must admit, has a gorgeous pair of melons. She is lovely. Unlike your wife—the hag."

"Well, I've seen your wife going at it with the neighbourhood dogs. And your son, well, his virility is yet to be proven. If there is no child within two years, I want a return of the entire dowry. Is the boy actually your issue? Or did your wife, you know"—Arlecchino made an obscene gesture with his left hand—"with another man?"

Pantalone was more concerned by the comment about the dowry than by the slurs and insults. "What do you mean? You cannot demand the return of the dowry! Only a portion. And then only if it is justified."

"It's in the contract." Arlecchino gestured at the vellum.

"Well, I don't care. I will never return the entire one thousand florins."

"Have you read the contract at all, at all? Oh my God, the idiot can't read. What hope for the son, then?"

Arlecchino and Pantalone squeezed their hands together ever tighter, their tangled fingers gone from scarlet to white.

"Let go!"

"You let go first!"

"Let's both let go at the same time."

"Do we need that in writing?"

"Fool!"

"Imbecile!"

"Now!" they both shouted, letting go and stumbling about the stage.

"Well, we've done it. The contract is agreed and they'll soon marry."

"Yes, a happy day."

"Let's hope so."

Both characters exited the stage, and a moment later Pantalone came running out, dressed again as himself, frantic, looking back and forth: "I'll pull out my hair! I'll beat my own face till it bleeds! I'm going mad! I'll kill myself! This can't be. I never thought they could agree on a contract. They hate each other. But they did it! My God, I'll lose Aurora, my last chance . . . Where's that damn fool with my violin? Why is it taking so long? Ah, there's the go-between. Signora? Please, I must speak with you."

A matronly character with a full round face, three fuzzy warts on her left cheek, stood before Pantalone, smiling. "Yes?"

"I will be direct, signora. What will it take to make you change your mind, as the official go-between, concerning the impending marriage of Aurora to Ottavio, and to suggest me in his place?"

She laughed heartily. "Arlecchino asked me the same question yesterday. I'll give you the same answer I gave him. More than you have or are willing to give up, crazy old man."

"Don't mock. Everyone can use a few extra bezants, my dear—I would reward you handsomely."

"There is only one way you can get me to talk the fathers into changing things—especially at this late date—and that one way has nothing to do with money." She sidled up to Pantalone and, lifting her skirts, rubbed up against him.

He put his hand over his face and shook his head. "Whatever, whatever shall I do?"

She looked at him beseechingly, hanging off his arm. "You don't know how lonely it is, being the go-between for every lover who wants me to arrange his dreams, my husband gone all these years, you don't know how it is. I can see you still have it, Pantalone, and if you want any hope of getting it from her you'll have to give it to me first."

Arlecchino wandered onto stage. "It, it, it—what are you two talking about? Oh, I see." Arlecchino addressed Pantalone. "You know I wanted to be the go-between for the go-between, you know I can use the money, but no, you go sneaking behind my back and make your own arrangements. What kind of a snake are you?"

"A smart one—you think I want to pay you to do something I am fully capable of doing myself?"

"Well, we'll see about that. If you don't pay me, I will tell Ugo that you no longer have any need for the violin, which is almost ready, by the way. He sent me to tell you."

"Don't! Don't do that! I need that violin."

Arlecchino strutted about. "Well, let's see now—you want the violin but you can't have it unless you pay up for my services. Sounds like you are trapped—by your own lust, I might add."

"I can do without the moralizing. What are you, a priest? Aargh! Not only do I have to screw this witch but

I have to pay for the opportunity. It appears I have no choice." He pulled out his leather purse, fished about in it and took out two large coins which he passed to Arlecchino.

Arlecchino bit the coins, placed them in his own purse and bowed. Turning to the matchmaker, he declared, "Would you be willing to entertain Pantalone in a manner appropriate to the occasion?"

"Delighted." The go-between grabbed Pantalone by the ear and dragged him from the stage.

Arlecchino mused, "All is well and sufficient tonight in the little kingdom of Cremona. After some roast meat and a flagon of wine, it's back to Mantua with me to retrieve that violin. Ah, good, good is life."

# CHAPTER ELEVEN

*Two more miracles attributed to Cambiati. It is said that one day the stone lion to the left of the cathedral entrance disappeared. The statue was found two days later in the reeds near the Po, as if about to take a drink of water, with lion pawprints in the mud nearby. An old lady from the country-side claimed to have seen Don Fabrizio on the lion as they came riding out of the morning fog. In the second miracle, a human footprint was found on the first step of the torrazzo, imprinted in stone. "How do you know it is his?" I asked the balding bell-ringer who had found it. "Who else could it be?" he replied.*

## A   LETTER   FROM   THE
## GENERAL   OF   THE   JESUITS

On returning to his rooms after his visit to the ducal palace, the advocate was met at the door by the housekeeper. "A letter was delivered while you were out, Your Excellency." She handed it to him, half-bowing.

It was from Rome, from the general himself. He hurried to the privacy of his rooms to read it.

*Monsignor Michele Archenti, Promotor Fidei,*
*Our Lord's most benevolent blessing upon you.*

*My dearest son in Christ, I write you with some urgency today. There are events taking place lately here in Rome among the Curia and our colleagues about which I believe you must be advised immediately.*

*But first, I do not know if you have yet heard. We have a new pope. It took over two months for the cardinals to decide but on the sixth day of July, Cardinal Rezzonico of Venice was elected. He has chosen the name Clement XIII. It is not known yet which way he will lean but time will tell. In any case, he has begun his reign under a cloud, as you will see.*

*Without going into the details and the complexities involved, which are legion, suffice it to say that alliances have been shifting quickly here and the results do not bode well for you, or for me, for that matter. I have it on good authority that your colleague and supposed friend Carlo Neri has come*

*across some intriguing information while doing research
on your behalf. He has gone to Cardinal Cozio with this
information and—the cardinal being a noted hater of Jews
and other infidels, as you know—this information is already
being used to poison the atmosphere here.*

*I can see you nodding your head with the surety that
this information pertains to your case regarding the holy
Cambiati of Cremona. Nothing could be further from the
truth. Neri, an intelligent and dogged scholar—was it not
you who named him The Burrower?—has discovered something else while looking into the candidate's past. Personal
information regarding your own background. It has already
been whispered in our august halls that you, as well as the
little-known Cambiati, share a bloodline that is less than
pure. How did the Cardinal word it? "Sullied by tainted
blood," I believe he said. I for one spoke out against this
besmirching of your reputation in your absence. I was not
completely alone, but nearly, nearly. The good Cardinal
stated that it was a blasphemy that the devil's advocate
should have impure blood in his veins, and now he has the
ear of Clement himself.*

*A man in your position is bound to make enemies,
and now they rise against you. I strongly supported your wise
decisions of the past—against much revered candidates in
Brindisi, Venice and elsewhere. These are now being seen in
a different light. Your own success works against you. Several
disappointed bishops, and at least two more cardinals, are
calling for your censure, and demanding that decisions*

*against their favourites be revisited and reconsidered. This,
as you might imagine, is a complication both the new Pontiff
and I do not want to be burdened with—but rather than
blame the instigators, His Holiness appears to be blaming
you (at the urging of Cardinal Cozio, of course).*

*Trust that I have not turned against you. I have my
own reasons for acting as I do and, unfortunately, can be no
help where you would most likely have expected it. As always,
I must keep the Society of Jesus uppermost in mind, even to
the detriment of any of its individual members. I trust you
will understand that I am in a most difficult position.*

*At this juncture, my son, I wish I knew how to advise
you. To return here now would be foolish, if not dangerous—
you would have few, if any, who could afford to stand as your
allies. In any case, I know you have told me on occasion that
you consider Vatican politics a cesspool; "an impotent harem
of bickering eunuchs" I believe was the phrase you used. At
the time, even I winced at your strong language. However,
you have been proved correct and your worst fears have
come to pass.*

*It is clear, at this point, that Carlo Neri will be
appointed as the new devil's advocate in several days. You
will be relieved of your duties and sent as a missionary to
Japan. I regret I was unable to stop them or even obtain a
hearing for you. The wild dogs of ambition have gathered
and are devouring a ghost—yours.*

*I return tomorrow for several months to Florence. I will
indeed be happy to quit this place in its season of disquiet.*

*Once again I must warn you against returning now—I believe it would be madness.*

*I regret having to be the bearer of bad news—but I sensed that you knew it had to come someday. You are far too independent a mind for this place. I have the greatest confidence that you will know what to do and will act in accordance with God's wishes.*

*In God's infinite mercy,*
*Society General Lorenzo Ricci*
*The Society of Jesus*

The advocate stared at his palms. *The blood of the Jew.* He sat slumped in his chair, gazing blankly into the distance, the letter still held loosely in his left hand. He couldn't believe it, could not believe he had never clearly recognized Neri's ambition. Archenti thought he now knew when it had begun—the moment Neri had been passed over for the position of devil's advocate five years before, when the previous general had made his choice. *Neri hid his envy well. It was entirely invisible to me. I cannot believe I grew to trust him wholeheartedly. What a fool I am, a fool! The plot, steeped in anger and ambition, must have been fermenting for those five years as Neri hid his face, bowed low over his tomes. And now he has the final, damning piece to use against me.*

Clearly there was no use returning to Rome—all was done and finished there. In his absence he had been tried, found guilty and executed. He no longer existed.

*All my work, my efforts, mean nothing now. What am I to do? Where can I go? Crawl back in a few months to Rome and beg for a sinecure, to be put to use somewhere, in distant Japan likely, a kind of death sentence? I don't think I could stand the blow to my pride. My pride . . . it sickens me. Not to mention that I would be forced to beg from the very people who have destroyed my reputation. It is bad enough to have enemies, but far worse to find that one you trusted as a friend has been working in secret against you.*

Now that he saw it, he saw it clearly—Neri did not just want the prestige of being named devil's advocate; he was putting himself in line for the position of general of the society! And he would get it, Archenti realized. Previously he had been blind to Neri's machinations but now a flood of memories came back, and it was apparent that Neri had been planning his moves for years, building alliances there and there and there. And now it had all clicked, gears meshing into other gears and catching Archenti in their crushing wheels. *He will have complete control over my life!* He was sickened by the realization, and by his own stupidity. His mind was racing but each thought was more numbing than the last. There was no ground under his feet. The letter slipped from his hand and fell to the floor.

Standing, he grasped for the back of the chair. He felt as if his legs had disappeared, the earth had lost its solidity; his lower regions were sinking away, he was dropping through space like a comet in freefall, like an infant plunging down a bottomless well and out the other side of the earth, about to be born.

## THE DREAM OF
## WRITING NOTHING

That night the advocate's sleep was tortured; he kept waking up in heavy sweats as he thought obsessively about Neri, as anger and disappointment churned in his guts. Exhausted, he finally fell asleep, like sinking down into bottomless waters.

In the dream, he was drawing a bucket from a well. He looked into it and saw that the bucket was brimming with ink—thick, rich, viscous. Leaning over, he took the quill from the hand of a faceless scribe seated next to him and glanced at the page. The scribe had been writing the word *falena,* meaning both "moth" and "paper ash." It sounded to him like a girl's name. Falena. The scribe's hand kept moving over the page, writing nothing.

Suddenly, lying asleep on the desk before him was Elettra, though in his dream he kept thinking her name was Falena. She was entirely wound in a cocoon of raw silk, which he could see through, as if she were floating just below the surface of a river. Archenti dipped the quill in the bucket of ink and swished it about, but by the time he brought the quill to a place above her forehead he had grown so distraught at the possibility of its point causing her discomfort that the quill had changed into a pointed brush with soft bristles.

He wrote in elegant strokes that suggested Arabic but were in fact Italian. An *e,* a single eye and open mouth; an *n,* a gate in a wall; an *i* like a tower with a star above it; a *g,* a snake, a cobra poised, its head raised in curiosity; an *m*, waves on a river; and an *a* like the head of a woman with long hair.

At the base of her throat he wrote *polso,* and the ink gathered there in a pool. He soaked the brush again and wrote *sangue* above her chest, and the ink ran in streams in all directions. It looked to him like a map of Cremona, the streets radiating from her heart. At the appropriate place he wrote *cuore,* and it was as if the ink soaked down through the silk and into her chest.

He began to cover the cocoon with words: *breath, musk, river, mist, dew, sleep, dream, silk, light, fountain, shroud.* Over her left cheek the word *maze;* above her right foot, *milk.* He covered the cocoon the way a fast-growing vine covers a wall, the way the tributaries of the Po in spring-time swell into low-lying fields.

And then he sank, drowning in a deeper sleep, one without dreams.

## RODOLFO'S PLAN FOR THE RELICS OF CHRISTENDOM

Archenti loaded up the sack, threw it over his shoulder and headed for the Po gate. It felt much heavier than it should have, considering the contents, and he had to stop often to rest. He walked with a slight indecision—stopping occasionally and glancing back—but kept on anyway. An hour later he stood by the river, the sack on the ground next to him. He looked into the water, its greenish reflections. He could see himself wavering there.

Turning the sack from the bottom, he dumped papers and documents out onto the ground. The *positiones* that he had been given in Rome, and everything else he had gathered and noted on Fabrizio Cambiati. There was no one around— just a couple of fishermen on the far shore, farther along. With a flint he was able to strike a spark that caught on a sheet of paper. He stared a moment at the weak flame, blew on it until the fire was fully alive and placed the paper under the pile of documents. In five minutes the flames were six feet high, dancing before him as if the man himself, Cambiati, were being immolated.

The smoke drifted eastward.

Out of the smoke appeared Rodolfo, clanking along with his skeleton on his back. "What are you doing, priest?"

"Burning the papers that concern the candidacy of Cambiati."

"Ah, a good idea. They were weighing you down, a burden for you, best to be rid of them."

Archenti grunted.

Rodolfo pointed towards the city. "Look, bits of paper ash are falling into the hair of the girl. As if she is going grey, growing old before our eyes."

Even though she was too distant to be seen by normal means, Archenti glimpsed the same vision that was in the eyes of Rodolfo—Elettra standing at a high window, the ash from the fire of Cambiati's papers falling lightly on her head. "Falena," Archenti said, and Rodolfo nodded.

"Let's sit down. I have a story to tell you." Rodolfo gently pushed the priest on the shoulder to make him sit on the ground. He pulled a bottle of wine from his satchel and passed it to Archenti, who took a swig and passed it back. Rodolfo drank deeply and wiped his mouth with his sleeve.

"A long time ago," he began, "when I was recovering in Cambiati's rooms, I found something in his library—in one of his many books on alchemy. It was a secret incantation, a complex chant of many ancient languages. It gave the user the ability to reanimate life, if one employed the spell with the proper attitude. You might not believe this, but I was able to revive a dead sparrow. I accomplished this magic a number of times. Of course, I never told Cambiati. He was such a sweet pure soul, I did not want to burden him with so great a power. In any case, I was tortured by guilt for the murder of my brother, so I decided I would try to bring him back to life.

"But then it occurred to me—why would I want to? My brother was forever complaining about life, he really didn't want to live at all—the first time! Why would I bring him back? A supremely unhappy fellow.

"A magnificent idea then came to me. I was in our cathedral and saw the Sacred Spine of Christ and I decided on a plan that was so incredible that I could not resist its sheer brilliance and audacity. I would steal all the bits and pieces of Christ's relics from all the churches of Italy and reconstruct Him, putting Christ together like the fifty-eight pieces of a violin, and then I would reanimate Him. Christ would live again! I would start by stealing His spine from Cremona and His blood from Mantua, and I would pour the blood into the spine and then I would build from there—adding femurs and tibias and knuckles and fingers and other bones and such from the thousand and one churches of our realm. I travelled everywhere and talked to hundreds of priests and scholars to find out where the relics were held and how to get at them—and you know what I learned?"

Archenti shook his head.

"I learned that the Christ I recreated would be a monster. He would have nineteen fingers, five legs, thirteen toes, a twelve-foot spine—He would stand over twenty feet tall—there were that many of His relics." Rodolfo laughed. "It's a story, priest. You like my story?"

Archenti knew it was just a fable, but there was something about it, something about this Rodolfo, that both attracted and unnerved him.

The fire was dying down. They finished the wine and Rodolfo stood. "I will see you again, friend. Till then," and he walked off along the river.

*THE PLAY—ACT SEVEN*

U G O   T H E   M A N T U A N
D E L I V E R S   T H E   V I O L I N

Arlecchino arrived at the Mantuan's palace in late afternoon and, following the mastiff's barking, was able to
find the hunchback. The little man sat in a high-backed
chair, staring out a window into an enclosed courtyard.
The violin rested near the end of a table of dark wood. The
instrument glowed, and almost seemed to pulsate like a
living thing.

"It is ready?"

"Yes, fool, it is ready." Ugo turned and looked at him.
"It is a masterpiece, I tell you, a masterpiece. I cannot let

you deliver it. It is much too precious to me now. It is imperative that I deliver it to Pantalone myself."

"Yes, of course. But I thought it was difficult for you to leave the palace of the Gonzagas?"

"With your help, it is not a problem. When alone, I have difficulty finding an exit. Do not ask why."

"When shall we go?"

"In the morning. I will show you to your room and you can rest until I send for you in the early hours."

Arlecchino slept, fully clothed, on a bed in a room narrow as a monk's cell. A plain wooden table, an armoire with a mirror, a bed with its straw mattress sagging sagging sagging like a swayback horse. Indeed, he was awakened from a dream of riding, the horse rolling under him, clouds streaking across the sky, waves undulating below. But what had woken him? A sound. The music of a violin. It drifted to him from a distant corner of the palace. A murmur, haunting and irresistible. Arlecchino sat up in bed, swung his legs out, stood and opened the door. He slipped into the hall lit by a candle in a high sconce. He stood a moment listening, then walked in the direction of the music.

After numerous wrong turns and dead ends in rooms crowded with gargoyles, succubi, incubi, and fat Cupids looking like overstuffed pink sausages, he passed an ossuary room packed to the ceiling with yellowed bones and skulls. He shuddered but despite his fear and disgust he continued, drawn on by the crepuscular music.

Finally he came to a doorway from which he could see through three succeeding archways. Ugo stood framed in the arch of the final room, playing the violin, the mastiff lying at his feet entirely consumed with crushing a thick bone. Ugo stopped and, holding the bow with the fingers of the same hand that held the violin, bent to rub the dog's neck, then leaned over and kissed the crown of the beast's head. The mastiff, busy with its gnawing, ignored him. Ugo stood up, sighed heavily, returned the bow to his right hand and began again to play.

Arlecchino was entranced. The music was a dark current flowing through the rooms, a rich, meaty sound that smelled of intimate flesh and sickly sweet powders. It unleashed an unseemly desire in him, a need to ravage something, someone, anyone. Frozen to the spot, he noticed a fresco on the wall behind the Mantuan. A scene he recognized—a kind of apocalypse, hell's gates yawning wide, a city in flames, humans and animals rutting among the ruins, skeletons chasing hysterical children, a man carrying his head in his hands, a dozen crucifixions, a soldier winding a tortured soul's intestines around his neck. The music of the violin brought the fresco to life in a single moaning cauldron of manic activity and black energy: incendiary, diabolic raving.

Suddenly the mastiff raised its head and barked once without rising to its feet, unsure if it wanted to leave its prize bone to go search out the smell that had drifted to it. Ugo stopped playing and peered out.

Arlecchino did not hesitate. He hurried from the room, back the way he had come, threading his way through the halls by the weak light of dawn that had begun to filter through the high windows. Once back in bed, he pulled the blanket over his head.

When the knock came at his door an hour later, Arlecchino, still in bed, realized that he had not once closed his eyes since returning. Ugo's driver had come to fetch the player to the carriage. The breath of the horses steamed as he entered the courtyard behind the man. He noticed then that Ugo and the mastiff were behind him, following, as if being carried along and out of the palace on the harlequin's shadow. The two men climbed inside the carriage, the mastiff at their feet. Across from Arlecchino, the violin rested on the seat beside the Mantuan, who was rubbing the ears of the dog.

Ugo glanced at the violin, as if unsure that he should talk about it in its presence. "I tell you it is a masterpiece. It is terribly difficult for me to give it up at all. The most excellent, the most perfect violin ever created. I believe Pantalone will be pleased. Not that I care one way or the other. It is mine, will always be mine, my creation, my child." The carriage shunted through the gates of the palace; the mastiff yawned, rose, turned about once in the tight space and settled down again to sleep.

Ugo handed Arlecchino a hunk of bread and a dry sausage. They passed a jug of thin watered wine back and forth. The Mantuan kept turning to stare at the violin. After a while he picked it up and began to play.

In the confined space of the carriage the sound of the violin gave Arlecchino intense claustrophobia, even though Ugo was playing it lightly, quietly. Again its voice seemed to have a haunting moan behind it—the guttural throb of dark passions—as it drew black thoughts to the surface of Arlecchino's mind. He began to sink, as if falling backwards, into the reverie of his waking dreams and fantasies.

For hours Ugo played, while Arlecchino drifted in and out of sleep and the carriage clattered across the Lombardy plain under a sun hidden by coursing smoke-coloured clouds.

By the time they arrived in Cremona in early evening, the full fury of a thunderstorm was upon them. Rain driven by the wind washed down in sheets, and water coursed down the stone walls and between the cobbles of the streets. The carriage halted before an alley too narrow for its passage. At the end of the passageway was an inn where the Mantuan would stay. Arlecchino opened the carriage door and jumped out into the weather while Ugo placed the violin under his cloak and stepped out behind his mastiff.

At the mouth of the alley, a horse had been tied to a post. Arlecchino recognized Cruna, the dam of the duke's slaughtered foal. As the mastiff and its master exited the carriage, the horse reared its head in nervous recognition. As dog and man hurried through the rain for the door of the inn, the horse pulled with all its strength against its tether, snapping the rope. A long roll of thunder across the plains and over the city hid the horse's first clattering steps as it charged the Mantuan from behind. By the time Ugo turned and saw the enormous white beast bearing down on him, it was like an apparition. In his shock, he dropped the violin as he leapt out of the way. The horse swept past to trap the growling mastiff against the wall at the alley's end. The violin, caught by the hoof of the horse, went skittering along the wet cobbles to rest at the feet of the mastiff. The dog was snarling and snapping as the horse reared high, its front legs kicking out. In a single powerful thrust, the horse came down hard on the mastiff. The dog burst like a bag of meat and bone, blood gushing from its mouth, the violin crushed beneath it. Again and again the horse trampled on the mastiff, blood mixing with rainwater, while Ugo stared wide-eyed from behind. Finally Giorzio, the duke's servant, came running down the alley and grabbed the remaining length of rope, bringing the mare under control.

Arlecchino stood in the mouth of the alley, unable to move. As Giorzio led the horse away, Ugo ignored them, his eyes fixed on his mastiff, a white rib shining through its fur. Approaching the shattered animal, the Mantuan knelt down, rainwater running off his hair. He touched the dead dog lightly on the head, lifted a piece of the broken violin as if it were something he did not recognize. Arlecchino continued to watch his bowed back, but after a while drifted away, leaving the Mantuan kneeling in the rain.

# CHAPTER TWELVE

*Another miracle, this one from the* duchessa
*madre. One I am inclined to believe, I know not
why. In fact, something has changed. I have lost my
will for skepticism entirely. I started out believing
none of their stories, thinking all the miracles were
dreams, hopes, imaginings. And suddenly now
I believe them all. Each has the ring of truth to me.
This state of mind was clearly precipitated by the
miracle the* duchessa *recounted. I am lost utterly—
or perhaps saved, who knows? She told me that she
and the duke owned an ancient violin built by
Master Niccolò in the time of Cambiati, one he had
played for the priest on occasion while he painted.*

*On Fabrizio's feast day in 1713, she recalled, this old dry violin had sprouted a fresh green leaf from deep within the spiral of its scroll.*

## A   G R E A T   L E A P

Without anyone noticing, high in the heavens the comet was coursing through star-fields, spiralling through time above the heads of players, priests, lovers, saints and demons. For seventy-six years the comet had streaked through the ether, and now it was returning to the stage of man, to once again come sailing out of that bank of fog, late one night, early one morning, pulling its glowing tail full of events and happenstance and coincidence, sprinkling lights and sparks over all.

The day of Elettra's wedding began with a thick predawn mist. The girl awoke with a start and leapt out of bed. After dressing, she opened her door and listened for the snores of the servant guarding the heavy front door of the palazzo. She slipped easily past him, out of the house into the street and hurried towards the main square. At the last moment before leaving she had swallowed a touch of belladonna to enlarge her pupils and make her more beautiful—a trick she had learned from her great-grandmother.

As she passed between the eight-sided baptistery and the cathedral she noticed, through the banners of fog that undulated on the piazza, a figure trudging across the square, shoulders hunched, staring at the ground. She was surprised to see that it was Michele. She almost called to him but caught herself, deciding to watch. He halted at the entrance to the tower, turned around and looked back the way he had come without noticing the girl. Then, as if he had resolved something in his mind, he bowed his head, swung about and disappeared into the tower.

She wondered what he could be doing. Late the previous afternoon she had asked her most trusted servant to carry a note to him in secret. In the note she had asked him—no, told him—to meet her this morning in a spot nearby, hidden deep under the portico across from the cathedral. Their time of assignation was only ten minutes off. She planned to announce her love for him then and there, and she was sure he would join her in the elopement she had plotted. In fact, she could not imagine him not responding, was so sure of her love that she could not even consider the possibility that he might feel otherwise, or that he might have mixed emotions about the proposition. They would run to the stables, find the purse of money she had hidden there, then take her horse and ride together for the river. They would be far away by the time anyone noticed that her bed was empty. Beyond that, she had not wondered what would happen.

She hesitated, standing hidden in the grey and mist of false dawn. She knew she was taking a terrible chance, but this was her wedding day, and she could not bear the thought of spending a single night with the loathsome Pasquali. She had no doubt that Michele Archenti was in love with her. She could read that in his heart and her own—it was clear. Hadn't the nightingale sung, two nights before, at the very moment she said his name aloud to herself in bed? It was a sign. But this—why was he going into the tower? Why now? That was not the meeting place she had designated in the letter.

She hurried across the square to the *torrazzo,* entered and, raising her skirts, rushed up the stairs, spiralling towards heaven.

When Archenti reached the top of the tower he stood panting for a few moments. The countryside and the city stretched far below. The fog was thickest along the Po, a white serpent twisting and billowing out of the river. He held his head in both hands a moment. Then, pulling off his cassock, his everyday clothes underneath, he threw it from the tower. He mused that he was no longer the devil's advocate, no longer Monsignor Archenti. Once again he was simply Michele Archenti, as he had been in the beginning, as he had always been. A man, nothing more, nothing less. He watched the black cloth, an empty shroud, drifting to the ground.

Climbing up onto the balustrade, he teetered there. From his pocket he drew the envelope from the girl, still unopened. He sensed that it was of crucial importance but he feared opening it, could not bring himself to read the words there, whatever they were. Angry at himself for his weakness, he ripped the letter into pieces and flung it from the balustrade. He looked out at the distant Po, which he imagined throbbed like a vein in the neck of a river god. He pictured himself flailing against air like Icarus as he fell from the tower into his own reflection on the surface of the river.

*I can't do this. But I must. I must!* He couldn't explain why. The most rational of explanations meant nothing in the heat of his disappointment with life and himself. Where would he go if not back to Rome, which now was impossible? Why could he not act on his feelings for the girl? Or, alternatively, why could he not just forget her? *One or the other—anything but this fever of indecision.*

Suddenly he remembered that, as he was leaving his room earlier, in his agitated and distraught state, he had gone to his desk, taken out the cerement cloth of Cambiati and shoved it in his pocket. Now he took it out and held it. A prayer came unbidden to his lips: "Holy Fabrizio, please help me in my time of need." *What? Now I'm praying to a man I'm still uncertain was a saint. And yet, despite everything, I begin to believe in his miracles. Please help me, good Fabrizio. Yes, help me decide. Reach out for the girl? Go back to Rome, to a vile emptiness and poisoned atmosphere? Strangle Neri with my bare hands? Jump? Do something, anything!*

He felt utterly empty—he could not come up with any good reason not to jump.

"Michele? What are you doing?"

He twisted about to see the girl standing, out of breath, at the top of the stairway, her eyes fixed on him.

Turning from her, he pointed. "Do you think I could dive into the Po from here?"

"Only if you had wings. The river is far off."

He stared into the distance, swallowed. "I received your note. I was . . . I was afraid to open it."

"It does not matter now. Come down. Talk to me."

He was dumbfounded that what she said, as always, felt like a command. A gentle one, but a command nonetheless. Due to her station, she granted herself power over him, and he acquiesced. With hardly a question. He climbed down, slipping the cerement back into his pocket, and they sat with their backs to the wall.

"Look," she said. "In the sky. That star is moving. Like a shooting star, but it doesn't burn out."

The comet, like the tip of a brush wet with silver pigment, was still visible in the slow-rising light of dawn. They said nothing. Simply watched. Eventually he turned away, placed his hands over his face and began to tremble. She leaned her head against him as he shook, his face still hidden. After a while he stopped. He began to speak but she placed her finger over his lips. "Just listen," she said, leaning close to him.

Moments later, she had finished whispering into his ear her secret plans for the two of them, her breath like a wind of light sailing through him. As the two hands of the clock below came together at 6:30, she took his hand and placed its open palm upon her cheek. With her other hand behind his head, gripping his thick, rich hair, she eased him down on top of her.

High in the heavens, the comet flashed, and grew brighter, a star of singular beauty tumbling through space.

By the time they finished, the fog had lifted from the city entirely and the light was raining down. It was a strikingly clear morning—a perfect day for a wedding.

## A PERFECT DAY
## FOR A WEDDING

A short while after Elettra had spilled the contents of her heart at the feet of Michele, she was leading Cruna from the stable while a chorus of songbirds greeted the day. The early morning sky was the purest eggshell-blue she had ever seen. The stable boy was not entirely surprised to see her—Elettra often went riding in the early hours. In any case, it was hardly his place to question anything she did, however unusual. Shyly, trying not to look at her, he saddled the horse and helped her mount. She rode off and did not look back.

At the Po gate in the city wall, already open for the fishermen who had earlier descended to the river at dawn, Michele waited in the shadows. As he waited he considered all the earth-shattering things that had happened in their short while on the tower, how everything had changed. She had revealed the secret about Cambiati and the *duchessa* that he had long suspected. Cambiati was, he realized, the girl's distant ancestor.

Elettra approached and he swung up behind her. In moments they were out the gate and coursing across fields of sparkling grass, breathless and unable to speak. As she urged the horse on with her thighs and they rode hard, Archenti, unsure how to hold on, wrapped his arms around her waist. Holding the reins with one hand, she placed the other over his hands and pulled them tight into her belly.

They headed for the river, and when they came to it, they travelled by a pathway that curved alongside. Archenti could see their reflection in the water, he and this beautiful, determined young woman flashing by on a horse. It was like a dream in full sunlight.

He felt dizzy with excitement and fear, wondering if anyone was following them, and wishing they could ride faster still. Glancing back, he saw nothing. Then he glimpsed a finger of smoke from a distant chimney, and he knew that the city was waking. They would soon be missed. He sensed something hardly born already slipping away. Turning, he saw the river, the fields, morning rising out of the earth, spirits of mist spiralling up from the water.

## STREAM OF SILK MOTHS

The ancient *duchessa* hardly ever slept any more; in fact, she found it difficult to make a distinction between when she was awake and when asleep. It seemed she spent many a night lying in bed from dusk till dawn and never once closed her eyes. At other times, it seemed, she would walk through entire days as if sound asleep and dreaming the day's events.

As she lay in bed staring at the window, where the first diffused light of dawn turned the sky grey pink white, she saw a disturbing black object, like a broken crow or a flailing headless ghost, go floating slowly past. *God in heaven, what was that?* With all the attendant slippages and creakings of bone typical of a woman in her nineties, she forced herself out of bed and shuffled to the window, where she looked to the street below. She stared at it a full five minutes before she realized what the object was. *A cassock. A priest's cassock? In all my years I have seen many things, but . . .* She looked up into the sky and saw a blurred streak of light coursing across the high heavens. *This is indeed an unusual morning.* She returned to sit on the side of the bed and think.

She must have fallen asleep a few moments, for she awoke with a start and there standing before her was—an apparition? a ghost? a memory?—she wasn't sure what to call it, but she was sure it was speaking to her.

"My dear, dear duchess."

"Fabrizio? Is that you? After all these years?"

"Yes."

"You've hardly aged at all." She paused. "They want to make you into a saint."

"Imbeciles."

"I didn't tell the advocate about our, our . . ."

"I know. You were true to your word. You have a wonderfully kind heart and I thank you. But I am here to request a favour."

"A favour?"

"Yes. You mention the advocate—the favour I request concerns him and your great-granddaughter, Elettra."

"Ah yes, she is smitten with him—but today she is to marry the Pasquali boy, and all her girlish dreams must come to an end. It is sad, but that is the way of the world.

The boy is not so bad, really. I know she will come to love him, in time."

"I am afraid she is a bit more headstrong than you bargained for. She and the priest have run off."

"*Dio mio!*" She bowed her head. "But why am I so surprised? I suppose it is at least partly my own fault."

"The duke has just been informed by the girl's maidservant that she is not in her room, and soon a guard at the Po gate will tell him that the girl and the advocate were seen heading for the river. I have no doubt they will be caught. I would ask that you set out now in your carriage. Your cool head will be needed to keep this bit of *opera buffa* from turning tragic. Just tell your driver to follow the duke's trail, for he will catch the eloping couple shortly and you must be there. Michele will need your help. Go now."

"Wait, Fabrizio. There is something I must know. Was it only the elixir, the love potion, that brought us together, or was there something more?" She looked at him with searching eyes.

"My dear *duchessa*—I loved you long before the elixir, and long after. The potion, the music, the magnetism of the stars—they all merely helped us to act on our deepest feelings." He smiled. "I have always loved you."

With that, Fabrizio Cambiati disappeared.

The *duchessa* sat but a moment, Fabrizio's smile seeming to linger in her heart, and then she called to her maidservant to set about dressing her quickly. Once dressed, she headed out of her room, her cane tapping on the marble floor as she cried, "Carlo, Carlo," for her driver.

After the long run, Cruna was sweating heavily and panting, in need of a drink. Elettra and Michele dismounted and let the horse slurp from the river. They then began walking the horse along the well-worn path that ran beside the water, as the sun was beginning to crest the horizon.

They thought it would be a while yet before Elettra's absence was noticed, and they believed that the duke would have considerable difficulty learning the direction they had taken. They never considered the fact that the second rider would slow Cruna.

Duke Pietro and six of his men were upon them so quickly that they had no time to remount and ride off. Archenti and the girl stood staring in disbelief as the pounding horses rounded a bend and appeared not a hundred yards away. Elettra recovered before Michele. "Into the river! Jump!"

"I can't . . . I can't swim."

The girl hung her head. "Everything is ruined now. Ruined!" The riders surrounded them. The duke dismounted and signalled for his men to do the same. He said nothing but glared at the priest, and walked in a circle around him. Michele Archenti stood still, his eyes downcast, mortified.

Finally the duke spat, "My daughter. On her wedding day. And you a priest." He drew his sword. "On your knees."

Elettra ran in front of Michele. "No, Papa! Please."

The duke pushed her roughly out of the way, keeping his eyes on the priest, who was now kneeling and staring at the ground, his head bowed. "I will run you through for this.

Priests!" The sword glinted with sunlight as he raised it and pressed the point against Archenti's chest. One of the duke's men held the struggling girl.

The sound of a carriage made everyone turn. The carriage halted, the door swung open and the *duchessa madre* struggled out, one of the soldiers coming to her aid. The duke watched her as she approached, his sword still planted over Archenti's heart.

The old woman looked at the priest and shook her head. Elettra moved behind her great-grandmother and peered out. The duke continued staring at the *duchessa,* as if hoping that she would leave so he could go about his bloody business. But she looked unflinchingly at him, and when she spoke Archenti noted that her voice suddenly had strength, her words carrying the same authority that he had often heard in Elettra's pronouncements. "I will take the girl back now. You are my grandson and you will do as I say. You will show mercy and let the priest go, once he has promised never to return to Cremona. Do you understand?"

The duke hesitated. He looked from the *duchessa* back to the priest and grimaced.

"Do you hear me?" she asked, quieter but more insistent.

The duke angrily kicked dirt on the priest, but he lowered the sword from his breast and slammed it back into its scabbard. Without another glance at any of them, he mounted, and he and his men rode hard back towards Cremona.

The *duchessa* walked to the carriage with the help of her cane and waited by the door in silence for the girl, who climbed in with a whimper. The old lady turned and considered the priest, who was still kneeling. He looked up for the first time as she sighed and shook her head again. Reaching into the carriage, she grabbed something and tossed it to him. His cassock.

Then she smiled at him, from her depths. But it was the smile of a young woman, as if she were forgiving someone else, another priest, a long time ago. At that moment, Archenti found her magnificent. She turned and, with the help of Carlo the driver, climbed in beside Elettra, who hid her face in her hands.

Michele Archenti knelt until the carriage was out of sight. Struggling to his feet, he turned in a circle, searching the four directions, regarding the fields, the river, the empty sky. In some strange way he felt liberated. Unsure which way to go, he could go any way at all. He picked up the cassock. Birds were singing in the Lombardy poplars that lined the river. He looked back at the city and shut his eyes a moment.

As he opened them again he saw Rodolfo approaching along the path.

"Priest," Rodolfo called from a distance, "come walk with me."

Archenti held the cassock. He stared at it, thinking, and then he put it on backwards.

They walked along the Po in silence for a while. Hearing a sound, Archenti spun around. "What?" The duke and three of his men had returned. They rode up and leapt off their horses. Archenti and Rodolfo stood awaiting them.

The duke drew his sword and approached. "She may have saved your life, priest, but you're not getting away that easily."

The three soldiers grabbed Archenti as Rodolfo stepped back, watching. One soldier held the advocate's left arm and hand against a tree as the duke approached. "That finger," he said to the soldier, and pointed with the sword. The soldier spread Archenti's hand, and with a flick of his sword the duke sliced off the ring finger with ease. Released, the priest fell to his knees and screamed, clutching his hand to his stomach as the foursome remounted and rode off without looking back.

Rodolfo told Archenti to hold his hand in the cold water of the river while squeezing hard above the cut to stem the flow of blood. Meanwhile, Rodolfo returned and picked up the finger from the ground where it had fallen.

He held it before Archenti. "I will bring it to a church and tell them it is the finger of the holy Cambiati."

"That's foolish. The naming of saints is a futile business, Rodolfo. Throw it away."

Rodolfo didn't throw it away but held onto the finger, wondering what to do with it.

By now, Archenti had pulled his hand from the river. Recalling the cerement in his pocket, he pulled it out, hoping to use it to wrap his wound. Before he could do so, Rodolfo took the cloth and tore off a piece. Handing the rest back to the advocate, Rodolfo wrapped the finger and shoved it in his sack. Meanwhile, Archenti took his portion of the cerement and wound it carefully around and around his hand, bandaging it in the cloth that had once been the shroud of Fabrizio Cambiati.

Hours later, as they walked eastward in silence along the Po, the river pulsing with light, a cloud of newly hatched silk moths began to stream from Archenti's pocket.

# *THE PLAY—ACT EIGHT*

## THE PLAY CONCLUDES:
### LOVE ALL AROUND

On the stage, the musicians were playing a series of violin sonatas. As they stroked their violins, guests arrived in pairs for the wedding of Ottavio and Aurora, entering upstage right, their names announced by a crestfallen Pantalone, crossing the stage and exiting upstage left. The players each wore five layers of clothing, removing a layer as they passed behind the stage to return and be announced anew by Pantalone. No one in the audience was astute enough to notice that the fat guests arrived first, the medium-sized came in the middle and the thin came last.

In order to swell their numbers further, the players had invited several townspeople as guests on stage—including a number of children, the go-between and Ugo the Mantuan. Ugo, who had planned to attend, was however otherwise occupied—for something completely unexpected had happened to him.

As at all weddings, love was in the air. That ever-dangerous emotion infected everyone near and far, even as distant as Ugo in his cold palace. Ugo had sighed, looked in his mirror and decided that, before leaving for the wedding celebration, he must set eyes on his own fair one, immortally captive in her room of dust and ancient *objets d'art*. He hurried down the long halls, panting, always amazed that he could look on her and see not the desiccated mummy-like body before him but the beautiful girl she had been, still alive in his memory. At last he came to the room and stood outside, staring. After a few moments, he decided he wanted to move closer. Knowing the danger of hearing the poem and being caught by its rhythms, he removed from his pocket a pair of soft wax balls which he poked in his ears. He entered the room, taking his lit candle with him. Walking up to her, he shone the light on her face as she read the poem. For him she was still lovely, would always be lovely—her sumptuous lips, her creamy skin, her icy blue eyes. He pulled up a straight-backed chair and sat gazing at her, placing the candle on a table next to him. Lost in his reverie, he was unaware that his head had begun to tilt. Without his noticing, the heat of the candle flame started to melt the wax in his ear. It happened in an instant—one moment it was soft wax, and the next it turned liquid and ran out.

*Her voice! Her voice! I can hear her voice!* Ugo rejoiced. Enraptured, he sat listening—caught forever.

Back at the wedding, the musicians played on, love emanating from the stage in curlicues of cloud that dissolved in the luminescent blue sky. The bride came forward, dressed in a gown of scarlet samite, with a train that stretched halfway across the stage and a collar of white ermine at her throat. Ottavio, handsome and gallant in a hat with a bountiful white feather, was aglow with happiness. A marriage ceremony was quickly performed, the bride received her silver belt legitimizing the conjunction and a great feast began.

The guests helped themselves from a long table heaped with loaves of bread, hard-boiled eggs, a round of cheese large as a carriage wheel, roast oxen and mutton, fish from river and sea, capon, chicken, boar's head, boar's-foot jelly, pigeons, sea-fowl, grapes and sweets. The wines came from as far away as Toscana and Piemonte and every point in between, as well as from every corner of Lombardia: Barbaresco, Barolo, Grignolino from Monferrato, Chianti, Ruche, Dolcetto, Freisa, sparkling Carmignano, Sassella, Grumello. And none of the wine was watered down, except for the children, of course. Jugs were passed out to the audience, and when the musicians began the irresistible second allegro from Arcangelo Corelli's Sonata Ottava, Arlecchino, in a polka-dot suit, grabbed the bride and initiated the dancing, and all on stage and in the audience joined in.

While they danced, servants from the duke's household brought out a great pie that contained ham, eggs, chicken, pork, dates, almonds, sugar and saffron—all the ingredients in one grand pasty in order to avoid the sumptuary laws, which allowed only three dishes at a wedding feast. Of course, they had already broken the sumptuary laws right and left, but the duke could not be seen to be contributing to the lawlessness typical of players.

Downstage left stood a downcast Pantalone. Arlecchino danced over to him with Aurora in his arms, and as the old dog reached out for her, Ottavio arrived and danced off with his bride.

"Do not be sad, Pantalone," Arlecchino said, panting and patting him on the back. "The magic violin was destroyed anyway—a horse from the duke's stable trampled it. It never would have worked out for you. Have fun, celebrate with us, come."

Pantalone turned to berate the fool. At that moment, the matronly go-between swooped down on the old man, swept him up in her arms like a featherweight skeleton, crushed him against her huge soft bosom and danced him around the stage. "Dance, my friend," Arlecchino shouted after him. "It's good for you. Enjoy, enjoy, life is short. Enjoy." He worked his way through the crowd back to the feast table, took a huge slug of wine and, laughing, buried his face in the great pie.

At that moment, Aurora glanced heavenward, pointed and exclaimed, "Look, everyone! Even in daylight we can see it!"

All the players on stage, and all the audience members from past and future, stopped and gazed into the sky high above.

# CHAPTER THIRTEEN

*Time is the first miracle. And the last.*

## THE PATRON SAINT
## OF WONDER

*Dawn—26 August 1682*

Fabrizio and Omero, at the top of the tower, continued looking out over the city of Cremona. The comet had disappeared in the dawn, light into light. A moment before it vanished, Fabrizio had said, "Look, Omero, how the comet reflects in the river." And then it was gone.

Staring through the telescope, Fabrizio watched as the devil's advocate walked with Rodolfo, the skeleton on his back seeming to tag happily along. They were idling beside the Po, talking. As Michele Archenti passed a line of Lombardy poplars, Fabrizio saw white silk moths flutter in a stream from his cassock pocket. Archenti and Rodolfo sauntered along together until they disappeared into the dusty blue mist in the distance.

Once again, Fabrizio removed the telescope from his eye and stared at it. "A most formidable instrument, all in all."

Sometime during the long night of waiting and the comet's passing, the sirocco had ended, gone to wherever it is winds go when they die.

As Fabrizio scanned the city, he whispered to himself. Omero could just make out the words, which he remembered hearing before. "Stone which is not stone, a precious thing which has no value, a thing of many shapes which has no shape, this unknown thing which is known of all."

Omero sat down and leaned against the inner wall of the tower, shifting his position. In doing so, with his elbow he knocked loose several bricks, which fell in. Fabrizio looked back at him and saw something whitish in the newly created cavity. "What's that in there? Behind you?"

"What?"

Fabrizio approached and, reaching past Omero and into the hole, removed a skull, his two fingers through an eye socket.

Omero snapped his head back, "*Dio mio!* If we have climbed the Holy Spine of God, then this must be His Sacred Skull."

"Intriguing suggestion, but no. I'm afraid this is the rather mundane skull of some poor soul who may have died around the time the *torrazzo* was built, or perhaps he even died in the building of it, fell down to knock heads with one of those marble saints below. Or perhaps it is a minor relic of the period—some martyr or other—purposely installed here as an offering to heaven."

"Perhaps it is the patron saint of comets." Omero took the skull, held it at arm's length and contemplated the blank sockets.

Fabrizio looked at it too. "Once that head was filled with desires and dreams, Omero, like yours and mine, sad stories and glad memories. All flown now, all wind—into the ether."

"I wonder what it signifies?"

Fabrizio shrugged and returned to his telescope. "I don't know. Everything? Nothing? Something or other? It is as it is. What do the stars signify?" He spoke with the telescope at his eye again, pointing it at the square below. "Wonder, Omero. Awe. That is all."

After the long, tiring night of watching the sky, Omero fell into a deep sleep at dawn, the skull resting on his lap. Fabrizio, who continued to gaze at the heavens and the city, thought his manservant was still listening. "The real truth about comets, Omero, is that they carry the power of love, a power that always returns, the power to bring together beings who are seemingly distant from one another. Ultimately, a comet brings in its wake the power to make life out of nothing. Where nothing but emptiness and endless dark once were, a light appears out of nowhere and the world is refreshed and begins anew."

On sensing Fabrizio's words in his sleep, Omero surmised that he was hearing a buzz of voices, bees and sparks ricocheting back and forth inside the skull he still held in his lap. He was unable to understand the words, but he knew that they constituted the telling of a long, involved story without beginning or end. And then the dream changed colour and from far off a voice was calling to him. *Of course,* he thought. *I know what it means now—the riddle of the Philosopher's Stone. "Stone which is not stone, a precious thing which has no value, a thing of many shapes which has no shape, this unknown thing which is known of all." It is the child about to be born, the unnamed fetus in its womb.* He couldn't wait to tell Fabrizio.

For the last time, Fabrizio took the telescope from his eye. He glanced up as a flight of doves from the tip of the tower over his head shimmered into the blue, like heat rising from an alchemist's furnace. "Omero, my friend, I have seen much; much of heaven and earth. Perhaps more than any man should see, and yet all men see much the same—enough sorrow to sadden a glad heart and yet much of joy too. Birth and death and birth again, in the great round of time." In the shadows, Omero continued to sleep. "Look. The sun releases its first arrow, and the Po, free of all mist, has begun to glow."

With the first ray of sunlight, someone below, lower in the tower, rang the bells, and beneath that the clock ticked and turned round, while down in the heart of the city a girl child was being born. Meanwhile the seed of life began its journey again, in the belly of another girl riding through the Po gate in a carriage with her great-grandmother years later, as day began again with the crying of cocks, the scent of woodsmoke, and the tuning of violins.

"We will go down from the tower now, Omero. I am no saint, you know. No saint. I believe I have been lucky enough to glimpse the face of heaven, its inconceivable brilliance, the same as the face of those I love and my own face reflected in a river of light, but we must once again become ordinary men and return to do what we can to help. We must go down now. Omero? Omero, awake!"

## A NOTE ON FIBONACCI NUMBERS

*Fabrizio's Return* is a story told in thirteen chapters and eight acts. Known as Fibonacci numbers, 8 and 13 have a ratio of approximately 1 to 1.6, which is the mathematical proportion of the Golden Section, commonly used in art, architecture and music in Italy from the fourteenth to the eighteenth century.

A Fibonacci series is formed by starting with 0 and 1 and adding the previous two numbers to find the next one: 0 1 1 2 3 5 8 13 21 34 55 89 144 and so on. As the numbers increase, the 1 to 1.6 ratio of consecutive numbers moves closer to the absolute Golden Section proportion.

Fibonacci numbers—discovered by Leonardo Fibonacci, or Leonardo da Pisa (1175–1250)—are found throughout the natural world: in the typical number of petals in flowers, in the way trees branch and leaf, in sunflower seed patterns and other common spirals.

ACKNOWLEDGMENTS

A number of friends and colleagues had a voice in the making of this book. I am deeply indebted to all of them for their excellent insights, helpful suggestions and encouragement. In particular, I would like to thank Nicola Vulpe for multiple readings of the manuscript at various stages in its long gestation. His patience and generosity go well beyond the call of friendship. Also, I appreciate the felicitous annotations of Chris Scott, who read the work early on and made significant contributions to its direction. His supremely intelligent notes could stand as a wonderful commentary on the novel.

I am also pleased to thank John Blackmore for his reading of the novel and his contribution of several fine suggestions. As well, readings and notes from my brother, Ren Frutkin, and his wife, Ann Berger Frutkin, were a signal contribution to the final text. In addition, much thanks to Bozica Costigliola and Biagio Costigliola for their discerning eyes, especially on things Italian, as well as Henry Chapin, Alan Cumyn and Suzanne Evans for perceptive readings. Also, thanks to Jeff Street for suggestions about starry nights, and Samuel Kurinsky, Executive Director of the Hebrew

History Federation in New York City, for providing valuable information. Thanks as well to Gaspar Borchardt of Cremona, Italy, for providing his perceptive views on violins and their construction, and to the city of Cremona for its gracious hospitality.

Perhaps no one had a greater influence on the book than Diane Martin, my editor at Knopf Canada. Her hard work, insight and enthusiasm for the project gave it wings. And, of course, the attention to detail and sense of precision of copyeditor Gena Gorell are also much appreciated. I would also like to thank my agent, Carolyn Swayze, who offered generous support for the book from the beginning. Finally, as always, I must thank my closest reader and favourite editor, Faith Seltzer. As always, her undying support was essential. Thanks also to Elliot for being there and helping to consider titles.

I'm sure there are others who could be thanked for their input, comments and information. My apologies if I have missed anyone. It must be added that any errors of fact or judgment are mine alone, and not the doing of the good friends and colleagues mentioned herein. Thank you all.

MARK FRUTKIN is the author of three books of poetry and six of fiction, including Atmosphere Apollinaire, which was a finalist for the Governor General's Literary Award for Fiction, the Trillium Book Award and the Ottawa Book Award. He lives in Ottawa.